THE LOST CULT

By E. E. Knight

THE WAY OF THE WOLF
THE CHOICE OF THE CAT
LARA CROFT: TOMB RAIDER: THE LOST CULT

THE LOST CULT

E. E. KNIGHT

BALLANTINE BOOKS • NEW YORK

A Del Rey® Book
Published by The Random House Publishing Group
 Published in the United States by Del Rey Books, an imprint of The Random House Publishing Group, a division of Random House, Inc., New York, and simultaneously in Canada by Random House of Canada Limited, Toronto.

www.delreydigital.com

ISBN 0-345-46172-X

Manufactured in the United States of America

OPM 9 8 7 6 5 4 3 2 1

First Edition: August 2004

To HPL,
for grabbing my imagination
and never letting go

ACKNOWLEDGMENTS

I give thanks to my wife, Stephanie, my parents and family, Paul Witcover, Steve Saffel, John Silbersack, Kate Scherler, the 254s, and the Inkplots for their time, advice, and support. Finally, I'd like to thank the people at Eidos Interactive and Core Design Ltd. for many (arguably too many!) hours of great gaming, following Lara's shapely form in and out of peril.

THE LOST CULT

PROLOGUE

The Tomb Raider fell through darkness.

She dropped, as she did all things, purposefully: back slightly arched, arms tight to her sides, feet shoulder-width apart, shivering. The air was far below zero at this altitude. She inhaled the mask's oxygen through her mouth, as she had since she'd started flushing the nitrogen out of her blood in the Royal Australian Air Force C-130J transport an hour ago.

Getting the nitrogen out of her blood saved her from the bends. Breathing through her mouth saved her a nosebleed.

A high-altitude low-open jump is nothing to sneeze at—or during.

She watched the flashing red telltale projected onto the inside of her visor by a tiny laser cylinder near her temple, corrected her course by extending an arm. The distant lights of the island of Mauritius, now twenty thousand feet below, comforted her. The Indian Ocean was a big dark place . . .

Terminal velocity. Glorious! The free fall equivalent of rapture of the deep, helped by warmer air as she passed into a more comfortable thermal layer. If it weren't for the masked HALO helmet—it made her look a bit like Darth Vader, or so the Aussie aircrew had joked—her eyelids would be peeled back to her hairline about now.

The rugged volcanic mountains of the southern half of the island could now be distinguished from the horizon. The drop aimed for an expansive estate on the coast that had once been a sugar plantation.

She watched her telltale, slowly spreading her arms and legs to retard her fall. Her jumpsuit cracked in the wind. As the altitude ticked down, she placed her gloved hand on the rip cord in case the auto-deploy failed. It didn't. Her employers issued good equipment, she granted them that . . . *Blast, I've overshot.*

After the hard, internal-organ-rearranging jerk of the black chute opening, she swung herself in a tight 180 to get back on course. Not many seconds now. A flashback to standing on the electric swings at the amusement park as a child, her father glowering, her nanny shouting imprecations, played through her head. She corrected course again, fighting the breeze coming from the interior of the island . . .

. . . and saw the rooftop cooling unit on Lancaster Urdmann's estate below. The industrial-sized air conditioner was her DIP: desired impact point. She got her first good view of the Renaissance-style main house. It was uglier than the satellite pictures let on. Urdmann had all the taste and restraint of a sybaritic Saudi prince.

Why anyone needed two outdoor pools *and* a spa . . . But then Lancaster Urdmann—ex-arms dealer, ex-Cold War military financier with a penchant for working both sides of the Iron Curtain—could afford them. When Urdmann retired from the grit and danger of gunrunning, he'd indulged a passion he had developed as he roamed the global hot spots: collecting and selling antiquities. Now he was in possession of some Iraqi artifacts acquired from the fleeing gangsters of Hussein's regime, and the Americans and British weren't interested in meeting his price for stolen goods.

So she'd been hired to handle the retrieval.

The Tomb Raider landed hop-skip atop the van-sized air-conditioning unit, thinking that satellite guidance was a Very Good Thing. Feeling a bit giddy, she fought the urge to bring her heels together and stick the landing, gymnast style. The exhilaration of a jump would blur her focus if she let it, and she had to stay clearheaded and on task. Instead of posing, she whirled her hands to take in her chute, unbuckled the harness, and let the packs of gear fall. With that done, she unzipped the jumpsuit.

She felt uncomfortably hot—ironic considering that the tight black overall covering her from crown to corns was a piece of insertion technology colloquially known as a *coolsuit*. Another gift from her employer, it prevented body temperature being detected from the outside. Inside, you sweated.

No rooftop guards. She crouched, did a few experimental stretches. No cramps, no joint pain. She began to fill pockets and belt pouches with gear, touched the ear transmitter beneath her head sheath. "Osprey is at alpha."

"Copy Osprey," her guardian angel said. "Proceed."

She snapped open a tool kit on her chest. Its tiny light revealed the latest in high-tech burglar equipment. Ignoring the jimmies, skeleton keys, alligator clips, and minicomputer, she selected an Allen wrench and began opening the access panel on the cooling unit. It came away easily.

She dropped inside. The dunnage bag with the rest of the gear waited among the whirring fans and cauldronlike condensers, placed by the prep team a few days ago. A scribbled drawing duct-taped to the end of the bag caught her eye. A childish stick figure that was—how had her biology teacher at Wimbledon put it?—*mammiferous* looked back at her. It read:

HI LARA!

"Oh, grow up," she muttered.

She lifted off the panel to the intake duct. The prep team had done a good job; the metal didn't look cut. She stuck her head inside. The meter-long blades of the intake fan roared below.

Her insulated snips cut the connection between fan and control unit. She stopped the fan with the bottom of her boot, dropped her backpack to the duct below the fan, and wriggled between the blades.

It took a little over thirty seconds for the fan to come back on. By then the Tomb Raider was negotiating the elevator junction. She passed one of the heat sensors on the way. The little gauge did double duty: checking the function of the air conditioner and triggering an alarm if an intruder, animal or human, tried the air shafts. She crawled past, hoping the coolsuit was doing its job, following the schematics she'd committed to memory.

Two turns later, she looked through the wall-mounted air-conditioning duct cover and down into Urdmann's display room.

Now for the fun bit.

A new oxyacetylene minicutter came out of a pouch on her arm. She began cutting, careful not to let the cover fall; the floor was one big pressure sensor . . .

"Osprey here. I'm at objective. Going for the alarm box."

"Copy Osprey."

She took a tube out of her pack, screwed on another piece, which she then unfolded into a rifle stock. The line thrower was a one-shot weapon; she had to do this right the first time.

Turn on the laser, find the target, exhale halfway, press the trigger button—

With a shoulder-bruising *foop,* the compressed air cartridge exploded and the harpoon with its trailing line covered the twenty meters in an eyeblink, burying itself just above the alarm box. She coated the metal side of the launcher with quick-acting glue and anchored it to the side of the shaft.

Then she slid headfirst down the threaded nylon line, gloves and inner-thigh padding absorbing the burn.

Patching the bypass into the alarm was hard enough under normal conditions, but she had to do it upside down while hanging from her crisscrossed knees. She'd practiced it in Baghdad with a virtual reality helmet, but that alarm had been only similar to Urdmann's, not an exact replica. She broke open the alarm panel with her knife, had to read the cryptic electronic notations on the motherboard by helmet-light—and the distorting visor wasn't a help. She popped a memory chip out of the board, and flashing lights went on in the display room. Out came two miniature alligator clamps attached to the spoof board in her kit. She fitted them, mentally timing down the seconds she had until every alarm in the house went off. Five, four, three . . .

Green light on her spoof board.

She dropped to the floor, drew a .22 pistol fitted with a silencer. With three quick shots she killed the alarm lights; there were no local switches to turn them off. She hoped the guards on the grounds hadn't seen the lights through the glass doors leading to the patio for the few seconds they'd been flashing.

"Osprey. Bypass completed. Are we clean?"

"Copy Osprey. The house sent out a tamper alarm to the security company. Not your fault; we anticipated it. We smothered the call."

"Please convey my thanks to the White Hats." Hackers on

your side were also a Very Good Thing. "Any sign of the guards?"

"Negative."

She peeled off the coolsuit hood and mask, shook her hair out. She mopped sweat out of her eyes with the tight-folding towel she always carried in her pack.

Urdmann displayed his treasures more brazenly than Lara did her own. Urdmann's category cards romanced the art, whereas in her own collection she kept description to a minimum. The walls held tapestries, rugs, and friezes; the waist-level cases containing artifacts were arranged in mazelike concentric squares, so that one had to do a good amount of twisting and turning to reach the central display. Here and there larger pieces, everything from urnlike Chinese burial caskets to statues and busts in varying degrees of deterioration, stood on pedestals.

All of the highest quality. Urdmann's prices pushed the envelope even for four-thousand-year-old artifacts, but the man sold no forgeries. The one redeeming quality in an otherwise disgusting character was his professionalism. She grudgingly granted him a modicum of respect for that.

She resisted the impulse to browse and found the Iraqi artifacts in a slightly taller case in the center of the room. Urdmann was proud of his new acquisitions. She popped the locks with a glass cutter and began to sort the items, separating the choice from the dross, the legally obtained from the stolen. This was why they needed a Tomb Raider instead of an agent: Not just anyone could distinguish Old Babylonian cuneiform from neo-Assyrian, or a holy symbol of Marduk from a whimsical bit of decor.

One of her targeted items, the rarest and most valuable, wasn't with the others: a briefcase-sized set of legal tablets that were in a very real sense the world's first comprehensive law book—a codified set of Hammurabi's laws. She'd have to explore the house, starting with Urdmann's study, so she'd better secure what she already had.

She reached into a satchel at her belt, unfolded and carefully filled two bags with tablets, a pair of painted vases, jewelry, and religious icons, then removed a cylinder from her equipment vest and triggered the built-in packing balloons to inflate and cushion the pieces. Then she took a second cylinder the size of a shaving-cream canister from her pack and squirted its contents into the bags. The Styrofoam-like packing would lock the items in place.

With the alarm disabled, it was a simple matter to cut out a pane in the glass doors, remove it with a suction cup, and step out onto the patio. She tossed the bags behind a shrub, tied them with a nylon line, and began to scale the Renaissance-style exterior. Baroque architecture looked impressive, but it gave her any number of hand- and footholds. She picked her path to the roof using Juliet balconies and cornices.

Back on the roof, she reported in to Roost. Then she hauled up the bags, keeping an eye toward the guardhouse at the rear of the grounds. She retrieved the rest of the gear from the air conditioner.

"Condor is on the way, Osprey," her guardian angel reported.

She tossed her two cushioned sacks of swag into a bigger bag. This one was bright orange. She turned a knob that inflated more cushioning within the semiluminous pickup container. With that done, she inflated the last item, a miniature dirigible complete with a wind-guiding tail. As it filled automatically with helium, she let go of the wire-cored line, and the dirigible shot up into the air, still inflating.

Even if the guards had seen the balloon take off, it was too late now.

Two hundred meters of line later, the orange pickup bag lifted off the roof. Condor, a fixed-wing recovery aircraft, would snatch the line in midair between protruding, antlike jaws.

It was all over, save for a few ifs, ands, and buts.

If Condor's pilot flew as well as the Australians who'd dropped her, Iraq would get its treasures returned quietly.

And Lara Croft would get a chunk of her life back without having to give endless depositions to the lawyers of three different countries following the murder of Von Croy in Paris and her bloody pursuit of the cabal that had killed him.

But the Tomb Raider wanted those last, missing tablets. Not just because they were part of her mission. And not just because they belonged to the Iraqi people. She would be fully within her rights to pull out now, take no further risks. The mission parameters gave her that option. But she knew she wouldn't take it. To leave the law tablets behind would be to grant Urdmann a small victory, and she found that she wasn't prepared to do that.

Urdmann's upstairs study and bedroom were accessible from the other end of the roof. She went to the edge of the roof and peered down at his balcony. A curtain flapped in the breeze through an invitingly open French door. The study balcony was beside that of the bedroom.

As she climbed down to the study balcony, she heard the mellow burr of the Condor's engines. Far above, signal strobes began to flash on the rising balloon, line, and recovery case.

Good work, lads.

Now on the narrow balcony, back against the wall, she heard a sonorous snore from the bedroom.

She used an old-fashioned jimmy on the French door and crept into the study. Ambient light from the exterior illumination gave her enough to go on. She could still hear the snoring from the connecting bedroom.

The tablets sat on a library table beneath a picture of a dark-eyed, comely woman with Betty Page bangs. Urdmann was hiding them in plain sight, like Poe's purloined letter, using them as bookends to a set of Gibbon's *Rise and Fall*: first editions, by the look of them. She reached out and gently touched the tablets on which some nameless scribe had set down the laws of another age.

The wonder of it fed the Tomb Raider's soul.

The snoring in the next room stopped. She held her breath until the noise came back louder than ever.

She took one of the tablets from its wooden stand, ignoring the first-edition Gibbon, and examined it with her kit light. It was a solid sheet of clay. Rows of wedge shapes had been pressed into the wet clay with a stylus; then the tablet had been baked and glazed. If there'd been a binding, it had long since rotted away.

The lights came on. She startled, but didn't drop the tablet.

"Lara Croft," came a smooth, BBC-pitched voice from behind. "So they cared enough to send the very best."

The snoring still echoed from the other room.

With a glance, she checked Lancaster Urdmann's reflection in the window. He didn't appear to be holding a gun. The Tomb Raider carefully replaced the tablet.

Then she turned on her heel, swinging the .22 up and pointing it at Urdmann. His eyes were brown, a slightly darker shade than hers. They held no fear, no emotion at all.

"Oh, please," he said. He touched a button on the wall, and the snoring cut off.

Lancaster Urdmann had a lush fringe of salt-and-pepper hair running from the crown of his tanned, mostly bald head to his thick sideburns. He wore a silken Turkish robe. A landslide of hairy fat descended from his chin.

Urdmann ignored the pistol and looked into the Tomb Raider's eyes. "I knew an attempt like this would be made, so I added a couple of extra alarms. It was that Kunai fellow showing up with that cock-and-bull story about needing a translation of symbols from some Babylonian law book that tipped me off. His whole story stank from here to the Yukon."

The Tomb Raider had no idea what he was talking about, but then she wasn't familiar with all the preparations that had gone into this operation. Perhaps an agent going under the name Kunai had attempted an earlier reconnaissance and been rebuffed.

"I'd love to chat, Urdmann, but I've got an early meeting," Lara said.

"Then leave, by all means. I've no gun; I'm not stopping you."

"Very reasonable of you. I'll just take these tablets and be on my way."

He took a step closer. "Leave me my souvenirs, Croft. I had to negotiate with some very unpleasant people to acquire them."

"Those 'unpleasant people' were thieves and worse."

"Yes, well, as I said, unpleasant. But I did what I had to do to safeguard the tablets. You should be thanking me."

"The tablets are part of Iraq's heritage. They belong in Iraq, not in the study of Lancaster Urdmann."

"As if the bloody wogs gave *that*"—he snapped his fingers—"for their heritage before we dug it up for them and told them that it was worth something!"

"Cut the John Bull, Urdmann." She reached with her free hand, grabbed one of the tablets.

Urdmann took another step closer. "No, Croft."

"I'll shoot," she warned.

He shook his head, his jowls trembling like jelly. "You're no killer, Croft. You won't shoot an unarmed man."

She grinned wolfishly in response.

"We can come to an arrangement. Some money for the upkeep of that drafty old manor of yours. Perhaps—"

For an obese man, Urdmann moved fast. The Tomb Raider moved faster. Her pistol spat even as he lunged at her, and a track of red scored Urdmann's fleshy right forearm. He fell back, clawing at his desk.

"Don't say I didn't warn you," she said drily.

"You shot me," Urdmann said, blood running from between his fingers as he smothered the wound. His brown eyes held shock now. And anger. "That bloody *burns*!"

"It's only a scratch," Lara said. "If I'd really shot you, you'd know it." As she spoke, keeping the pistol trained on him all the while, she stuffed the tablets into her pack. Then, as an afterthought, she tossed him her travel towel. "I suppose you realize you're dripping blood all over a thirteenth-century rug."

"Eleventh!" Urdmann protested, grabbing the towel and pressing it to his arm. A film of greasy sweat had appeared on his brow.

"I'll take your word for it. But you might want to look at those pikes again. Please drop dead at your earliest convenience."

She stepped past him onto the balcony. Behind her, one of Urdmann's guards burst in, rifle at the ready.

"No, don't shoot, you fool! You'll damage the tablets," Urdmann bellowed.

She swung over the side of the balcony and dropped to the ground. A Klaxon sounded. Lights went on all over the grounds.

Oh, bother.

She hit and rolled, then ran downhill, heading for the west wall. A peacock squawked as she leapt a decorative hedge. She climbed up an iron fence topped with sharpened spear points.

"Osprey!" her guardian angel broke in. "Condition check."

"Running for my life," she gasped.

"Why aren't you with Condor? They just picked up the cargo. Why did you break plan?"

"Contingency."

For the first time, the guardian angel's voice showed signs of stress. "There is no contingency. You were supposed to go out on Condor. Now—"

"Listen," she interrupted. "Can we talk about this later? I'm kind of busy now. I'll see you in the Seychelles by the seashore."

She ripped the coolsuit going over another fence. She made note of the extraction point and jumped down into the outer grounds.

Lancaster Urdmann employed a full-time security staff of eight. Labor in Mauritius was cheap. But they stayed on the inner grounds, in the house, and at the road gate.

She heard a police whistle blow from Urdmann's balcony. Flashlights bobbed at the side of the house, then swung in her direction.

She crabbed into a stand of brush. Beyond the estate's outer wall, a hundred meters away, the night sky loomed. She crawled toward it, hoping that whatever firearms the guards possessed didn't come equipped with light intensifiers. The coolsuit would hide her from an infrared scope.

The outer wall was concrete with shards of broken glass embedded at the top amongst coils of razor wire. Lara angled for a thick palm near the wall. Urdmann's landscapers had cleared everything on the other side of the wall, trying to keep people out, not in.

The Tomb Raider saw the lights of a jeep roaring across the outer grounds. She climbed the palm, got amongst the fronds at the top, saw a clear a spot on the other side of the wall, and jumped. She brushed wire on her way down, but her falling weight carried her through. She didn't think she'd been cut too badly.

As she hurried down the steep slope, she marked the little inflatable boat waiting for her among the oceanside rocks.

Gunfire from behind—she threw herself sideways. Urdmann's guards stood on the roof of their vehicle, muzzles blossoming yellow as they fired automatic weapons at her over the top of the wall.

Trigger-happy amateurs. You get what you pay for, Urdmann. One man with a scope would have got me.

She dropped to her bottom and slid on the loose soil as bullets zipped all around. She bumped and thudded, smashing body and gear on volcanic stone, cushioning the precious items in her pack with flesh and bone, until she was out of the line of fire and among the giant boulders at the edge of the ocean.

The com-link was gone; the headset had come off somewhere on the slide. She waded out, felt the sting of seawater on her battered thighs and backside, reached a hand down. It came back up bloody.

Scratch one coolsuit as expended in the line of duty . . .

Djbril, her freelance ex-military gearhead, helped her into the boat with a smile but said nothing. It was his kind of mission: a week's worth of lounging on a cocktail-service-included beach capped off with one night of noisy excitement. When she had settled into the boat, Djbril tossed her a first aid kit, still not saying a word. That was one of the things she liked about him.

Then the Zodiac's two-hundred-horsepower engine roared to life, and the boat shot away from shore, heading for the open ocean.

Ten hours later, Lady Croft tested the water temperature in the spa-sized tub in the bathroom of her room at the Stansfield resort hotel in the Seychelles and dumped the second of three boxes of lavender-scented Epsom salts into the sudsy water.

She glanced at the full-length mirror in the shower door next to the tub, turned, lifted her robe, and winced. The pummeling she'd taken on her slide to the sea had left a series of black-and-blue souvenirs of Mauritius. At least the cuts and abrasions were healing nicely, thanks to applications of antibiotic cream.

Now for a glorious soak, then a real sleep. Upon arriving at the hotel, she'd stuffed herself with poached eggs, fried tomatoes, and toast—she never skipped breakfast, but contingencies sometimes forced her to enjoy it at seven o'clock at night. Then she'd limped down to the hotel druggist for the Epsom salts.

Speaking of which, the tub was nearly full. She topped it off with the third box of bath salts. Then she stuck one leg in up to the knee, relishing the painfully hot water.

Exquisite. She stuck her other leg in and prepared to lower herself ever so slowly into the steaming bath.

Her suite door buzzed loudly. *Go away*, she thought at whoever was out there. Whoever was out there wasn't listening; the door buzzed again. Sighing, Lara left the tub, rewrapped her cushy robe about herself, and went to the door. She looked through the peephole, saw an oversized nose and watery blue eyes.

The American. The guardian angel in her ear. She opened the door.

"Hey, Lara." A thin veneer of Yale lay over an accent from the Georgia pinewoods. "Hope you weren't sleeping." She liked the American; he was so awkwardly polite.

"What now? Did you miss something at the debriefing?"

"No. We missed something on Condor. The Hammurabi tablets. The Iraqis are screaming."

"And why do you think I've got them?"

"Because you're Lara Croft, that's why."

She had to smile at that. "Supposing I do know where they are, when is my record going to be cleared? That was our deal, wasn't it?"

"It's been done."

"Not according to my lawyers."

Her guardian angel frowned, reached for his cell phone. Lara crossed the room to the bulging Viennese dresser for hers. They faced each other like two gunfighters across the burgundy-colored carpeting and punched in numbers.

The American held up his index finger, spoke into his phone. Waited. Spoke some more.

"A fax is coming through," said the associate working the graveyard shift at her solicitor's, her voice tinny in Lara's ear.

The American closed his cell phone with a click. "You should be good now."

Her phone: "Yes, here's your Interpol file, Lady Croft. All the stops are gone."

"Thank you so much," she said and hung up.

"Well?" asked the American. "Where are the tablets then?"

She walked over to the tub, went down into a very unladylike squat, reached one hand into the still-steaming water, and pulled up a waterproof case. She opened the seal and extracted her lucky backpack.

"You take that with you into the tub?" the American asked, looking at the battered backpack.

"Never out of reach when I'm out of England."

She pulled out the tablets in their own cushioned, waterproof wrapper. Handed them over. "That concludes our business, I believe."

"It does. Sorry about the delay. Unintentional, I assure you."

"I never thought otherwise," she said. "Now, if you'll excuse me. I'm sore, and very, very tired."

The American flicked a strand of straw-colored hair out of his eyes. "We've got a cure for that where I come from. Some good Kentucky bourbon, a strong set of hands, and a big ol'—"

"I don't drink," she said. "And if you want to cure something, I suggest you focus on your prep team. That was sloppy work. Urdmann spotted the Kunai fellow right from the start."

"Kunai? We didn't send anyone in with that cover."

"My mistake." She took a scrunchie out of her robe pocket and began to put up her hair. "Be an angel and close the door quietly on your way out, would you?"

PART ONE

1

Chaos reigned in the converted farmhouse during the last morning of Dr. Stephen Frys's life. Dresser drawers hung open in his bedroom—dark, thanks to the still-closed curtains, except for a guttering candle. Dropped towels lay all over the bath, but no water speckled the tub; he'd washed in a basin so he could hear any suspicious sounds coming from outside the house. The bed stood as tidy as on any normal morning, but only because the professor hadn't slept in it.

Dr. Frys even skipped his beloved morning tea, taken with lemon, sugar, toast, and the incomparable view of the Scottish Highlands, a tradition that dated back to the first morning he and his late wife had spent in Whistlecrack House thirty-one years ago.

Blood—thanks to a trembling hand during his shave—spotted his chin and the mole on his left cheek as he lumbered down the narrow stairs. He listened to the silent, darkened house and heard only the wind outside.

He dropped his dusty suitcase to the kitchen floor with a thud, then removed his thick, black-framed eyeglasses and rubbed them clean with his handkerchief, a gesture any of his senior students knew meant a pause in the lecture while the professor turned something over in his mind. As he put the handkerchief back, he patted his pocket, reassuring himself that his cell phone was still there.

Any visitor to Whistlecrack House stopped and looked at the fireplace first when they arrived in the kitchen. Almost big enough to climb in if one crouched, it filled one wall, a great arch of brick with iron-mongered doors, a spit, hooks, and shelves for baking, roasting, or frying foods.

Last night the fireplace had been roaring. Paper after age-yellowed paper, notebook after notebook, reams of photocopied research, even old-fashioned carbon copies had flamed yellow-orange, curled, blackened, and then turned to fine gray ash almost as quickly as he could feed the fire.

Dr. Frys checked the blackened mass. A substantial part of his life lay in the still-smoldering heap. He prodded the pile with a poker, and the fire burst into new life as he exposed the last few unburned reams of typescript. He stirred the mass to make sure of the destruction.

Life does save its best jokes for last. The ashes were all that remained of research that had once made him a bit of a joke in his profession . . . until he gave up trying to pry open closed and comfortable minds. But now that same research had turned out to be of unexpected interest to hard-eyed, ruthless men. He'd always been half afraid of the secrets he'd discovered, but after three decades in which not even a graduate student had asked about his *Méne* work, he'd half forgotten about it as well. He and Von Croy should have abandoned their research without publishing any of it, left the frightful revelations where no one would ever find them.

But the cat was out of the bag now—and she'd had rabid kittens.

He checked the clock, pulled out his cell phone, and tapped in a number. It wasn't even eight yet, but there was no harm in checking.

Just the answering service again, and he'd already left a message.

Dr. Frys stepped lightly past a cream-colored wall covered with family photos—an empty hook and an oval a slightly lighter shade than the rest of the wall marked the place where a photo had hung—and went to the front sitting room. Without parting the curtains, he looked through the narrow gap between glass and fabric, wincing as the morning sun hit his eye. He repeated the process at the other side of the window.

No sign of them.

The note for the police—or *them*—to find sat on the mantel. An identical copy rested folded inside a little plastic 35 mm film canister he'd put down the kitchen drain, blocking the plumbing. Even if the police didn't find it, the new owners would.

He picked up his suitcase and walked to the garage, the final change to the house that his beloved wife, Emme, had lived to see. He opened the connecting door with a swift motion. His eyes swept across the dim garage, checking the condition of its sole window before he entered.

The powerful old Merkur beeped an acknowledgment as he deactivated its alarm. He placed his suitcase in the boot and pushed it shut with a soft click. He popped the bonnet and picked up his attaché case from where it lay atop the fluid reservoirs, hidden there since last night. Grit smeared the weathered leather.

He climbed into the car, pulled the door closed as softly as he had the boot, and took a deep breath as he slid the key into the ignition.

Then came the temptation. Again.

Wouldn't it be easier to just chuck the contents of his attaché into the fire and wait, engine running, in the closed garage until he escaped into the sleep he so desperately needed? Oblivion. No more strange eyes watching him as he bought his groceries, no more funny looks from the police as he spoke of burglars who took nothing, no more fearful listening at each creak and crack in the old house. A younger heart might be able to summon the courage to fight them, but his old pump with its bad valve . . .

Almost too much effort to run. He resettled his glasses on his nose. No. It wasn't just his life and sanity they threatened. When he'd seen that accursed monocle, realized how near the rot had spread . . .

Reaching into his coat pocket, he pulled out his cell phone and placed it in its dashboard cradle, checked the battery indicator, and started the car. With luck, and he couldn't have expended all his share in sixty-eight years of living, he'd meet her in London before his flight. Von Croy had always spoken highly of her. Personally, Frys had always considered her to be a bit of a loose cannon, to say the least. There was no question of her talent, her knowledge, her bravery. But her methods were so . . . *unorthodox*. Those pistols she wore—and, according to the magazines, was not shy of using—he did not consider them to be the proper tools of a serious archaeologist. But now the very qualities that had caused him to view Lara Croft with suspicion had made him seek her out for help.

The electric garage door answered to the sun-visor button.

He didn't wait for it to open all the way but backed out as soon as he thought he had clearance. But he thought wrong. He tore away the plastic weather strip at the bottom of the garage door, heard splintered wood scrape across the roof of his car as he backed out and turned around in the gravel driveway.

The glitter of sun on a windscreen down the road panicked him. A sedan was coming from the north. He forgot about shutting the garage door again as he backed around and shifted into drive, then stomped on the accelerator. Gravel flew as his tires spun. He fishtailed at the end of the driveway and knocked over the white-painted rural delivery postbox with “Whistlecrack House” painted in green, friendly script on each side.

A silver roadster appeared in the road south of his driveway, pulling out from cover as it moved to block the narrow mountain road. The driver stared straight at him from under a cloth cap, daring him to smash into the side of the little sports car. Frys swerved into the leafless bushes the little car had been concealed behind and barreled straight through, then swerved back onto the road that snaked along the side of the fells.

The sedan and the silver roadster were right behind him. With a burst of speed, the roadster shot ahead, coming around his right side too quickly for Frys to do anything but swerve into the gravel it kicked up from the slender verge. Then it was past him. Its brake lights flared, and he stomped on his own brakes as the sedan pulled next to him, the sound of its tires like the yowling of an alley cat. He dragged the Merkur against the mountainside, caught a flash of the sedan driver’s pox-scarred cheek in the second before his air bag deployed, smacking him in the face and flipping his glasses off the back of his head.

Fighting dizziness, Frys clawed the white mass of the air bag down, saw blurred images of men getting out of the sedan and roadster. One coming around his side of the car carried a tire iron . . . or perhaps a gun. It was impossible to tell without his specs.

There was still a way out.

He shifted the car into reverse, ignored the horrible squealing from the left front tire, and floored it. *Bang!* He jumped, unsure if the noise had been a gunshot or a tire exploding. But the car was still moving, and he was still alive . . . He held the steering wheel purposefully straight, directing the Merkur across the road and off the steep mountainside.

Life does save its best jokes for last, Professor Stephen Frys (*emeritus*) thought again as the car began to slide down the hill to the discordant tune of the suspension tearing itself to bits. Then it tipped and rolled over backwards and began to tumble. It occurred to him that he hadn't gripped his attaché case to his chest, and he groped for it blindly. But then a hard *whump*, like a cricket bat striking the back of his head, brought the oblivion he'd rejected only moments before, back in the garage.

2

Lara Croft rose out of the water with her guns up and ready. She wore her usual shoreline training gear: a torso-covering dry suit, surf shoes, her two-gun rig, and a radio-mike headset that allowed short-range communication in three ounces of ear-fitted plastic.

With one addition.

A hard plastic shell clung around her hips like an over-sized black fanny pack. Two short crablike arms with socket ends extended forward from the shell to her hip points.

The December Irish Sea air hit her like a slap. She inhaled; the seawater in the tide pool she'd swum through had left an iron taste, almost bloodlike, in her mouth, thanks to the wash from all the rusting metal lying about the pierside. Gantries and loaders dating back to before the Great War loomed all around this coastal piece of postindustrial Lancashire.

She squelched through the mud under barnacle-encrusted pilings, lost her footing, recovered, spotted a plastic keg with a large "4" spray-painted on it.

The Heckler & Koch USP Match pistol muzzles angled in toward the number, blasted out their .45-caliber staccato.

The ejected cartridge cases hissed as they struck the wet mud. The fléchette shells did their job, fragmenting into a dozen lethal slivers on impact. Plastic splinters flew out the rear of the keg.

"Four down," she said into the radio mike as she holstered her guns.

She made for a wooden ladder, climbed it. She peered over the top, studied the abandoned wharf. Well, not quite abandoned. The Special Air Service and the Royal Marines used it for training. Sometimes they let her breathe some of its Irish Sea air for weapons training. Lady Croft was a generous giver to funds that supplemented the income of the relatives of men who never came home from missions that could never be publicly acknowledged.

A rusted corrugated shed sat atop a pallet in the middle of the wharf. A "5" the height of a surfboard was painted on its side, facing her.

No challenge doing it the easy way. Using the strength in her inner thighs, she let go and hung on to the ladder by main force, pressing her knees outward against the sides of the ladder. She unholstered her guns.

"VADS: double nitro," she said into the mike.

The new voice-activated, variable ammunition delivery system on her back recognized it was being addressed and responded. As it should: she'd spent enough hours patiently "training" it. It clicked softly as the tops of new magazines appeared in the arm sockets. She pressed the ambidextrous magazine release levers, ejected the empty fléchette magazines, and lowered her guns to her hip points where the fresh magazines waited in the crab arms. The fresh magazines slammed into the USP grips with a satisfying *tschuck*.

She aimed her custom guns, though if the shells did what Djbril promised, aiming wasn't *that* critical. She squeezed the triggers.

The shells hit, exploding on impact, blowing fist-sized holes in the shed. She kept firing, enjoying the thunderous sound of the explosions magnified by the interior of the shed. When the military-only twelve-round magazines were empty, there was nothing left of the shed but its roof, resting in the torn metal nailed to the pallet.

"Five down," she said into her headset.

"Was that a chuffin' rush, or what?" crackled Djbril's voice in reply.

"No comment. We're not done yet."

"Into the rabbit hole, Alice."

An old warehouse stood at the other end of the pier. She holstered her guns and trotted along the wharf toward it.

It was dark inside.

"VADS: left *lumen.*" VADS didn't care if she used Latin or Swahili; it was all the same to the computer . . . as long as Lara Croft was the one doing the talking. A magazine popped out at her left hip point. She slammed the gun down on it. Brought the H&K back up, released the safety with her trigger finger—one of the reasons she loved this pistol was its custom functionality, the right/left operation of both the safety and magazine eject without a change in grip—and did a scan of the junk-filled warehouse from catwalk to rat traps.

She got out of the door frame fast, checked three and nine o'clock. The old windows were boarded over and covered with tarps that the SAS put up and took down to simulate a variety of lighting conditions.

"Long way off yet, Croft."

She fired the illumination rounds into the darker nooks and crannies of the unlighted warehouse, jumped to the side as something whizzed past, and leapt over a pile of scrap, still firing.

Basically chemical paintballs, the illumination rounds splattered phosphorescent dye where they hit. Looking for suspicious outlines, she sprinted across the cracked concrete.

Lara slid under a stack of rusting oil drums just as a second rubber bullet fired from somewhere on the catwalk hit where she had stood an instant before.

"Nice try," she said.

"Keeping you on your toes, Croft."

She looked through a hole in the oil drum shielding her, saw a pile of loading pallets with an old rag painted with a "6" taped to it.

Four more illumination shells went up into the catwalk. Djbril probably had hid himself somewhere up there; it was both too obvious and too good a place to watch her from.

"VADS: right pyro, left rubber."

The magazines popped out, ready for loading into her pistols. She slid on her back, working herself behind a pile of scrap metal, the smooth, hard plastic of the harness gliding over the floor.

Rubber bullets bounced off the wall behind her.

"If I can see you, I can kill you, Croft."

She rolled behind an old stripped forklift up on blocks, fired her right pistol into the pallets. Phosphorus glowed bright in the bullet holes, and the pallets began to burn. She removed the VADS, wiggled under the forklift.

"Okay, Croft," Djbril whispered over the radio. "You got it. Draw."

She waited. Smoke billowed up. She brought her head and left arm out from under the forklift. She heard a cough from the catwalk. It came from an old rug and a portable radio. The three glowing red points of the tritium TRU-DOTs on her USP Match sights floated over the fabric. She fired rubber bullets into a suspicious, foot-shaped bulge.

"Bugger!" the voice in her ear said. "Lay off, luv."

"What was that about a draw?"

"Yuh got me, pilgrim," came the mock–John Wayne drawl.

"I respect your confidence in your workmanship. But supposing this contraption had put armor-piercing in?"

"I'd need a new ankle."

Her strictly-off-the-books armorer threw the top of the rug off his body, unloaded his rifle, slung it over his shoulder, and slid down the access ladder sailor style, using his feet to slow himself.

"Thought for sure you'd go up the ladder first to get a look around," he said, pulling back a navy blue balaclava and taking off his long-sleeved gloves. "I could have had you in the doorway, you know."

"Knowing exactly when and where your target's going to show helps," she said, crawling out from under the forklift and getting to her feet.

"You could have found another entrance. The roof is full of them."

"I'm on a schedule today."

"Oh, yeah. The lecture. Sorry to keep you waiting, professor."

It had been a long day. Djbril had started before dawn with a detailed briefing on the new gun system, how the VADS held and distinguished a dozen clips with whatever mix of ammunition she chose. He showed her how to open the "turtle shell" to replace the magazines in their racks that led to the crab-arm "feeders" and the control unit, a tiny pocket PC built into the buckle-cover at the front of the harness. Wireless technology linked the microphone headset to the control unit. He had created VADS almost from scratch, with a little assistance from some college engineering students and a twelve-thousand-pound check from Lady Croft.

The bullets themselves came in six flavors: armor-piercing for hard targets, fléchette for soft targets you wished to turn into sausage stuffing, pure explosive, incendiary, illumination, and less-lethal rubber bullets. For maximum destruction, he recommended a mix of armor-piercing, explosive, and incendiary. "A killer cocktail," he'd said that morning, demonstrating it on a mannequin in body armor placed within an upright freezer.

The mannequin had gone into the defunct appliance looking like a stud from one of those American reality shows set on a beach resort, complete with suntan and impossibly white teeth. After twenty-four rounds, it had come out in charcoal-colored chunks.

Then he'd let Lara try out the different loads in her personal, custom-made H&K .45s. The ammunition impressed her.

At nine she took a break from gunsmithing to check her voice mail. Calls to her London office from everyone from her accountants to a retired Scottish archaeologist named Frys, who claimed to have known Von Croy, had to be answered. She had no luck reaching Dr. Frys, but got the day's other business out of the way while Djbril filled some magazines with his special ammunition.

Then Djbril had talked her into trying the VADS autoreloader. After ninety rather repetitious—and therefore tiresome—minutes mapping the software to her voice, she had tried the system out on the course.

Now she was sold.

"Wish I'd had this behind the green door."

Djbril raised an eyebrow. "What, a copper door in some vault that you—"

"Czechoslovakia. The Strahov Fortress. A biological facility."

He waited for her to say more. She didn't, so he let it drop, changing the subject.

"Well, what do you think? Will the Ministry of Defense, or better yet, the Americans, buy it? We can adapt it for battle rifles, scout-snipers—"

"Visions of defense contracts dancing in your head already?" she said, leafing through the documentation.

"It started out as a bit of a lark and a giggle, yeah, but if there's money to be made . . ."

"Think again. You'll run into a lot of 'airplanes have no military purpose or value' types, you know. Try it on your mates in the regiment. Maybe you can get someone's ear that way." She rubbed her right shoulder. She'd fired over two hundred rounds, one-handed at that, and the ache was setting in.

"You can keep the prototype," he told her. "It's the least we can do after you funded our beta. Plus, we made it to your measurements."

"And where did you get my vital statistics, I wonder? I don't post them on my CV."

Djbril brought his heel down hard enough on the concrete for Lara to feel it. He set his eyes straight forward, gave a formal salute. "Sir! Sworn to secrecy on sources and methods. Sir!"

Lara rolled her eyes. She loved military men the way she loved dogs and horses: They were noble, reliable, and very comforting to have around at times, but they had their limitations.

"I'll take the prototype, seeing as how you went to so much trouble. Wrap it up and send it to Winston at the house, would you? The documentation, too. Now I've got to run. My lecture's at seven."

He followed her to her motorcycle, a Triumph Speed Triple. It glittered silver and black in the afternoon sun, 955 cc's of warp speed.

"London in two and a half hours? That's going to be some ride, even on that."

"Two. I need to stop and wash the cordite off."

"It's your license."

She unbuckled her holsters and handed them over. Djbril looked at the scratches on the all-weather coating and the dent in the left trigger guard and clicked his tongue in disapproval. "I'll put new O-rings in while I'm at it. They don't make this variant anymore; you should take better care of them."

She needed to get out of the training rig. "You think I'd use my field pistols on experimental ammunition? That pair is safe at home."

"Good. We in the regiment would hate to see anything happen to your pair, Lara." He puckered his lips, flirting like a disco swain.

"He 'who dares' gets slapped in the face sometimes, you know."

Djbril smiled at the play on the regimental motto, *Who dares, wins*. Taken, of course, from a much older Empire's *qui audet vincit*.

* * *

"Lara Croft?" the crackling voice said over the bad connection.

"We verified it with Frys's phone," Tisdale said. He felt a migraine coming on. He stood at the Heathrow airport phone, worried at his teeth with the edge of the plastic calling card, utterly drained from the botched Frys job in Scotland.

"Lara Croft." The Prime's voice was the same monotone it had been upon hearing about the death of Professor Frys.

"Well, Croft Foundation offices," Tisdale replied.

"Same thing. Wait a moment, would you?"

Tisdale waited, looked at the cracked cell phone. The contents of Frys's briefcase were now nestled in the carry-on of a courier and would be in Peru in twenty-four hours. The Merkur had tossed both phone and briefcase onto the hillside as it rolled. He and Dohan in the roadster had stayed to investigate the wreck and phone the police to report the accident while the sedan limped off with the others. Dohan, a Scot, handled the officers smoothly while Tisdale stood silently beside him, sweating at the thought of Frys's property in the boot. When the police, having recorded all the particulars, sent them on their way, Tisdale had barely been able to light his pipe at the thought of how close he'd been to using the needle. He was a chartered accountant, albeit one with a peculiar set of interests, not some hardened drug lord used to being questioned by the police.

Moving, and occasionally hiding, money was Tisdale's forte, not car wrecks and bodies.

The Prime came back on: "You're in luck, Twenty-eight. She's in London tonight. If you move quickly, you can catch her off her guard."

The blood pounded at the back of his eyes as the headache hit full force. "What—tonight?"

"Talk to Sixty. He'll get you men."

Sixty. Egorov. The driver of the sedan. More surveillance, stolen cars, pistols, danger—and headaches. Tisdale briefly considered declining, but to do so would forfeit a position built up with years of quiet, devoted service. "How do you want her handled?" he asked.

"Alive would be better," the Prime replied. "But she can't get so much as a hint of our existence. Not until the Awakening. Then it won't matter."

Mention of the goal straightened Tisdale's spine. "I'll handle it, sir. No worries. It'll make up for the death of—"

"Forget about it. Just think about Croft. Your future position depends on how you handle her."

"Sir . . . sir?"

"Yes?" The tone suggested that the conversation should be over by now. But Tisdale had to let him know, ask for understanding.

"I've had my dreams."

"Fantastic!" More interest in the voice now. "What were they?"

"Murky. Floating. I swam, swam in and out of tunnels. Smooth-sided tunnels." Tisdale warmed to the subject; he had to pass on the vision, pure and powerful and as breathtaking as a glassful of vodka, neat. "Reminded me of one of those documentaries about the circulatory system, where they put a fiber-optic camera up someone's leg."

"Congratulations. You've taken your first step toward immortality."

"Were they like that for you?"

"Goodbye, Twenty-eight. We'll talk more after you get Croft. I don't want a call saying you've failed. Understand?"

"I understand."

Tisdale replaced the phone on its hook with a trembling hand and pocketed Frys's cell phone. His head hurt worse than ever.

3

Lara Croft's King's College lectures were always well attended. The departments closest to her area of expertise, history and classics, would have nothing to do with her—the feeling was mutual—but oddly enough, the geography department was happy to sponsor her whenever she had the time and inclination to give a talk.

The late autumn rain steamed off her hot Triumph Speed Triple as she detached her hard-shell carryall from the back of the bike and hurried onto the Strand Campus. The carryall held a change of clothes and her computer.

She strode past the two Greek statues, their marble eyes seeming to look with disapproval upon her wet biking attire as she went to the information booth to verify her room number.

She was late. A tight-mouthed woman who introduced herself as Miss Wallesley reminded her of that fact. Lara apologized as best as she could, then asked if there was a place that she could change clothes.

"*Hmphf.* I should hope so. Follow me, please."

The women's WC outside the theater gave her room to change and warm up her computer while Miss Wallesley stood with crossed arms outside. Lara reorganized her hair before putting on a blouse and did her best to smooth out the wrinkles in the lightweight sports jacket she unrolled.

Her shoulders ached from all the shooting she'd done and the long ride into London. The Triumph was a lightning-quick bike, but the stiff suspension had taken its toll. She tied a Sudanese scarf loosely about her throat—its sandy color complemented the greens and browns in the sports coat nicely—and surveyed the results.

Now she could get away with clomping about in high boots. She looked more Ralph Lauren than Road Warrior.

"We're *fifteen minutes* past now," Miss Wallesley reminded her as she left the WC.

She handed the woman her motorcycle jacket.

If anyone knew the value of time, it was Lara Croft. Her life had hung on seconds more times than she cared to think about. And if there was one thing being a tiger's whisker from death had taught her, it was to filter the essentials of life from the trivial.

Tonight was trivial.

Besides, she'd already apologized, and the participants knew she was on the way.

She strode to the front of the lecture hall to a smattering of applause. The shell-shaped hall was a mixture of old and new: new technology grafted onto blackboards, stairs, and walls as old as the college itself. The audience, ranked stadium style in their fixed plastic chairs, was a mixture of college students and adults. The background chatter quieted as soon as she entered.

Miss Wallesley, for all her fussiness, knew how to set up a computer. Lara worked the presentation slides from her lectern, going point by point through her lecture. Geography, history, ethnography, some interesting myths of the Sudanese . . .

She knew from her recent experiences with the Mahdists that some of those myths weren't myths at all. But she kept those memories to herself.

"—and let me end this presentation with a plea. Though it sounds like something from two centuries ago, the Sudan, and indeed the entire horn of Africa, is still a center of what's left of the international slave trade, not to mention the trafficking in women that still takes place from Indochina to the European Union. Great Britain led the world once in a crusade to lift the burdens forced on innocent shoulders. I ask that your voices persuade her to do so again."

She turned to her final slide, a photograph she'd placed after her summary. It was a telephoto of a line of black figures—men, women, and children chained neck-to-neck in bonds that had changed little since the days of the Romans—being marched in a line down a dirt road in Somalia.

The students looked at the picture with frowning, lip-biting, brow-furrowing concern. She would have preferred anger. Of course, they hadn't her experience.

The question-and-answer session was short. There was only one adolescent crack about her love life, instantly booed down by the rest of the audience. She fended off a question about the Paris "Monstrum" murders with a frown and a prepared spiel: "Much of the press is wrong, as usual. I had the misfortune of being the only name involved in the investigation that returned a few photos and hits from the archive searches, so my involvement was—how should I put this?—'sexed up,' to use the current idiotic idiom. Apologies to any of the Fourth Estate present, of course.

"Any more geographical questions? No? Then I thank King's College, Strand Campus, the geography department, and all of you for your invitation and interest."

The applause was warm, which she preferred to enthusiastic. Enthusiastic was for celebrities—and she hated celebrity.

Naturally, a few diehards clustered about the lectern as she packed up. Are you going to write a book? What's the most beautiful place you've ever been? Where's your favorite place to dive? Are you going to accept the invitation to try out for Britain's biathlon team?

The last she answered with something other than a shrug.

"If I were to be an Olympian, I'd want to be in a combined event. You get to compete against men. But I don't have the time, or a good enough horse." She noticed a woman with a camel hair coat over her arm tape-recording her answer, but before she could say anything, a magazine was thrust toward her.

"Please, Lady Croft, would you sign this?" A pretty girl who looked a bit too young for college, Lara judged from her accent that she was a Hong Kong native, was holding out a road rally magazine with a shot of Lara at the end of her punishing race from Tierra del Fuego to Alaska.

"Where did you dig up this old thing?" Lara asked. The magazine was from six years ago.

"I'm a huge fan," the girl gushed. "I bought it on the Internet."

The idea of having fans struck Lara as a bit absurd—she wasn't a pop star, after all—but people sometimes picked strange idols. She signed the magazine, and the girl snatched it out of her hands with a squeal and rushed off.

Next up was the woman with the camel hair coat and the

tape recorder. "Lara Croft?" she asked with an American accent. "I'm Heather Rourke. It's great to finally meet you."

Heather Rourke was close to Lara in height and frame. While she was not a beauty, her immaculate makeup made the most of her blue eyes and Celtic cheekbones.

"Yes, Heather? I hope you enjoyed the lecture. I have a rule against tape-recording, however. As I believe I stated clearly at the outset."

The woman looked disappointed, as though she'd expected to be recognized. "Yes, but surely that doesn't apply to me."

"Why wouldn't it?"

"Haven't you received my letters and calls?" she asked in turn.

Lara searched her memory. *Rourke . . . Rourke . . .* "You're some kind of journalist, aren't you? With a magazine?"

"I've written for several. And appeared on TV. I was hoping to do a story on you."

"Sorry, not interested. I do apologize for not recognizing your name. My reading only occasionally gets past the fifteenth century, and I rarely watch television."

"Perhaps we could—"

"I'm afraid not. I haven't had much luck with journalists."

"I'd still like—"

But Lara had already turned to the next person in line. The press frenzy following Von Croy's murder had only made her more determined than ever to steer clear of reporters.

The man she had turned to in escaping Heather Rourke was built like a security wall. He wore a cable-knit sweater over a turtleneck. His chest and shoulders resembled a modern art sculpture made out of cannonballs and structural steel pillars. Shaggy—not artfully shaggy, but wet-weather-on-an-oil-rig shaggy—honey blond hair brushed Nordic features. He had black leather gloves on his hands and a matching black waist pouch large enough to carry a knife or a gun.

Lara felt a tiny alarm go off in her nervous system and involuntarily tensed. Only men who didn't want to leave fingerprints wore gloves indoors.

But his soft blue eyes didn't belong to a killer.

"Please, Miss Croft," he said. He was bulky, and awkward about it. She realized he hadn't been at the lecture; a man his size would have been impossible to miss.

His accent placed him as Norwegian or Danish. Not her night to talk to Londoners, evidently. There was a stiffness about him; he held his arms pressed to his sides like a soldier standing to attention.

"No way!" a student said.

"Quick, get a picture. Lara Croft and the Borg. Beyond cool," another added.

A flash went off. She was tired and hungry; everything was going out of balance and fuzzy.

"I am Nils Bjorkstrom. May we speak together?" the giant asked. He had anxious anguish in his eyes. "It is important."

She'd never heard of him. He looked stolid, but didn't have the feel of a military type, and no agency would employ him as a field operative. He stood out too much.

"Let's step into the hall."

"XXXtreme rules!" one of the students yelled as she shut the door behind them.

The hallway was no good either, with students stepping up and back like nervous pigeons.

"Lady Croft, would you sign my program?" a very correct jacket-and-tie type asked.

Lara signed it absently. Another college boy wanted a picture with her.

“I’m sorry, the flashes are giving me a headache,” she said. She shrugged away the students and ducked around the corner that was the Norwegian and pulled him to the stairs. He had strong arms; they felt like banisters.

“What is it, Mr. Bjorkstrom?”

“An hour of your time is all I ask.”

He didn’t look like he was selling anything, and the marketing stick-at-noughts who wanted her to be pictured with their dreck always brandished presentation folios. “What is this about?”

With some difficulty, he retrieved a photograph from his waist pouch. Lara realized that the stiffness she’d noticed in his arms came from the fact that they were both artificial. He had artificial hands, the thumb and forefinger working like pliers within the leather gloves.

Heather Rourke chose that moment to appear at the top of the stairs, card in hand. Lara glared at her, and the journalist shrank away. When she glanced back, she was looking at a photograph of the man before her standing on an Alpine prominence with his arm—flesh and blood, by the look of it—around . . .

Lara felt an emotional stab. A piece of her youth stood grinning into the camera. Blond hair, high cheekbones, frosted blue eyes, and creamy white skin red from windburn, it could only be Alison Jane Harfleur. She looked up at the man. “You’re a friend of Alison’s? I haven’t seen her in years. How is she?”

“I do not know; Ajay has disappeared,” he said, using her old nickname. “I am afraid she may be in danger. Please, Miss Croft. I need your help.”

Lara nodded. Ajay, her old friend, in danger . . . “We could grab a bite, if you like, and discuss this in more detail.”

He smiled with a nice set of teeth, whitened in the American fashion. "I do not know London well, but I saw some places between the tube station and here."

"London food's terrible unless you know where to eat. I'll give you a ride, if you don't mind a motorcycle."

"I will follow you. I have a car—specially made."

The ice broken, Lara let her curiosity out.

"What's Ajay plunged herself into now?"

"If I knew for certain, I would go myself and not . . . trouble you. She is my intended . . . my fiancée."

Good for you, Alison. He seems an interesting man . . . I bet your parents hate him!

"Congratulations, Mr. Bjorkstrom."

He winced. "Please, Nils will do. My friends call me Borg. Something of a joke. I do not mind, and I would be honored to call Lara Croft my friend."

"Then it's Lara, Borg." She offered her hand.

"No, please."

She kept her hand out. Finally, he extended the artificial limb. She grasped the gloved fingers and they shook.

"Now that the formalities are over, let's eat."

Heather Rourke watched her prospect leave the building with the himbo. Correction: celebrity himbo.

If Lady Croft thought Heather Rourke could be brushed off so easily, she would soon learn otherwise. She spotted one of the students who'd cheered for "the Borg" and taken pictures; he looked to be no more than seventeen. She checked her hair and lipstick in the door glass, put on her best smile, and approached the young man.

Nils Bjorkstrom followed Lara in his car as she made her way through London's eternal traffic stoppages. As she drove,

Lara turned the name, the association, over in her mind. Ajay. Alison Jane Harfleur. She'd entered Gordonstoun a year behind Lara.

Like Lara, Alison had been something of an outsider, but while in Lara's case it was because of her interest in archaeology and history, in Alison's it was because of her family's financial circumstances. The Harfleurs were an old name without any of the old money, reduced to living in a decrepit Regency manor house. What funds they had went toward getting their only child a proper education.

The friendship had begun when Lara returned for her second year. At mealtimes, while the other girls chatted about Saint-Tropez or Marbella or Corfu, sixteen-year-old Lara spoke of Angkor Wat and showed off a backpack she'd discovered there. On a corpse!

"Not even Coach," Elizabeth Lloyd-Patterson sniffed.

"Where were you in August, Alison?" another girl asked.

The Harfleur girl lowered her eyes. "Back home."

"Oh," Elizabeth said, attaching immense significance and condescension to the single syllable.

"Is your mother feeling better?" Lara broke in. She remembered Alison mentioning that her mother had been in the hospital for a foot operation. Minor surgery, but the others didn't bother with details unless they came off a Paris runway.

Relief flooded sixteen years of keeping up appearances. "Much better. Very kind of you to ask, Lara."

Alison was interested in the backpack story, Von Croy, Angkor Wat. Lara had started calling her Ajay because there was another Allison at Gordonstoun, and in return Ajay called Lara "LC."

Lara had liked her in an older sister sort of way. She'd

known all too well what it was like to be at the bottom of a feminine pecking order. It had been the same for her when she arrived at Gordonstoun. But unlike her, Ajay lacked the spirit to fight back. When Ajay—something of a late bloomer—burst into a woman's figure, Lara had happily donated some of the "prissy" outfits she hated to Ajay.

The friendship wasn't all one-sided. Ajay was brilliant at chemistry and knew how to parse a literature paper to garner top marks. Lara didn't bother with flowery phraseology; she tended to say what she thought in three brief paragraphs. Drove her lecturers batty. *What do you mean, "Hamlet whines like a desperate, self-centered drip," Miss Croft?*

Lara had exchanged letters and an occasional call with Ajay after she'd moved on to finishing school in Switzerland, but they'd seen less of each other. Lara spent her summers in Greece, Italy, and Egypt. Once in a while they reunited, but they were like two allies who no longer shared a joint war, speaking more of old times than the future. What Ajay provided for Lara as she matured was an appreciative audience for her vacation exploits, something that Lord Croft went out of his way to deny her.

The girls were reunited when Ajay won a scholarship from a science foundation and joined Lara at the same Swiss finishing school that Lara so despised. Lara hated to even remember its name; she had spent as much time as she could sneaking off the grounds. The skills, habits, and forms the school tried to instill had struck Lara as anachronistic. Though looking back now, she supposed she'd mellowed—a little. At least, the lessons in fencing and horsemanship that she'd taken had come in handy more than once in the years since.

Ajay had been a breath of fresh air in that stuffy atmosphere. They became roommates, and their friendship rekindled. Until Mexico.

It had seemed a simple enough trip at first, a between semesters jaunt to Cancún. The two friends had had fun in the airport, fun on the plane, fun at the hotel, and then fun on the jungle's step pyramids. But then Lara had decided to wander away from the tourist paths, looking for some Olmec burial mounds she'd seen mentioned in an old conquistador diary. Instead of burial mounds, they'd stumbled onto an airstrip with camouflaged bush hoppers.

Drug runners . . . or so they assumed. They never got near enough to the cargo to check before the shooting started. Lara had been in danger before—perhaps without quite so many bullets flying around—but she knew how to handle herself. Not so Ajay. The girl had panicked, run screaming into the jungle. It had taken Lara hours to find her. They had been lucky the drug runners hadn't found either of them first.

Back in Switzerland, Ajay started reading Lara's archaeology books, determined to redeem herself in her friend's eyes by becoming as much like Lara as she could. Ajay's precise mind, superb memory, and indefatigable energy now turned toward the arcana of lost civilizations that Lara found so fascinating. Suddenly Lara found that instead of having a friend, she had a disciple.

They'd finished school and gone their separate ways for a time. Lara had suffered her disastrous accident in the Himalayas and through it found the strength to chart her own course—even at the cost of being disowned by her father. And then Ajay had contacted her about an expedition to the Black Sea that she'd heard Lara was planning. She wanted in.

On paper, it made sense. Lara had her eye on a Sarmatian

artifact—the Pearl Breastplate. She felt a tickling affinity for the old barbarian tribe, terror of Rome's eastern frontier and allegedly the descendents of the Amazons—and Ajay could speak Russian better than she. Not only that, but Ajay had been studying archaeology and anthropology on a Cambridge Fellows scholarship, specializing in ancient Sarmatia, of all things. Lara put her memories of Mexico aside and welcomed her old friend on board.

Together, they pieced together a map from details in an old Roman geography treatise by Strabo, then headed into the Caucasus Mountains, looking for the ruins of an all-but-forgotten Sarmatian temple. Despite the trouble in Chechnya, it was a strangely peaceful expedition. Lara didn't use her guns once, though she kept them ready beneath the cloaks and scarves of the native dress. The temple turned out to be mostly collapsed and emptied on the surface, but it extended deep below the ground and required a good deal of spelunking to explore. Not a problem for Lara.

But once again, Ajay fell short. Lara's would-be protégé managed to get lost while crawling through the catacombs. First her light had failed. Then she burned herself with a flare and dropped it down a fissure. Finally, alone in the dark, she hadn't had the sense to use the backup chemical lights that Lara had demanded she carry, and instead had started screaming.

By the time Lara dragged her out, Ajay was quiet, ashen-faced, and trembling with fear and humiliation. But moments later, she insisted on going back in. Lara, who had been ready to send her home, melted a little at that: She liked a "get back on the horse" attitude and was impressed with Ajay's courage. But the rest of the expedition turned out to be as tiresome as a date gone wrong. Lara spent too much time nannying Ajay and not enough thinking about the temple. She felt as though she'd missed something.

It turned out she had. The Pearl Breastplate ended up in the hands of Larson and Pierre, who'd followed her and done a more thorough job of investigating nooks and crannies. The only souvenirs Lara brought home were a Russian foot fungus and a dispirited partner.

Shortly afterwards, just prior to leaving on a trip to Peru, she'd taken Ajay to dinner at an Italian restaurant near Cambridge and did her best to explain why the two of them wouldn't be working together in the field again.

"You're being unfair," Ajay said, pushing her spaghetti Bolognese away.

"Unfair? Because I care whether a friend of mine lives or dies?"

"It's my life to risk."

"You lost your head, Ajay. Just like you did in Mexico."

"That was different."

"Was it? Next time it could get us both killed."

"Then I'll work on my own, so I'm the only one in jeopardy."

"Don't, Ajay. You've so many talents that put you head and shoulders above the crowd. Above me, if you're thinking this is some kind of rivalry."

"Not a rivalry. Partners don't compete."

"There's lots of places to do fieldwork safely. If you think you have to contribute by getting dirty, I can name—"

"I want the same thing you do. To know what no one else knows, to touch something no one else has touched since Pharaoh dreamed of his fat cattle eating the lean."

Lara startled at that. "That was in my journal. You read my journal?"

"No . . . I—"

Lara's eyes made her admit the truth.

"I'm sorry, Lara. After you pulled me out of the dark and started going back in without me . . . I needed to see what you thought of me. If you still respected me."

"Chase your own dreams, Ajay. Chasing mine is"—Lara caught herself on the verge of accusing Ajay of a personality disorder—"dangerous."

"You were about to use another word," Ajay said. "What was it? Sick? Is that what you think of me, Lara?"

"I think it will be better for both of us if we work separately, that's all."

"Fine." Ajay pushed back her chair and stood, throwing her napkin down on the table. "I know when I'm not wanted." She turned her back and stalked out of the restaurant.

Lara hadn't seen Ajay, or heard from her, since.

Lara drove into Soho and parked the bike in a Tottenham Court alley off of Frith Street. Borg parked in a garage nearby. They met outside a pair of glass doors that read "Little Italy." As they entered, upbeat jazz came over the restaurant's speakers.

"Lady Croft," the maître d' said, beaming. A few patrons leaned to get a better look at the newcomers.

"The back room, Johnny," Lara said.

"Of course." He led them up a flight of stairs.

Little Italy's close-walled back room looked as though it should have organized-crime wiseguys leaning over their plates of squid and pasta beneath the closely hung pictures of Italian landscapes and doorways. Instead, well-dressed couples chatted over savory-smelling dishes and bottles of wine. Beneath some of the tables, bags from London's famous department stores bulged with holiday purchases.

"The tuna's really good," Lara suggested as they sat at a table tucked into a private corner. "The house Chianti is one of the best you can get in London . . . or so I'm told. I don't drink alcohol myself."

"Red Chianti, please," Borg responded as their waiter asked if they would have anything to drink. The waiter cocked an eyebrow at Lara. She ordered a seltzer water and lime.

"Dinner is my treat," she said, noting the look of alarm that had passed over Borg's features as he glanced at the menu.

"Thank you," he said with a smile. "Ajay always said you were generous. Her parents thought a great deal of you."

"I wasn't the influence Lord Harfleur hoped I'd be."

The waiter returned with their drinks and poured a taste of the wine into Borg's glass. The big man took a sip, then nodded. "Very good."

The waiter filled Borg's glass. He took their dinner order, then left them alone.

"What's happened to Ajay?" Lara asked. "What is it that you're afraid of?"

Borg emptied his glass in one swallow and refilled it from the bottle; there was, Lara noticed, a rough but very real grace in the way he manipulated the mechanisms that served as his hands. "I met Ajay when she came to me for training. I was already in the papers; 'extreme' sports were becoming popular. I was known for climbing, base jumps, and some cave exploration. *Die Welt* did an extensive article. She found me through it. There I was, in Iceland, at a photo shoot for some hiking boots, and suddenly she is there.

"She was so upfront and brash. 'Teach me to do everything

you can do,' she said. It was before my accident, when I could do what few others could. At first, I laughed. She asked so many questions. Rappelling, oxygen gear, altitude disorders, lighting for scuba cave dives."

"Learning about a subject was never difficult for Ajay," Lara said.

"Oh, but she worked hard."

"So you took her on."

"More than that." His eyes became wet. "I fell in love. How many women travel to Iceland just to acquire a personal trainer? How many women show such determination to improve?"

Determination . . . or obsession? Lara wondered. It wasn't the first time she'd asked herself this question with regard to Ajay. Of course, there were times when she'd wondered the same thing about herself.

"We became . . . treasure hunters. She determined . . . was determined to restore her family fortune through valuables found this way. I thought it was just a dream, but in my love for her said nothing.

"We did not meet with success. We could hardly cover our expenses, Lara. Though we had many good times together. Until . . ."

"Your accident?"

"We were on a climb in Bulgaria. She was convinced of the presence of a cliffside treasure trove from the days of Darius. I was in the lead; she was tied to me. She slipped. I anchored, pulled her up. She was winded, so I did something foolish. I unhooked from her, knowing that if I lost my footing on the next lateral we would both go down. I was driving another piton to help her across the lateral when I slipped. I landed badly, compound fractures in both arms. We abandoned the climb, but because of my injuries, it took us two days to get to help. The Bulgarian doctors . . . they meant well, but all they knew to do was remove the limbs. I did not know until I awoke."

Lara could imagine what was left unsaid. The agony of walking with broken limbs, the smell of sepsis as the flesh died, waking up in some provincial hospital where they washed the dressings and reused them. Waking up without arms. And always wondering if Ajay could have said something. Done something. Stopped the doctors from performing the unnecessary amputations . . . if they were unnecessary.

There was a moment of silence as the waiter brought their food. Lara dove into her chicken piccata with an appetite. Borg filled his glass again, then continued. "I despaired, but Ajay helped me through it. The story made me more famous than ever in the media. A fund was started in my name. I had a job as a, what is it they say, color commentator for an American extreme sports cable channel. They paid for arms, special arms, as a stunt, and filmed me using them. I traveled and narrated other shows they did. They called me 'the Borg.' I saw less of Ajay, but I thought I could make enough money with television or a book to help her family. But while I did this, she became involved with *them*."

"Them?" Lara's psychic antennae quivered at the inflection.

"A group. Also treasure hunters, I think. Thought. Now I am not sure. I have had only one conversation with Ajay about them. She disappeared soon after. I think they first contacted her when I was back in Norway, in a special hospital for physical therapy. Or perhaps she contacted them. She sought out treasure-hunting jobs. I know she did some work in the Mideast."

"If my fiancé were in hospital, I'd stay a little closer," Lara said, and instantly regretted it.

Borg averted his eyes, poured the last of the wine from the bottle.

"So she just disappeared?" Lara asked.

"Four months ago," said Borg. "I tried to find her myself, but I failed. I quit at the cable channel to look for her; they now say 'breach of contract' and will pay me no more money. I know the name and reputation of Lara Croft—most of us in these sports do—and I know you once were a friend to Ajay, so I have come to you. You have perhaps contacts and sources I do not have. Also, there is one other door that is not open to me; I think you can get through it."

"What door is that?"

"Lord Harfleur's."

Lara raised an eyebrow.

"He did not approve of me," Borg confessed. "He wished for Ajay to marry into money and society. I have little of either, by his measure, even with the television job. Our engagement is secret from him."

"You think he knows where she is?"

"She wrote him always, wherever she went."

"Then why not you?"

His artificial thumb and forefinger clicked closed on the stem of the wine glass again. "Her mind has been turned against me by this . . . group. Not a religion, not a political society. They are, what is the word . . . theosophists. Mythologists."

"I thought you said they were treasure hunters."

"That, too."

"Do they have a name?"

"I heard her call them the 'Many' once."

"The Many?"

"That is what she said."

"So that's what the Scientologists are calling themselves these days."

"No. The 'Many' is an old"—it took him a moment to find the word—"cult."

"I've never heard of them, and I know a lot about old cults."

Borg shrugged. He emptied his glass. "I was away too much. Perhaps if I had seen her more, she would have confided in me." A maudlin tone had crept into Borg's voice, and he was beginning to slur his words.

Lara tried to keep things on subject. "You still haven't explained why you think she's in danger."

"The Many have done something to her, Lara. Brainwashed her. Or perhaps kidnapped her. The Ajay I know would not just disappear."

The Ajay Lara knew had done exactly that. But she didn't tell Borg. Instead, she said, "Suppose I go to see Lord Harfleur, and it turns out that Ajay has written to him after all, and those letters are perfectly normal? Suppose they show that she joined the Many of her own free will and is happy to be there? What then?"

"Then I will leave her in peace," Borg said, though Lara could see the pain it cost him to say so. "But I do not think you will find that."

"The 'Many,' " Lara mused, leaning back in her chair. She was tired, sore. "It's late, Borg. After midnight."

He stirred a bit at that. "I did not mean to keep you out so late. I have talked too much. Please, if you decide to help, contact me at my hotel."

"Not so fast," said Lara. "You're in no condition to drive anywhere. When I'm in town this late, I usually stay overnight at my office. It's nearer than your hotel, and there's a couch you can use."

A near-freezing mist flowed through London's streets, creating halos around the streetlights. Lara pulled her motorcycle into the alley behind the Mayfair Croft Trust offices and parked it at the back. Borg unclasped his arms from about her waist and dismounted from the bike. He'd actually apologized outside the restaurant as he'd clasped his prosthetic limbs around her, as though they were something to be ashamed of.

Lara unstrapped her hard-sided case from the back of the bike and steered Borg, who was unsteady on his feet, out of the alley. A taxi crawled along the street, its headlamps slowly sweeping by as Lara guided Borg along the elegant iron railings that lined the sidewalk and the small front yards of the townhomes that had stood here since the eighteenth century.

Coping with her case, keys, and a slightly drunk, melancholy dinner companion prevented Lara from noticing anything amiss until the last second. She heard the click of a car door, and suddenly two men appeared from the clipped shrubbery to either side of the white-painted entrance to her office.

"Someone wants to speak to you," a pockmarked man said in a heavy Russian or Eastern European accent. He held a gun close to his side, pointed right at Lara. Next to him, a bronze-skinned man, spindly as a chimney sweep's brush, gripped a pistol tightly, as though afraid it might jump out of his hand.

Lara heard a step behind her and turned her head. A black, classic-style London taxi was waiting at the curb. A good-looking man, face pale and strained, held the door open. Lara looked inside the cab, saw handcuffs resting on the seat. The driver was a large but indistinct shape.

"Lara Croft," the pale man said. Like the others, he, too, held a gun. His grip on it was ominously shaky. "Please get into the car. And your friend."

Borg sagged against the rail, breathing hard and gulping. Lara wondered for a moment if he was having a heart attack.

"We don't need him. Put him down," the pockmarked Russian said.

Time slowed as the spindly man raised his gun. Lara readied herself to spring on him, wondering if the bullet from the Russian's gun would kill her before she reached him.

The Russian struck aside the gun barrel with his free hand. "No, *zjelob*. Knock him. In the head. With your gun."

The spindly man took a bowlegged step toward Borg, gun raised high to strike the sagging Norwegian.

A torrent, a waterfall, a tsunami of Chianti-scented vomit poured out of Borg and splattered across sidewalk and the splindly man, whose face took on a look of sheer horror.

Grimacing, the Russian stepped back to keep Borg's vomit off his shoes. Lara acted. She bowled her case at the Russian with a quick underhand throw. His gun fired with a bang and a flash. The case deflected the bullet, then bowled into the shooter's stomach, knocking him off balance. Lara was right behind.

She got a grip on the Russian's gun hand, encouraged him to let go by bringing her booted heel down hard on his instep. She caught a glimpse of the spindly figure turning his gun toward her before Borg clubbed him across the back of the head with a sweeping blow from his right artificial limb.

A knife appeared in the Russian's other hand, sprouting from his sleeve like a magician's trick flower. He slashed for Lara's throat, but she brought her shoulder up, and the motorcycle jacket absorbed most of the blade.

Lara twisted the pocket automatic, trying to wrest it from the Russian's hand. A muffled pop sounded between them, and the pockmarked man grunted. Then Lara was holding the gun, and the Russian was slowly falling to the ground. Judging by the blood that was pumping from his chest, the wound was fatal. In any case, she had neither the time nor the inclination to render assistance. Pivoting on one heel, she dropped to a crouch and pointed the gun at the pale man by the taxi door, who was trembling so badly that he looked as though raw electrical current was coursing through him. He closed his eyes and fired his gun. The crack of Lara's pistol came a split second later.

She heard his bullet whiz by her ear.

Hers struck him in the thigh.

He cried out, dropping the gun and gripping the leg as it collapsed under him.

The taxi roared off, its door hanging open, but not before Lara had memorized its license number.

Lara glanced at the spindly victim of Borg's strength, who lay stretched out on the sidewalk. His eyes gaped open, lifeless and dry.

"He is dead," Borg said, his voice no longer slurred.

"This one, too," Lara said as she quickly checked the Russian. Then she walked over to the man with the leg wound, who lay whimpering and writhing on the sidewalk. She kicked his dropped gun away, though he seemed in no condition to make a grab for it.

"Was that Urdmann behind the wheel?" she asked.

"Who?" the man groaned.

There were no witnesses to what had happened . . . at least no visible ones. Lara wondered if any eyes were peeking out through drawn curtains. A siren began to wail in the distance.

"Lancaster Urdmann."

The man turned so that his weight didn't rest on his injured leg. "Never heard of him, Croft. Three men with pistols . . . You would have done better to just get in the taxi. We'd have made it worth—" He reached into his suit coat pocket.

"Drop it," Lara ordered, aiming her pistol at his right eye. She felt blood running down her arm from where the Russian's knife had cut through her leather jacket.

"Take it easy, okay?" He produced a leather-covered notepad to which a pen was attached by a leather loop. "I'm going to write down a phone number." He removed the pen and clicked it open, but instead of writing, he stabbed downward suddenly and poked himself in the thigh with the point.

Lara kicked out, knocking the pen away.

"Too late, Croft." He looked up at her and gave an incongruous giggle. "At least the headaches will stop now." He stiffened, eyes bulging. His body jerked in one terrible spasm, spine arching above the pavement. Then he fell back and lay still.

Lara usually preferred to let dead bodies lie. The less involvement with police, inspectors, and prosecuting attorneys, the better. At least, such had always been her experience, and the recent business with Von Croy, as much farce as tragedy, hadn't exactly changed her opinion.

But this time the corpses lay on her doorstep. And there must have been eyes peeking out from behind curtains, because it wasn't long before the police arrived. As crime scene technicians and uniformed police hovered about the bodies and set up yellow crime scene tape all around, a constable escorted Lara and a sobered—if not completely sober—Borg off the sidewalk and into the Croft Trust offices: two tiny rooms and a WC, and one larger room with tall, thin windows, a cavernous old fireplace, and a long leather couch, into the comfortable embrace of which Lara and Borg gratefully sank . . . but not for long.

Lara was taken to one of the smaller rooms and questioned. She told the police everything she knew, which wasn't much. The only real clue she had was the license number of the taxi, and she had no reason to hide it. At last she was allowed back into the larger room, where she found Borg stretched out on the couch, sound asleep under the watchful gaze of the constable. She sat at the big desk from which Gwenn, her sole full-time employee—an ambitious Welsh woman raising a three-year-old daughter while studying for an M.B.A.—ran the day-to-day operations of the Croft Trust.

After no more than ten minutes, a uniformed Special Branch man with an expression that would have won him a role in a commercial for indigestion medication came stomping into the room. He removed his checkered hat with a snap, rested it atop a clipboard, and held it in place with a thumb. He nodded at the constable, then at Lara.

"Lady Croft."

She got to her feet. "Captain Dools." She was surprised to see Dools. He'd been peripherally involved in the investigation of Von Croy's murder, but his beat was international terrorism, not street crime, however bloody. "Am I under arrest?"

"Not yet. Come with me," he added softly, motioning to the snoring form of Borg. "No need to wake Sleeping Beauty."

Lara followed him back into the room where she'd been questioned. There was a fold-out couch, a small desk, and a full bookcase. In one corner was a midget refrigerator and, next to it, a rolling cabinet with a coffeemaker and an electric teakettle on top. Lara decided to remind Dools, gently, that he was on her turf. "Please, Captain, have a seat. Can I get you some coffee? Tea?"

"Just some answers, please, Lady Croft. What happened out there?"

Lara perched on the edge of the couch. "My dinner companion, Mr. Bjorkstrom, and I were at the door when three men accosted us. They were armed, we weren't, but I don't think they were expecting us to fight back. Borg—Mr. Bjorkstrom, that is—killed one of the men in self-defense. The second shot himself as I struggled with him for his gun. The third man shot at me, but he missed. I didn't. At that point, the driver of the taxi decided to make himself scarce, which he did. I tried to question the third man, the one I wounded, but he stuck himself with that pen you have in an evidence bag."

Dools was scribbling notes on his clipboard. "Did you recognize any of the men who attacked you?"

"No."

He glanced up. "Perfect strangers, eh? No idea who they might be?"

"You're the ones with the computers and fingerprint kits," Lara said.

"Quite." Dools consulted his clipboard. "The cab number you gave us checked out. A missing vehicle, presumed stolen. I'm sure it's been dumped somewhere. Odd set of bodies out there. One scrawny, bowlegged, unidentified male, possibly Middle Eastern, without so much as a penny in his pocket. We've just sent his prints on to Interpol. One dermatologist's nightmare with false ID but a face that matches Anatoli Egorov, who has stops for questioning on three different EU lists. Possible terrorist connections. Then there's Eric Tisdale, the bloke who stuck himself with the poisoned pen."

"Another terrorist?" Lara asked. "He didn't strike me as the type. Seemed more like an accountant, to tell the truth."

Dools flashed a grin at her. "And so he was. An accountant with a record as clean as a hospital sheet. Like I said, an odd set. Hard to imagine them sharing a bottle of sauce at a chip stand, let alone accosting Mayfair citizenry."

"Nevertheless," Lara said, recognizing a pregnant pause when she heard one.

"That pen of yours that stuck Tisdale—"

"Captain Dools, please. It wasn't my pen, or Mr. Bjorkstrom's. Save the quiz show traps for someone who is actually guilty of a crime."

"Humor me," Dools said evenly. "There are some strange stories associated with your name floating around the Home Office, Lady Croft. The Von Croy murder wasn't the first time you've come to our attention. I hear you've left bodies on every continent save Antarctica."

"I wouldn't be so sure of that. Blowing snow can cover a lot of—"

"Spare me your wit."

"If you spare me your innuendo. What does this have to do with Her Majesty's Special Branch, Captain?"

"The streets of London are difficult enough without multiple homicides filling the papers and setting up a row." He lowered his voice. "Privately, at least as far as Egorov goes, you've just saved the taxpayers arrest, trial, and incarceration expenses. Publicly, this is the second time I've had to clean up bodies you've left scattered on the London pavement. I'd like it to be the last, or I'll find something you are guilty of and make it stick. Friends at the Home Office or no."

Lara felt the hairs on the back of her neck rise. "If it's a choice between a jail cell and a cemetery plot, Captain, I'll take the cell. Now, do you have any more questions, or should I call my attorneys?"

"Yes, there is one more thing. We recovered a body from a car wreck at the base of a mountain this morning in Scotland. The victim was a retired doctor of archaeology at the University of Glasgow, name of Frys. Turns out he called your office twice this morning before the, er, *accident*. And here's a funny coincidence: Our chartered accountant, Tisdale, had a receipt for a petrol purchase in Scotland yesterday tucked into his wallet, as well as a cellular phone belonging to the late Professor Frys in his jacket pocket. Odd, that. If you can shed any light on how the lines are connected in the triangle between you, Tisdale, and Frys, I'll think better of you."

Lara felt the room sway for just a moment as the importance of what the Special Branch man had said sank in.

A picture popped into her head, a thoughtful university publicity shot. Of course. Dr. Stephen Frys. Now she remembered him. One of Von Croy's old cronies, part of the "Dawn Club" that met for breakfast once a year, archaeologists and anthropologists and classicists, mostly. The Dawn

Club had put out a quarterly journal in the fifties and sixties, but it had died off. The surviving members still met occasionally. She'd even gone to one of their meetings as Von Croy's guest . . . and been bored to distraction.

So this wasn't an old enemy like Urdmann trying to pay off blood with blood, as she'd assumed. Frys had retired years ago, and hadn't done any actual fieldwork for decades before that. What could Frys have wanted with her? Whatever it was, it seemed that someone had been willing to kill him over it . . . and to kill her, too. Yet she had no idea what it could be.

"Care to shed any light?" Dools invited again.

"No." Lara showed him the office phone log and played back the voice mail messages. Sure enough, Dr. Frys's calls were among them.

She put the dead man's voice on speakerphone. *Miss Croft, this is an old colleague of Dr. Von Croy's, Dr. Frys. I must meet with you at your earliest convenience. Please call me back as soon as possible.*

A moment of silence. Then: "If I knew what it was about, I'd tell you, Captain."

"According to the records, Frys called twice. Where's the other message?"

She skipped ahead, but there was no other message from Frys. "He must have just hung up the second time," Lara guessed. "Look, Captain Dools, I want to find out what's going on as much as you do. More. Someone just tried to kill me. They may try again."

"We'll keep an eye on the place tonight," Dools said, passing her his card. "If you think of anything else, call me." He turned to go. "Oh, and one more thing: Don't leave the country without checking with me first. I'm putting a stop on your passport, just in case. And on your friend's, too."

Lara sighed. It might have been easier just to let herself be kidnapped.

"Coffee, tea?" she asked Borg after the police finally left. They'd photocopied Gwenn's call log. It was after 3 A.M.

"Tea, please," Borg said. The fight and the police questioning had cemented something between them: In the space of six hours, he'd gone from stranger to ally.

Borg looked at a framed print above a small sofa, a silhouette of a woman engaged in an inverted climb up a question-mark-shaped rock, literally hanging on by her fingernails. Chinese characters drawn in cloudlike brushstrokes stood out against a polarized blue sky.

He glanced at her, waiting for the light on the electric teakettle. "This is you, correct? The ponytail?"

"Correct. It's one of those business inspirational posters. You know, picture of a skier or something, an exhortation involving excellence below. This one only sold in East Asia. Milk or lemon?"

"Milk. What do the characters say?"

"Chinese proverb: *Fall down seven times, get up eight.*"

"Ajay would have liked that."

The kettle light went out. Lara made the tea. "Do sit down."

She carried the tray over, placed the cup before him. He fumbled with the sugar packet.

"I'll be mother," Lara said. In a proper English tea, whoever poured and fixed was known as "mother." She smiled at herself. Breakfast at eight in the evening in the Seychelles, teatime at three-thirty in the morning: The only consistent thing about her life was its lack of routine. "Would you like sugar?"

"I can do it myself."

Perhaps being watched made him nervous. She walked over to the desk, flicked on the computer. "Are you going to be in London long?"

"I have taken too much of your time. I will drive back to my hotel as soon as I have finished the tea."

"You're not in any state to drive, Nils," she said. "You're staying right here, on the sofa."

"I do not wish to deprive you of your bed . . ."

"You're not. There's a fold-out couch in the other room. So that's settled. Tomorrow I'll drive out to the Harfleur House and see what I can find out about Ajay. By the way, you handled yourself well out there. Vomiting was an inspiration."

Borg winced, and his face turned bright red. "I'm not used to having guns pointed at me. I was scared out of my senses. And the wine . . . I apologize."

"Apologize nothing," she said. "You saved our lives."

Borg sipped his tea. "Those men. Alive one moment, and then dead. So fast. A friend of mine died once when we BASE jumped, but that was different. It was an accident, and I did not actually see it. Just his body, afterward. Now I've killed a man. I've killed someone. Will they arrest me?"

"I doubt it. If Dools was going to arrest either one of us, he would have done it already."

"You do not seem upset, Lara," Borg observed. "Have you killed men before?"

"I have," she said after a moment. "But I take no pleasure in it. We both acted in self-defense, Nils. Try to remember that. They would have killed us without hesitation."

"I know. But still, taking the life of a fellow human being, even a criminal . . . It is hard to bear."

"It is," Lara agreed. "But would you prefer that it was easy?"

"No," said Borg. "I would not."

"Neither would I," said Lara. "Now, let's see if we can get some sleep."

4

Ajay's family may have fallen on hard times, but Harfleur House still possessed a certain aloof grandeur. It stood behind a line of smaller, but somehow more ostentatious, houses; at some point, the Harfleurs had sold much of the lands of their estate, and only some hedges now separated the old country society from the new. The narrow windows at the front of the house, three rows of them, and the slightly higher square turrets at either end, put Lara in mind of one of Lord Nelson's battleships. It wouldn't have surprised her to see cannon emerge from hidden gun ports.

Lara had risen early that morning to find Borg already awake. He'd wanted to come with her to the Harfleurs, but Lara thought that would be counterproductive, given the feelings of Ajay's father. Borg had reluctantly agreed. Then Lara had called her usual car service and arranged for transportation to Harfleur House. She owned several cars, garaged at her aunt's old mansion and in London for her frequent trips in and out of Heathrow, but didn't employ a full-time driver. She liked to work her own gearshift. But her shoulder was sore from the shallow wound inflicted by the Russian the night before, and she felt that she deserved a little pampering.

A crowd of reporters was gathered outside the office,

waiting for her to emerge; news of last night's dustup had obviously gotten out. While waiting for the car to show, Lara called Gwenn to prepare her for what awaited at the office. When the car arrived, a Rolls-Royce, she waded through the throng, ignoring the shouted questions and popping flashes, and jumped into the backseat. She'd told Borg to wait five or ten minutes, then leave the offices by the back door; hopefully, no one would see him. She could just imagine what the gossip columnists would make of Lara Croft and "the Borg."

A graying gardener in a misbuttoned cardigan clipped at some tired hedges as the Rolls turned into the driveway leading to the house. Lara saw the outlines of old flower beds given over to hostas and juniper shrubs, or just replaced with grass.

The car pulled into the turnaround, and Lara stepped out. Someone had done a careful job of turning the central fountain into a fishpond. A torpid goldfish opened its mouth to her.

The window frames needed work. The wood was rotting under the paintwork, but a cheery holiday wreath hung from the imposing double front doors. Lara climbed the marble stairs with a feeling of déjà vu. It had been years since she'd come here, yet in a way, it felt like just yesterday. She half expected to see her younger self come running around the corner. She took a breath and pressed the bell. Three chimes sounded from within.

Ajay's mother opened the door, looking a lot older than the last time Lara had seen her. In fact, had she passed Lady Harfleur on the street, Lara doubted she would have recognized the woman. But Lady Harfleur, for her part, recognized Lara at once.

"Why, Lady Croft," she sang. "What a delightful surprise! It's been ages since we had the pleasure of seeing you."

"Lady Harfleur," Lara said, keeping with the formalities. "I apologize for just stopping by like this, out of the blue."

"Nonsense, dear. Please come in. What a lovely car. Don't have your driver trouble; it's fine where it is. Lord Harfleur is working his way through the *Times*, but I know he'll want to see you."

"I've come about Ajay . . . Alison," Lara began, but Lady Harfleur waved a hand airily as she led Lara through a grand hall almost devoid of furniture.

"I think it's wonderful that you two have stayed such close friends," Lady Harfleur chirped.

"Close . . . friends," Lara repeated, not sure she'd heard correctly.

"Oh, yes. Alison writes to us regularly about all your exploits together. I must say, you certainly lead an exciting life! Well, here we are." She knocked at a stout oak door, then pushed it open. "Dear, look who's come to visit."

Lord Harfleur was much as Lara remembered him: a thin-haired cross between George Sanders and Jacques Chirac. He wasn't reading the *Times*. Ajay's father was asleep at his desk in front of a portable television: Some Latin American variety show featuring girls dressed mostly in sequins and a host with mother-of-pearl teeth played silently on the screen. A thin wire ran from the TV to the earpiece that lay on his lordship's shoulder.

"Dear!"

Lord Harfleur's eyes popped open. Lady Harfleur reached across the desk and hit a button on the television as though she were killing a spider and making sure of it, and the TV died.

"Look who's stopped by to say hello."

Lord Harfleur rubbed his eyes and stood. He evinced not the slightest surprise at the unannounced guest. "Hmph. So nice to see you again, Lara. Ajay's told us so much about your work together."

"Yes, well . . ."

Lord Harfleur frowned. "Don't know as I approve entirely. The papers have the most lurid stories about you. Still, you've always had the decency to keep Alison out of the press."

Lara nodded and smiled, trying to sort things out. Had Ajay invented an entire relationship with Lara and played it out for her parents? It seemed unthinkable, and yet what other explanation was there for what she was hearing? Still, she thought it best to go with the flow for now. "How is your brother, your lordship? I remember him very well from my visits all those years ago."

"He's puttering around in the garden somewhere." His face broke into a smile. "Always manages to find his way home by dark."

Lara thought of the man in the misbuttoned cardigan. Not the gardener after all, apparently . . .

"Tea, Lara, dear?" Lady Harfleur put in.

"No, thank you. I can't stay long. I've come about Alison, actually."

Lord Harfleur reached into his shirt pocket and extracted a pack of cigarettes with a book of matches stuck in the plastic. "Dear, I'd like a cup, even if our guest doesn't. Why don't you bring tea for three in here? She might change her mind."

"Our help has to be off sometimes," Lady Harfleur confided to Lara with a trill of laughter that sounded practiced. Then she turned back to her husband. "If you're going to smoke, at least open a window. And put on your jacket, so you don't take your death."

Lady Harfleur hobbled out, and his lordship went to the window, opened it with a grunt, and lit up. He shook out his match with a smooth, thoughtless gesture, then tossed it out the window. His lordship must have been very attractive in his prime, Lara decided. Even if his family's fortune had run out, he still had the grace of those to the manner born.

He offered the pack to Lara.

"I don't smoke," she said.

"Thought all you young things smoked on the sly to keep yourselves so thin."

"I prefer to exercise," Lara said.

Lord Harfleur grunted. Clearly, he disapproved of exercise, at least for women. "So you've come about Alison, eh, Croft? What's she got herself mixed up in now?"

"I'm not quite sure, but I think she could be in some trouble."

His lordship blew a lungful of carcinogens out the window. "And whose fault is that?"

Lara sighed. "Look, Lord Harfleur, I don't know what Alison may have been telling you about the two of us, but—"

"Lies," said Lord Harfleur bitterly.

"I beg your pardon?"

"You heard me. She made it all up, or most of it, anyway. A father knows." He gazed sadly at Lara. "Alison . . . is not quite right." He tapped the side of his head. "Took a wrong turn somewhere. Known for years. It's the money, you see. Don't give a tinker's cuss about it myself, but it matters to her more than anything. I tried to get her help, but she wouldn't hear of it. Stormed out. Haven't seen her since. Just letters. Letters filled with lies about the two of you going off on your expeditions together. A lot of rubbish about restoring the family fortune, the family name."

"I-I'm sorry," Lara said. "I didn't know."

"Not your fault," Lord Harfleur said, but he looked at her as if he didn't quite believe that. "Lady Harfleur doesn't suspect a thing," he added, dropping his voice to a whisper. "And I prefer to keep it that way. It would break her heart if she knew."

"I understand. I won't say anything. But if Alison has written you lately, there may be a clue in those letters about what she's up to."

Before Lord Harfleur could reply, his wife arrived with tea on a tray. She poured a cup for her husband.

"Thank you, dear," he said. "Lara was just telling me about her latest project with Alison."

Lady Harfleur smiled. "I expect you'll be going down to join them soon. Buenos Aires is beautiful this time of year! And that doctor friend of yours, the jungle surgeon: What a brilliant man! So thoughtful, too. He autographed one of his books for us, didn't he, dear?"

"That he did," said Lord Harfleur.

Lady Harfleur crossed the room to a coffee table cluttered with an assortment of magazines and books. She picked up a large book and brought it to Lara.

Lara took it. The book was titled *Rare Flora of the Amazon Basin*. The name of the author was Dr. Tejo Kunai. There was something familiar about that name, but Lara couldn't place it at first.

"He's Portuguese, I believe," Lady Harfleur rattled on. "Studies native medicines and all that. Quite famous in his field, apparently. Been in *The Lancet* and *The New England Journal of Medicine*. But then, you know all that!"

Then she had it. *Kunai . . . Not* Urdmann's *Kunai?*

Lara opened the book at random. Photographs of silver white blossoms in close-up against a dark background filled the page. "Beautiful," she said.

"Yes, isn't it?"

Lara turned to the back flap and looked at the picture of Dr. Tejo Kunai. An older man with delicate, dark features looked back at her in black-and-white sagacity. She'd never seen him before.

"Perhaps you'd like to see Alison's old room, dear?" Lady Harfleur asked.

"I'd love to," Lara said, putting the book down on the edge of Lord Harfleur's desk.

"I'll leave you women to it," Lord Harfleur grunted. "Think I'll join Roddy in the garden."

Upstairs, Lady Harfleur opened the door to Ajay's room and ushered Lara inside. It hadn't changed much in the years since Lara had last seen it. Pictures of out-of-date pop idols were on the walls, along with some framed photographs of Lara and Ajay from their various schools and the trips to Mexico and the Caucasus. But there were none more recent.

"Lara, I brought you up here so we could speak privately," Lady Harfleur said after she'd shut the door behind them. "Just between you and me, I realize that much of what Alison has told us over the years about your partnership is, shall we say, an exaggeration."

Lara couldn't hide her surprise. "You know?"

"A mother always knows. But Lord Harfleur, bless his trusting heart, doesn't suspect a thing. For his sake, I pretend to believe all that she writes us."

"But Alison went to Buenos Aires for a reason," Lara pointed out. "She didn't make that up."

"No, she didn't. And to be perfectly frank, I'm worried about her."

"Why?"

"There's a bit of her grandfather in Alison. Not my father, but his lordship's. He was a gambler, liked long odds, didn't know when to quit. He kept trying to win back the family fortune. Wound up squandering what little was left of it."

Lara nodded. "There's a bit of that in the Croft family tree, too. And now you think that Alison is following his example?"

Lady Harfleur nodded grimly. "Only it's her own life she's gambling with. Or that is my fear." She fixed a steely gaze on Lara. "Tell me the truth, Lara. Is she after some bit of jewel that you are, too? Is that why you've come to see us?"

"No." For a moment, she considered telling her about Borg, but then decided to keep silent about his involvement for now. "I heard from mutual friends that Alison might have gotten into something over her head. My sole concern is for her well-being. You have my word on that, Lady Harfleur."

Lady Harfleur nodded and glanced out the window, where Lord Harfleur could be seen talking to the man whom Lara had taken for the gardener. "Alison idolizes you, Lara. She's tried to remake herself in your image. I saw it happening, tried to get her to see what she was doing, but she wouldn't listen. And now, these letters and postcards from Buenos Aires, all filled with promises of a rosy future, the family fortune restored. You don't suppose she's been brainwashed, like that Hearst woman, do you?"

"Brainwashed by whom? Judging from his book, Dr. Kunai doesn't seem like the type to go in for that sort of thing."

"No, I suppose not . . ." Lady Harfleur bent to straighten a tousled comforter that lay at the foot of Ajay's bed. "Oh, how did this get here?"

Lara leaned closer.

Lady Harfleur pulled a thick and obviously ancient

leather-bound Bible from beneath the comforter. "Been in the family for centuries. All sorts of notations about the Harfleurs, going back to Henry VIII."

"What's bookmarked?" asked Lara, interested as always in old things. The tip of a satin ribbon, faded to the color of thin tea, peeked from between the closed pages.

"It's bookmarked? Why, so it is. I don't have my glasses; would you mind?"

Lara took the Bible and opened it to the marked page. It was in the Book of Daniel. A line of italicized text caught her eye, the fearful magic words that foretold doom for a nation:

Mene, mene, tekel, upharsin.

"Numbered, numbered . . . ," she translated the phrase from the Aramaic.

What had Borg said? The Many? The Mene? The Numbered?

"What's this?" Lady Harfleur pulled at the edge of a piece of paper that had emerged from between two pages when Lara opened the book.

On the paper was a pencil-rubbed etching that reminded Lara of the Greek letter Omega: Ω

Written beside it, in Ajay's precise handwriting, were the date and location of the rubbing: the ruins of Smyrna, sixteen months ago.

"Why, look at that date!" Lady Harfleur exclaimed. "Lara, she must have been here! Snuck in and out without ever telling us, like a common thief!"

"Except she didn't take anything," Lara said. "Instead, she

left this behind. Almost as if she wanted you to find it." Or wanted *me* to find it, she added silently to herself.

"But why would she do such a thing?" Lady Harfleur asked.

"I don't know."

Omega was the last letter in the Greek alphabet; it often had the metaphorical connotation of the end, an ending . . . In electrical engineering terms, omega signified resistance. Might Ajay's mysterious new associates in Buenos Aires have a political agenda, a resistance movement dedicated to ending the current Argentine government? But then again, the symbol wasn't even a proper omega. It was thicker in the center, like a worm, and thin at the tips—which curled up slightly, something Lara had never seen in representations of the Greek letter.

So perhaps it wasn't Greek. She recalled that Urdmann had told her Kunai had asked him about an ancient *Babylonian* text. Did the Babylonians employ a similar character?

There were too many possibilities. She didn't even know if it was the same Kunai.

"Lady Harfleur, did Alison ever mention a group called 'The Many' or something similar in any of her letters?"

"I don't believe so," Lady Harfleur replied after a moment's thought. "Why? Is it important?"

"It may be. I just don't know." She glanced again at the symbol. "Do you mind if I keep this?"

"Take it, please. Whatever you need to find Alison and bring her home. You are going after her, aren't you?"

"I'm going to do what I can," Lara promised. "Ajay and I were best friends once. I still care about her."

"Bless you, dear. If you find her, will you give her a message from me?"

"Of course I will."

"Tell her, 'Bugger the money, bugger the family name, bugger whatever destiny she thinks she has to fulfill . . . Bugger all of it. Just come back home.' "

5

"Give me a few days to run all this down," Lara said over the phone to Borg as she told him about her interview with Lord and Lady Harfleur. "It's got to fit together somehow. We might do better to chase this Tejo Kunai than Ajay. If we find him, we'll probably find her."

"I want to go with you, if you're going after her."

Lara turned it over in her head. She preferred to work alone, but then she tried to put herself in Borg's shoes. "Don't leave or switch hotels without calling me, okay?" she directed. God, she was sounding like Dools.

"Of course."

Back at the manor, she breezed in and immediately gave Winston the rest of the day off. The last thing she needed were wheezy exhortations to be more careful on London's streets. She almost missed her days as a recluse.

She needed some time in her library and archives.

Croft manor had, deep within its foundation, a secret room that dated back to the English Civil War. One reached it through a wall panel and a narrow staircase; it was easy to imagine Cavaliers sitting there over a candle plotting confusion to the Roundheads. In the springtime quiet before the Blitz of 1940, her grandfather had turned it into a bomb shelter, adding a better ventilation system and electric lighting. About the time of the Berlin Uprising in the early fifties, it was upgraded again with its own stove, a diesel generator in a separate room, a thicker security door, and additional storage space for the household staff, which, at that time, numbered six people.

Lara made the next modifications, adding fiber-optic lines for a security system and converting the whole thing into a four-room, walk-in safe. Cold-forged steel cages held the treasures she'd picked up around the world.

The ones that were too dangerous, or too valuable, for public display.

The two larger, better-lit rooms held her private library. Well, not all of it was hers: Von Croy had willed her his collection, acquired in turn from other sources. She checked her index—an Oxford postgrad student had helped her with the dreary task of cataloguing—and found what she wanted, Von Croy's old copy of the *Dawn Roundtable Record*.

She brought up a folio containing letters from Frys to Von Croy. Lara had mixed feelings about Von Croy. She owed much of her identity to him; he had awakened her desire to rediscover what was lost to the world. Under his guidance, she'd looked at 100,000-year-old skulls in the Klasies River Mouth Caves in South Africa and found imprints of an ear of wheat from the seventh millennium B.C. at the Mehrgarh dig in Pakistan. He'd told her stories about the real-life King Pakal, elevated by the Mayan to the rank of maize god after his death and shown, on the imposing, carved lid of his sarcophagus, surrounded by elaborate, stylized religious icons. Great people, long forgotten and waiting to be rediscovered by the intrepid and intellectually curious.

But Von Croy could be so damned obtuse at times—a

source of wisdom but full of concealed knowledge and uncertain motivations, like the man behind the curtain in *The Wizard of Oz*. He'd often dropped dark hints that the world was not what *Homo sapiens* thought it to be. "There are powers and histories beyond our poor, insignificant perception," he used to croak, sounding like some leathery old crocodile god from the upper Nile. "Probe too far, and we may be swallowed up like a fish so intent on a wriggling worm that it doesn't see the snapping turtle coming up behind it."

The letters from Frys to Von Croy were in the same vein. Apparently, a paper titled "The *Méne* and Other Faiths of Proto-Ur" had troubled both of them in its original form. Von Croy had suggested at first that they publish everything their research had uncovered, holding nothing back, but Dr. Frys had responded from Scotland with alarm:

> Madness, Werner. Either we'll be accused of a hoax—the Piltdown man of the archaeological world—or, God forbid (ha!), we'll be taken seriously. It would be a revelation that could cause an intellectual cataclysm. What is man, that they aren't now mindful of him? If I may quote the gentleman from Providence: "The sciences, each straining in its own direction, have hitherto harmed us little; but someday the piecing together of dissociated knowledge will open up such terrifying vistas of reality, and of our frightful position therein, that we shall either go mad from the revelation or flee from the deadly light into the peace and safety of a new dark age."

Von Croy's next letter must have agreed, for Dr. Frys had calmed down by the following correspondence, dated a week later.

> I believe the new version, with just the sampling of proto-Ur text (we really must come up with a name for this language; how does Froyan sound?) is satisfactory. Just the suggestion that another civilization, advanced at least to the level of Rome's, existed prior to the last ice age will cause us more than enough grief. With the texts gone, we needn't worry that others will look into the guessed-at web that held together a civilization encompassing the entire Pacific Rim and beyond, even unto Arabia and Africa.

But in the letter after that, only a week later, Frys was hysterical again.

> No! No! and a thousand times No! We can't mention them. Not a footnote, or I'll destroy the collection.

Lara read it twice. There was no mention of what Frys meant by "them." But it was like listening to one end of a phone conversation. She wished she had Frys's half of the correspondence, the letters that Von Croy had sent to him, but Von Croy evidently didn't keep copies of friendly collegial correspondence.

Had this old research cost Frys his life?

And where did Ajay and Kunai fit in? She did a LEXIS-NEXIS search for the name Tejo Kunai, and variations thereof, but found no evidence of anyone by that name other than the author of the book that Lady Harfleur had shown her.

After dinner, Lara went to the indoor pool to relax. Her grandfather had built the pool to be big and deep, but inspiration from her mother had made it beautiful after Lara had inherited it.

Visitors always thought that Lara had designed the mosaics of Artemis and Helen, the dolphins and the seabirds, the soothing aqua, gray, and sea-foam tones contrasted with deeper browns. But she'd taken the images from a painting her mother had done while bedridden during pregnancy—her mother had been subject to miscarriages. Mum had once theorized that Lara's passion for the classical world was the outcome of her poring through books of Greek, Roman, and Levantine art for inspiration.

The water felt like melted snow. She didn't heat the pool; its chill gave her body a wake-up call. There were a number of questions she had to consider. She dove and swam laps and finally framed the questions properly.

1. What was it about the *Méne* that had so frightened Professor Frys and Von Croy?
2. Why did Tejo Kunai, and presumably Alison Harfleur, want this frightening piece of knowledge or information, presumably in the possession of Frys?
3. Why had Kunai gone to see Urdmann?

It was clear to her that Kunai wanted something having to do with the *Méne* cult. She listed the possibilities: an artifact; the reputation that would come with publication of the discoveries Frys and Von Croy had feared to reveal; even, perhaps, the resurrection of the cult itself. That was why Kunai had gone to see Urdmann: for his expertise, yes, but also because of his reputation as someone who could be trusted not to involve the police in anything illegal.

Afterward, he must have threatened Frys, and Frys had tried to contact her for help. But Kunai had gotten to him first.

And very nearly gotten to her as well.

Clearly, Kunai was a dangerous man. It was hard to square these actions with the dignified portrait of an elderly gentleman on the back flap of the book that Lady Harfleur had shown her. Still, Lara knew very well that appearances could be deceiving. How often had men underestimated her simply because she happened to be attractive?

But where did Ajay fit into everything? Why had she secretly returned to Harfleur House? And why had she left that strange symbol for Lara to find? Was it a clue, a cry for help? Or a taunt?

Was Ajay the innocent, brainwashed victim that Borg imagined her to be? Lara didn't share his confidence in that explanation. Her history with Ajay wouldn't permit it. She had to consider the possibility that Ajay was Kunai's willing accomplice.

It struck her suddenly that Borg might be part of the plot. How much did she know about him, really?

Sighing, Lara pulled herself from the pool. There were too many questions and not enough answers. But she had an idea where she might be able to find some.

First, though, she needed to call Dools and get the stop taken off her passport.

6

The sun and surf of Mauritius made a welcome break from England's dreary December.

Lara's reconnaissance of Lancaster Urdmann's estate from the wheel of a rented Land Rover found no obvious gaps in security. She parked the Rover where it couldn't be seen from the road and observed the gatehouse through binoculars. Anyone who approached the formidable closed gates had to pull up next to a bunkerlike station that housed a single guard.

Lara waited until the guard picked up a magazine, rose from his chair, and disappeared into the WC at the back of the bunker. Then she ran over to the gatehouse and jumped up on the ledge in front of the window to get a look through the armored glass. While listening for the sound of a toilet flush, she noted that the gate-open button next to the window required a key. Then she saw her photograph on a clipboard.

Urdmann had gone so far as to do a few mock-ups of her in sunglasses, a hat, even a man's beard and sideburns. In big letters at the bottom was a sum of rupees that would allow a guard to retire in style for spotting and apprehending her.

Why would Urdmann be expecting another visit from her? She'd told no one, not even Borg—whom she'd told to wait for her call—of her plans to return to Mauritius. No one except Dools, that is, and she knew better than to suspect that straight arrow of any mischief.

She'd entered the country quietly, under a fake French passport. At first she'd been tempted to simply call Urdmann and offer him a drink in the hotel bar. Perhaps the two of them could discuss Kunai and the *Méne* in a civilized fashion. After all, the bullet wound she'd given him—a scratch, really—had only settled an account that went back to her earliest days as a Tomb Raider.

Before the inheritance from her aunt, Lara had been supporting herself on a shoestring budget after her parents had cut her off for refusing to marry that awful prig, the Earl of Farringdon. Urdmann had offered to take a set of Aztec artifacts off her hands at a price she later learned had undervalued the Sun Stones of Quetzalcoatl by 20 percent. Nor had he turned them over to the Mexican National Archives as he'd promised.

But he'd taught her a valuable lesson. A brilliant mind and a first-class education didn't automatically instill character; that had to come from a surer source. She later learned that archaeological relics weren't the only things he traded; in those days, they were just a passion, and his real money had come from weapons.

Since then, their paths had crossed a number of times, and her respect for Urdmann as a human being had steadily dwindled . . . while her respect for his archaeological knowledge had, however grudgingly, grown.

Evidently, she'd taught Urdmann a lesson as well. His security, so lax on her last visit, was much improved now. Getting in wasn't going to be as easy as she'd hoped. But she had to find a way, because she knew that the fat man wasn't going to consider his wound anything but a fresh insult to be avenged.

The Tomb Raider lay still in her inflated cocoon, smelling the wood enclosing her and listening to the activity outside the crate.

"It's a special delivery, sir," the guard said after they'd set her box down. She heard a separate grunt, perhaps from the courier, perhaps from another of Urdmann's employees. "The dog didn't signal for explosives or guns, but he's interested in something. There's a letter for you with it."

Pause.

"Madame Tussaud's."

Pause.

"T-U-S-S-A-U-D-S, sir. London, England. The manifest lists a 'Lara Croft statue.' Yes, that's right: Lara Croft."

She heard the envelope open.

"A card, from the Croft House. It reads: 'Sorry about the blood on the carpet. I thought you'd like a little reminder of me.' It is signed. Of course, sir."

The crate was lifted again, and carried for almost two minutes before it was set down again, heavily. A few seconds later, she heard a crowbar applied to the wooden crate. At least they'd paid attention to the "This End Up" markings.

"The boss told us to be careful with it."

"*Oui*," a second voice responded.

The Tomb Raider froze herself into the selected pose, gun up and face turned to the right. She'd had to do some quick work with her computer and the hotel printer to get the documentation right. A suitable payoff to the airport courier service that morning had ensured instant delivery, no questions asked.

The courier service was an excellent example of a Creole proverb of Mauritius: *Si t'as du pognon, t'as du pouvoir*—if you've got bucks, you've got power.

Of course, the philosophy operated everywhere. The Mauritians just phrased it more musically.

They got through the crate and used a blade on the cardboard. Lara forced herself to look at the light coming through the widening cracks so her eyes would be adjusted by the time they had it open. From her limited view, it looked like she was in a garage. She saw groundskeeping gear hanging from hooks, a workbench covered with tools, and the bonnet of an automobile.

One of the guards let loose with a Hindi oath. Another pulled away the inflated plastic wrapping about her.

"Tussaud's—of course! The wax sculptures," the more garrulous of the guards said. They wore khaki shorts, with high white socks and Sam Browne belts. Neither had a weapon out. "They are very famous. Must have cost the boss a mint."

"No, you're wrong there. It was sent to him. Didn't you see the manifest?"

It was hard not to move her eyes. One reached up to touch her.

She brought the gun down, pointing it between the two guards.

Their reaction was worthy of a photograph. One took a startled step back and tripped on the lid of her packing case, falling to the floor; the other flung up his hands like a soccer goalie blocking a ball kicked at his face.

The Tomb Raider flexed her stiff legs. "Good afternoon, gentlemen."

"Y-you're alive!" stuttered the guard still standing.

"Very observant." She swiveled her gun barrel to the one

on the floor, who had been in the process of pulling his own gun. "If you're going to take out your gun, do it with thumb and forefinger. Grasp it by the bottom."

He complied, placing the gun on the floor.

"Kick it to me."

After the pistol had slid to her foot, her gun returned to the guard still standing. "Just like him," she instructed him.

The pistol joined its twin.

"Now we can relax," she said, holstering her gun and picking up the two pistols on the floor. "What are your names?"

"Dinesh," the one on the floor said.

"Harbe," the other said. "I don't understand. The dog . . . he detected no firearm."

"Because I wasn't carrying one," Lara said. "It's a toy. Very realistic looking, though, wouldn't you agree?"

With a growl, Harbe made a move toward her. She brought up the pistols. "Not so fast, Harbe. These are real enough. Whatever Mr. Urdmann is paying you, it's not worth a bullet."

Harbe wilted.

Lara grinned. "Now, Harbe, where's Urdmann?"

"Say noth—," Dinesh began.

Lara cut him off. "Quiet now."

"Third floor," Harbe said.

She looked around the garage, let her eyes linger on a beautiful Rolls-Royce, then looked further. The tool shelf held what she was looking for. The garage also had a pair of convenient support pillars, festooned with work lights and extension cords.

"Now, I'm only going to need a few minutes of your employer's time. Gunfire really makes conversation difficult, so I can't have you two running around setting off alarms. Dinesh, if you'd please get up and go to the column there.

You both have handcuffs? Good. If you both would stand back-to-back."

They complied, and she removed the handcuffs from their belts and carefully closed the bracelets so the pillar was enclosed in a ring of flesh and steel. She went to the workbench and returned with some clean rags and silver duct tape and went to work gagging the guards.

"As a reward for being so agreeable, I'm going to take care with the tape and make sure I don't gum up your skin and hair too badly." She wadded up two rags and stuck one into each of their mouths, then wrapped up their heads in duct tape.

"Breathing fine? Comfortable?"

Neither bothered to nod. Harbe had tears in his eyes.

"Worried about your paycheck, Harbe?" She tucked a card in his breast pocket. "I've got friends on the Seychelles. Much more beautiful there, and the pay would probably be better. I'll let Mr. Urdmann know you're in here; you'll be loose by teatime."

She turned out the light.

Urdmann's house looked different with the sun shining. Antique bombe chests with expensive vases atop them stood at intervals in the hallway with suits of armor, statues, and even ancient farming implements. She heard a vacuum from somewhere down the marble-floored hallway. Women's voices echoed from the other end of the house.

Lara's memory of the layout of the house was perfect. Avoiding the museum, she found the servants' staircase. She climbed to the first floor, looked out a window. The guard at the gatehouse was leaning out the window, chatting with a gardener working outside the walls. A third man, also a guard, rode up on his ATV and joined them, lifting a canteen from a gear bag at the front of the four-wheeler. It seemed that no one had yet checked inside the garage.

She left the stairway at the third floor and turned down the hallway that ran to the center of the house. Carpeting silenced her footfalls. A cleaning cart stood outside Urdmann's suite; a faint splashing echoed from the open door.

"Hew, hew, hew, hee," she heard. A masculine giggle.

The Tomb Raider felt her face tighten into a tiger's grin. She trotted down the hallway toward the splashing.

She walked past some simple black-and-white smocks and white crepe-soled shoes, discarded on the floor of Urdmann's bedroom.

She didn't bother with guns this time, just stepped through the doorway and stood in front of the phone next to the loo.

Bubbles hid most of what was going on in the master bath—a mass of stone and porcelain and mirror larger than some London hotel rooms. Urdmann shared the tub with two bronze-skinned women who, combined, probably didn't weigh as much as his hairy torso.

"Diddling the help, Lancaster?" she said.

"Croft?!"

The cleaning women squawked, slid around behind Urdmann's bulk. He was large enough to hide both, head to toe.

She offered him a towel and one of his wispy robes. "I was hoping for a quick chat."

"You've got to be fu—"

"Language, Urdmann. There are ladies present. I'm prepared to trade. Down in your museum I noticed you had Akhenaton's crook. How would you like the flail as well?"

The red left his cheeks and went into his eyes.

"The flail? I thought it was lost. Early grave robbers getting into the first tomb, or some such."

"Can we talk without the staff around?"

Urdmann without bubbles looked a little bit like a soused orangutan. She was relieved when he put on the robe and squelched across the floor to his bedroom.

"Excuse us, ladies," Lara said, shutting the door on the two maids, who clung to each other amid the bubbles of the bath. She followed Urdmann across the bedroom and into his office.

"Rumor has it you've left more than a dozen children scattered about the globe," she said, interposing herself between Urdmann and his desk, the stolen pistols casually displayed in her hands.

"What's the matter, Croft? Jealous?"

"Try disgusted."

"You can be as high and mighty as you like. The fact remains, I've got something you want, haven't I? What is it that's worth the flail of Akhenaton?"

"Everything you know about Tejo Kunai. What he was looking for, what you told him, any associates you met—"

"Kunai?" Urdmann sank into a papa-san chair by the window. Rattan crackled under his weight. "That CIA snoop who was working with you?"

"He's not CIA. He was here on his own."

"Toss me a smoke, won't you? In the box on top of the desk."

"And set off a radio alarm?"

"Croft, I want Akhenaton's flail. I'm not tricking you."

The top of the lacquer box was painted with a Taoist picture of Chinese philosophers tasting vinegar. The Tomb Raider opened it, extracted a cigarette and a book of matches, and tossed them to Urdmann.

"Better," Urdmann said, lighting up. Jets of smoke poured

out of his nostrils. He held his cigarette between thumb and forefinger. "My heart can't take these sudden appearances, Croft. You keep popping up over my shoulder like a guardian angel. If I didn't know better, I might think you were obsessed with me."

"I'm a born bear baiter," she said.

"I really should take you by the ear and toss you out the window, Akhenaton's flail or no. But you're armed, I see . . . and with two pistols that look suspiciously like the make and model I issue my guards." He fingered the suture swellings on his arm with his free hand.

"Yes, quite a coincidence, that."

He sighed. "And the statue from Tussaud's?"

"You're looking at her. But about Kunai . . ."

"Kunai . . . nervous fellow. High laugh. Kept toying with a little monocle. I must say I liked him, even though I suspected his story from the first. But nervous. Always seemed to be listening over his shoulder. He had some rubbings he wanted translated. Pre-Zoroastrian rubbish. The *Méne*. I assume you've heard of this myth from the mouth of your late teacher."

"I'm still learning. Werner Von Croy didn't think the *Méne* 'rubbish.' "

Urdmann shrugged. "Kunai's rubbings were some sort of decree. Seems the *Méne* upset the Babylonian king."

"What were they? A cult?"

"More like a full-blown religion of some kind. Kunai's record was a list of proscribed glyphs. Anyone found with one of the symbols on the walls of his dwelling, inscribed onto any device, or uttering one of a list of forbidden prayers was to be tortured and killed. Oddly enough, old King Bashphet of Babylon wrote into the law a codicil declaring that even a pardon from the king himself couldn't reverse the sentence. Perhaps he was getting senile and worried he'd be talked into reversing his own laws."

"The Babylonians had translations of the symbols?"

Urdmann smoked and looked skyward. "Yes. Let's see, there was seawater, freshwater, ice, mountain, cave, crops, animals, sacrifice, cataclysm, something called a 'judge god,' ruling man, supplicant man, slave man, wealth, property . . . some astrological stuff as well, having to do with the sun and stars and moon and comets and so forth. That list is by no means complete."

"You kept a copy?"

"No. I tried to get one, but Kunai wanted the translation done right there and then. His check was good—I called the bank—so I translated as best as I could over the course of an afternoon."

"How about the death-sentence prayers?"

"Mumbo jumbo. One oddity, though. Most religions have their worshippers lift their eyes up. This one had them cast their gaze *down*, within, to the depths. Don't know if they meant their souls or the earth itself: lots of '*in deep places of the heart, beneath still waters . . .*' That sort of thing."

The Tomb Raider drew something on a sheet of Urdmann's cotton-pulp stationery. The Greek letter omega, only thickened at the middle, with the ends turned up.

"Recognize this? And don't try to tell me it's just an omega."

"The Babylonians had that one first and last on the list. Don't know why they repeated it. It stood for 'god.' Or possibly 'gods.' "

The Tomb Raider felt a chill. "Anything else?"

"He asked if I'd ever come across any platinum panels in my

dealings. I was curious by then, acted as though something about platinum panels jogged my memory, and asked. He said they would have come out of South America, pre-Columbian. A little under a meter square. Thin, etched closely."

"Have you?"

"No. I told him I'd never heard of that sort of thing. And if I had, that sort of thing tends to get melted down by grave robbers. He didn't seem happy at the idea."

"Thank you, Lancaster. You've done me more good than you know."

"Only by accident, Croft. Won't happen again."

"Send me the hospital bill for the bullet wound."

"I'd rather have the flail."

"Yes, well, so would I, for that matter."

Urdmann's face purpled. "You said! . . ."

"I never said I *had* the flail. I just asked if you *wanted* it."

"You little bitch!"

She brought up a pistol sharply. "Now, now, Lancaster. I'm sure you don't want another scratch to go with the last one, do you?"

"I'll get you for this, Croft!"

"Very original. Now, before I tie you up, you're going to place a call down to the front gate and let them know that I'm about to be driving out of here."

"Driving out?" Urdmann looked close to a heart attack. "In what?"

"I saw a fine Rolls in your garage. I thought I'd borrow it, take it for a drive. Don't worry; you'll get it back in one piece . . . unless your guards try something stupid, that is."

PART TWO

7

Underground, finally at the Whispering Abyss, and his Tomb Raider wasn't up to the task. Even weighted with responsibilities as he was, the irony of it brought a smile to the Prime's face.

The Prime had been putting off that conclusion for a week now. Facing facts meant he had to act on them, and acting on them meant hurting Alison.

But the *Méne* Restoration was worth a few emotional bruises.

Now enlightenment—the explanation of his new dreams and desires—was finally within reach. Though his reach had been into the right part of the earth, the grasp had failed—repeatedly. Alison told him she'd seen the Panels of the Prophecies in the light of her torch, but every time she tried to pry them away . . .

The Prime could see Alison better now, making her way up the stairs. Relief washed down his spine. The breeze coming up from the Abyss smelled of gunfire, and his sensitive nose detected blood. From here the climb would be easier for her. He turned from the Whispering Abyss and paced around the room.

Leonid, at the winch, sensed his mood, retreated to one of

the air shaft alcoves around the circular chamber, and lit a cigar.

The leader of the cult of the *Méne* needed to pace.

The Prime checked his watch. It would be getting dark up on the surface. Another hour, and the cursed arthropods would be up and hunting again.

A variety of mutated creatures in this isolated stretch of Andean cloud forest had claimed the Abyss as their own.

Ironic that a variant of the Sacred Vine had so altered some of the local wildlife. He looked at a green frog that had found its way down one of the air shafts. A line of tiny eyes ran down its spine. He waved his hand over the frog: the eyes blinked, and it hopped. Frogs were like canaries in a coal mine; changes to an environment showed in them first.

The Food Chain, a Frangible Web. A line from the title of his doctoral thesis. Deep Gods, how could it be that he had ever been interested in such trivia?

He'd wasted years photographing tadpoles and counting toes before he had been enlightened to the true state of the world by Kunai. And now, thanks to that happy chance, he was standing in the spot where demigods had once ordered the affairs of men. At the cusp, as it were, of a new age that would come out of this ancient place.

The roof over the Abyss was old, a low dome like an enormous stone igloo. The masonry set into the walls was unusual, interlocking triangles growing smaller and smaller until they reached the centerpoint of the dome. One would expect some sort of design or emblem there, but there was none. With the smell of gunfire gone now, even the air wafting up from the Abyss felt ancient, damp and cool.

He wondered what sort of hands had worked the blood-colored granite millennia ago.

The circular chamber, a forty-meter expanse of shaped red granite surrounding the gaping Abyss, looked like a movie set now. A generator clattered in the corner, overwhelming the faint jungle sounds that drifted down the shafts ringing the room. Cables snaked their way to lights set on stands and the electric winch that had been set up among the old stonework. Modern girders had been fitted where once beams had lain for *Méne* priests to stand upon as they chanted the ancient rites, pushing captives into the Abyss as sacrifices all the while.

Long, long lengths of wire-cored rope ran from the winch down into the Abyss. His engineers had been through purgatory figuring breaking strengths and load weights with the makeshift gear they'd smuggled into the ruins past the Peruvians. It wasn't the person at the end of the line that mattered so much. It was the weight of all the cable descending into darkness. The ancient stairs running their corkscrew length down and down and down had disappeared in some long-ago earthquake, and now the only way to the panels was via an arduous and treacherous descent. They only used the winch in emergencies; the sound had been known to wake up the hive.

Though Alison had fallen short at the last jump, the Prime didn't regret bringing her along. She'd been good company during their hunt for the location of this ancient interface. What's more, she truly believed.

Some of his followers chafed about money, groaned and bleated at every setback. Not Alison. Ever since he'd shared his vision with her—the bits and pieces he'd picked up from Kunai, Von Croy, the Old Man—she'd been at his side every step, arguing down the malcontents, walking first into every danger. A German shepherd couldn't have been more loyal.

When he'd mused aloud that they would have to put Croft

out of the way through an assassination or kidnapping, she'd thrilled at the idea and kissed him. "I hope they get her alive. It'll drive LC mad, when she finds out who did it."

The Prime had gone along with it. He had to admit that Alison knew which tripwires were connected to which reactions in the Croft psyche. Besides, he'd already planned to use Croft to retrieve the tablets as a contingency in case Alison couldn't manage the job. And now, as it turned out, she couldn't manage it. But she would still be useful in handling Croft. They'd once been close. Alison knew how to read people—except, perhaps, herself.

And him, of course.

Best of all, she was a superlative lover. There was a lot of spare time to fill while waiting for men and equipment and information to arrive.

He'd actually become quite fond of her, in his way. He regretted the words he'd have to say to her now. But feelings couldn't stand in the way of the Restoration of the Old Order.

Alison came up the last stairs, unhooked her safety line, and sat at the edge of the Abyss, catching her breath. She'd been beaten, or frightened, and looked it. Gunpowder residue marked her cheek like a bruise; she'd taped a dressing to her forearm. Alison's glycogen-starved muscles trembled as she unslung the shotgun from her back and set it aside.

"They woke up," she said. "Angry, as usual."

"And the panels?"

"Couldn't get near them. Sorry. Let me try again tomorrow. I could really use another shot of juice. Do you have—"

"Too much isn't good for you, my pet." What he really should have said was that the supply gathered, at great time and expense from the atoll, was running short, but the concern he voiced was also the truth.

"Or, better yet, just dump a drum of DDT down there."

"Air currents. It would come back up in our faces, even if we could get the right chemicals. Obtaining powerful nerve agents in large quantities has gotten more difficult of late. And contrary to its name, the Whispering Abyss has a bottom. I don't want to hurt whatever might be down there."

"Then six men with shotguns—"

"After we lost Kurt and Yassim and Rafael? You want to ask for the next group of volunteers? No, going in noisy just aggravates them. Defense of the nest, I suppose."

"You're the expert."

"I'm the Prime. It's time for me to act for the good of the *Ména* Restoration. We'll get your old friend to retrieve them."

Alison bit her lower lip. "Bugger Lara. I can—"

"No. I don't want you down there again. You forget, I've got a stake in your well-being, too."

"Don't coddle me."

"Don't dispute my decisions."

He and Alison were both teeth grinders. Their jaws worked as they stared at each other, until Leonid put his cigar out at the center of one of the equilateral triangles and tapped his watch.

"We're both overwrought," the Prime said. "We need to leave before they come up. We'll talk about it once we're safe in the hut."

She fed shells into the shotgun. "I'll stay. I'll blast them as they come up. Whittle down the numbers."

The Prime took out the old monocle, looked at Alison through its distorting lens.

"Alison, look at me."

The shells went in *schuck schuck schuck* . . .

"Alison!"

She looked up, met his eyes through the lens. The red plastic of the shell with its metal cap dropped, rolled into one of the grooves in the floor.

The Prime began to spin the lens on its handle. It glittered, catching the generator-powered lights. "Alison, relax."

"Relax," she agreed.

"Let's talk about it in safety. Fair enough?"

"Fair enough."

"Now follow me. I've never played you false, or for a fool, have I?"

She followed. "Never."

8

Lara Croft had her research spread out on her aunt's old craft table in what had once been an aviary attached to the mansion. Brown leather-bound tomes opened to unevenly typeset pages alongside a modern microfilm reader covered the waist-high worktable's butcher-block surface. Two plates containing the remnants of quick baked-beans-on-toast meals stood nearby. A samovar next to tea things on a little table in the corner steamed away.

The glass-enclosed annex to the house had the advantage of being farthest from the telephone and the front door. It held happy memories, along with a variety of plants and small trees. Her grandfather had built it to indulge a passion for exotic birds. She liked the space of her aunt's huge worktable, the bank of fluorescent lights over the table for nighttime, and the variety of places to put her feet on the stool or the table rail.

Lara tended to fidget as she learned. Her muscles had to tap out each new fact.

During her aunt's time, all the birds but one had been donated to a local zoo, and the glass enclosure had been turned into a greenhouse. The remaining bird was an African gray parrot, a favorite of her grandfather's. Named Sir Garnet, he was older than Winston and just as much a fixture of the Croft estate as the butler. Sir Garnet enjoyed screaming matches with the local crows and tormented the cats from neighboring estates by running back and forth at the base of the glass wall as they stood outside watching helplessly.

As Lara read into the night, taking notes on her laptop, Sir Garnet caught her mood and ascended to the top of the tallest tree in the greenhouse, a sweet acacia, and went to work trimming twigs. If she was going to work, so was he. She ignored the *snaps* and *snicks,* accompanied by an occasional satisfied cackle when a twig full of tiny sets of neatly paired compound leaves fell to the floor. In another six weeks the tree would erupt in yellow-orange blossoms. Her aunt used to collect and dry the petals to put into sachets for the dressers and wardrobes.

She'd kept up the tradition. Her clothes still smelled faintly of honeysuckle in the spring.

Lara refilled her tea from the samovar. It was a thank-you gift from the Russian government after she'd cleaned house in Murmansk in pursuit of the Spear of Destiny. Michelov and his pet admiral . . .

Shivering from the cold.

She brought herself back to the microfilm reader and waited for the tea to kick in. Lara rubbed her eyes, opened the next book. She'd ordered volumes from libraries in Beijing to Buenos Aires, Sydney to Oslo, in an effort to duplicate Von Croy and Frys's original research.

It was heavy going. She was on her fourth cup of black lifeboat tea.

Winston's familiar shuffle sounded behind her.

"Will there be anything else, miss?"

He clung to his formalities like the balding parrot above clung to his acacia branch.

"You don't have to ask permission to retire, Winston," Sir Garnet called from the ceiling. In her voice.

"You don't have to ask permission to retire, Winston," she repeated.

She had told Winston this every night since coming into her inheritance, but to Winston formalities were as much a part of the Croft estate as the old bricks from the days of King James. It was part of his code not to drop the ritual, just as it was her code not to treat employees as inferiors. "Good God, it's eleven thirty. Don't bother with breakfast in the morning."

"One small matter, miss. Have you looked at your phone messages?"

She'd called Borg first thing upon returning, after having decided that the key to Alison's whereabouts was in Von Croy and Frys's old research. Her shadowy attackers needed something buried in the work the partners did decades ago. Borg had been eager to go right to Buenos Aires and pick up the trail, but she'd demurred. They didn't know enough yet.

By reading the references listed in their paper, perhaps she could piece together what Ajay was after. Lara had also been trying to reach Frys's only remaining family, a forty-five-year-old son who was, as it happened, a professor in his own right at Dublin University . . . though he wasn't an archaeologist like his dad. His field was biology. But Lara still wanted to talk with him. He might have memories of his father's earlier work.

"Anything important?"

"That journalist. Heather Rourke. She's called twice today."

Lara groaned. "I don't have time for interviews and photo shoots. As I've told her at least twice."

"She came to the door uninvited while you were in the Indian Ocean last week. Cheeky."

"I admire her determination. You've got a withering stare. Then again, steady drops hollow the stone."

"You remember your Goethe. Your tutor would be pleased."

"Herr Baltz would rather I'd said *Steter tropfen holt den stein*. Is she being a nuisance? I could speak to her."

"Have you hollowed?"

"No." She stretched. "I redirect the drip."

She returned to her books, driving herself to put in a few more hours.

The whole *Méne* business was like a fog, a fog where unsheathed stilettos waited in determined hands.

What she was learning from her global collection of books and microfilm copies wasn't making her feel any easier. Usually she slept long and soundly when home in England, but lately her dreams had been invaded. Falling . . . drowning, always in suffocating darkness. She'd awake and hurry to the nearest window to look for the sun.

She glanced into the glass wall of the aviary. Thanks to her dark jumper, a trick of the light made her face and arms appear to float against the night outside. It was like looking at one's own ghost.

"Don't wear yourself out, miss," Winston said. His voice was soft and soothing when he chose to make it so, very like her grandfather's.

"Good night, Winston," Sir Garnet called. He was used to that exchange as well.

There were smiles in the glances they exchanged. If she couldn't have her parents, Winston was the next best thing.

Her father's traditional conservativism and her mother's unstinting—but unvoiced—affection existed in that creaking old frame . . . without the qualities that had divided her from her parents.

Lara listened to the shuffling steps, promising herself that after her next trip she'd send Winston to Jamaica for a fortnight. Winston loved Ian Fleming novels. She'd put him up at the Fleming House at Goldeneye, where he could watch sun-bronzed girls run back and forth on the beach all day.

With a guilty pang she realized she'd promised herself that before her last trip. And probably the one before that, too.

She returned to the microfilm reader, turned the knob to advance a page: *"So the Méne hold the number three holy . . ."*

Now, why would Kunai, a botanist who'd published papers on the medicinal value of rain forest blossoms and tubers, along with more lucrative coffee table books of exotic blossoms, become interested in a dead cult?

Lara Croft awoke to the sound of a rosewood tray landing atop her research.

Sir Garnet gave an outraged squawk. He'd been asleep, too.

"Breakfast, miss."

She blearily took in Winston's morning coat. The inviting smells of eggs, fried potatoes, hot buttered toast, fresh jam, and sausages made her open her eyes. A neatly creased paper sat beneath the tray.

There were disadvantages to being too used to sleeping rough. She'd set her head down at 4 A.M. atop Von Junst's *Unaussprichliche Kulten* and nodded off. She felt a twinge in her trapezius muscles as she straightened.

You are not aging, Croft. It's just that you took no exercise yesterday.

"Sausages, Winston? I told you not to bother getting up to cook."

"They're fresh from the market. They were coming with eggs and milk this morning anyway—"

"Give them to your dogs."

"Only after you've had two bites."

Tempted to tell him what he could bite, Lara held her tongue. Winston would absorb a fit of morning crankiness with the same dignified aplomb as he would a knighthood.

She hated being babied. Winston knew it, but did it anyway, with the same obstinacy that made him ask to be allowed to retire, or iron the London *Times*, or perform any of the little duties that she didn't give a toss about. Unless, of course, she was sick. The last time she'd been seriously ill, as opposed to just wounded, was twelve years ago. But still. She remembered how much she'd appreciated his attentiveness to all the small details of her comfort then, and sighed.

Swallowing two tiny bites of sausage, she watched him fill Sir Garnet's feed bowl, knowing she was being watched in turn. The taste of the sausage awoke her appetite, and by the time Winston had finished with the damp rag used to mop up Sir Garnet's droppings, she had finished the sausages and poached eggs—the centers were perfectly gelled, Winston being the twenty-four-carat treasure that he was—and was starting in on the fried potatoes and toast.

Having seen to her stomach, Winston shuffled out of the aviary.

Her mood rose with her blood sugar. Feeling mischievous enough to upset Winston's morning routine, Lara picked up the aviary's hose. As she turned the tap and washed the buttery smear from the toast from her fingers, she decided that hearty breakfasts, a reliable postal service, and parliamentary democracy were England's three great gifts to the world. Probably in that exact order.

She glanced at the morning paper as she absently turned the hose on the nearby plants and Sir Garnet, who shook and turned on his perch under the gentle rain, clucking contentedly. She was considering a swim to work the kinks out when she heard the gate bell.

Sir Garnet ceased preening and fluttered to a higher branch so he could look down the lane for a visitor.

"Courier for you, miss," Sir Garnet announced, recognizing the white and red of the express delivery van.

Lara wasn't about to make Winston walk the length of Croft Manor with whatever was being delivered, especially not after her recent delivery to Urdmann. She wouldn't put it past him to pay her back in her own coin—or a deadlier one. Worried now, she replaced the hose and hurried through the aviary, into the house, and to the massive timber door of the front entrance.

Winston was already signing for the delivery. How had the old man moved so fast? She sometimes suspected him of having a twin, or of secret passages in Croft Manor known only to the staff and handed down from servant to servant like Masonic passwords.

"South America, miss," he said and handed her the letter-sized packet.

"Professor Alex Frys," she read. Mind and body were both wide awake now. "So my letter did get through."

She took it into her home office, a small converted sitting room, woke her computer, entered her desktop password—"Boxgrove," the dig where as a child on a school trip she'd found her first artifact, a flint edge—and opened her file on Alex Frys. It contained a copy of the letters she'd sent, one to the care of his father's attorney in Scotland and the other to his university address in Dublin. She'd also made a note that an e-mail sent to the university had received an "out of the country" auto reply. She turned on her scanner.

The courier pouch had originated in Peru. It contained a letter, some photos, and a map. She read the letter first.

Lady Croft,

It was with a species of relief that I received your letter. It took some time to find me; I have given the university a delivery-service address.

I would be happy to meet with you, but I fear your journey may involve more distance than your proposed visit to me in Dublin. It may involve physical danger as well, but I get ahead of myself.

Let me begin by saying you were correct to call Dad's death "untimely," but only partially so. In the months before his demise, anxiety had been growing in him. I've since learned that Dad had bought a new security system for his house and made a number of reports to the police about prowlers, and even one that said he'd been followed on the very road where he met his death! He gave me reason to fear for his safety not four days before his accident, during a phone conversation late at night. Dad was not a man to drink, so a slurred conversation shortly after midnight, complete with whispered warnings of a "conspiracy" against him (all this from a teetotaler whom I had only seen drunk once before, upon the death of my mother), caused me to worry.

I confess that I moved too slowly. I called his assistant at the university, fearing either rapid onset of senile dementia or trouble with students from a country Dad had removed artifacts from—there have been the odd threats before. The police met me at the plane, having been told by Dad's assistant that I was on the way.

They wished me to identify his body, or what the car crash left of it.

Among his papers I found your number. The police said that he'd called you on the last day of his life. I heard a report that you might be mixed up with his murderers, or I would have called you then. I've just now learned that you've been cleared, so I have decided to contact you.

I found the most astonishing note tucked in the kitchen drain when I was doing dishes and had a stoppage. Apparently Dad had reason to believe something was going on at an old dig of his in Peru involving research he'd done years ago. Frankly, I thought that he might have been slipping at the last and imagined the whole thing. I decided to fly down here and investigate on my own and take a look around. But what I found . . . It is beyond me.

Please come at once. As I write this, I am observing the old site at a distance with the aid of a Peruvian park ranger named Fermi at the ruins of Ukju Pacha, in the eastern beginnings of the Andes. There is a river man named Paulo Williams you may trust; he works out of Puerto Maldonado, though if you have your own method of getting to the location I've highlighted on the enclosed 1:10,000 scale map, do so.

I shall give you more details when we meet.

As to Dad's notes concerning the *Méne*, which you inquired about, they have entirely disappeared. He burned them at the last.

Come soon!

Alex Frys

Lara looked at the black-and-white photos printed on copier paper. Paulo Williams squinted out from a forest of lines at the corners of his eyes and mouth; he had the bleary, narrow-eyed look of a man who enjoyed his tequila. Juan Fermi stared proudly into the camera; a grin split the wide face of an upper Amazon native.

The photo of Alex Frys wasn't framed very well; he only took up half the print. Lara saw a river behind him, thick jungle vegetation at its banks. He was older than Lara had pictured, a middle-aged man with smooth skin, a narrow, pointed chin, and receding hairline. He looked at the camera out of the sides of his eyes. His face rather reminded her of a portrait of William Shakespeare . . . had Shakespeare worn a Vandyke beard and cotton khakis.

Peru. Serious terrain. Tough enough without a potentially murderous cult to deal with. She should call Djbril and ask about the VADS rig.

Kunai might be at Ukju Pacha. Ajay was probably with him. Her last known address had been Buenos Aires.

It was time to call Borg.

9

"So nice to see you again, Lady Croft," said the British Airways flight attendant as Lara took her seat aboard the flight to Peru.

"Hello, Mishez." She'd flown before with Mishez, an archetypical first-class attendant with mannequin-perfect looks and an even, white-toothed smile.

Mishez reached into the first-class cooler. "Your usual big bottle of water?"

"Yes, please."

Mishez's pretty eyes widened as Borg crammed himself into the seat next to Lara. "Oh, my," she said. "Aren't you? . . ."

Lara was amused. It took a lot to fluster a professional like Mishez. The woman was actually blushing. "Mishez, this is my friend, Nils Bjorkstrom."

"Please, call me Borg," said Nils to Mishez with a smile.

"I'll be happy to get you anything you like, Borg," Mishez said.

I'll just bet you would, thought Lara. She tuned out the preflight bustle and pulled the volume by Von Junst out of her carry-on.

* * *

There'd been on-again, off-again debates among archaeologists for years about just when civilization had started during the last Ice Age. A few obscure artifacts going back 100,000 years or more were the source of much controversy. Von Croy had been one of the proponents of a "proto-Ur" civilization that had come into existence during a warm period of a few tens of thousands of years during the last glaciation. A few wilder souls claimed there'd been a fairly advanced civilization up the Pacific Rim from the subcontinent and Indochina, perhaps even stretching to the Americas, and that it was this civilization, or the dim memories of it, that had given rise to ancient legends of Atlantis and Lemuria.

Lara never dismissed anything out of hand; she'd seen too many impossibilities walking the earth.

Professors Von Croy and Frys believed that they'd discovered the religion of the proto-Ur civilization, or rather inferred its existence, mostly through laws amongst the earliest recorded civilizations barring its practice. Symbols, prayers, gods, rituals . . . It appeared that the rites of the *Méne*, going under a variety of names, had been banned everywhere, from predynastic Egypt to the early Shang dynasty in China.

Of course, it was all conjecture. Supposition was the inevitable result of patched-together written records thousands of years old which were themselves based on oral history stretching back many thousands of years earlier. The common thread was the image Lara had first seen in Ajay's bedroom, the distinctively shaped omega symbol.

Anyone found carrying that symbol was to be killed by a variety of methods that in themselves cast an interesting light on the respective cultures involved. Burning alive, bloodletting, crushing . . . There was no shortage of ways to kill someone, Lara reflected. In all the data, she found only one explanation for the harsh policy: a Chinese fragment maintaining that "evil wizards" used the omega mark to summon up and control murderous floods and storms.

Lara paged through the Von Junst until she came to his discussion of the glyph. Beside her, Borg drowsed, his eyes closed, headphones over his ears.

> Certain ancient insignia inexplicably exist worldwide. Like the turned cross, or the *swastika*, the snaked omega of the *Méne* has been found from the Americas to Siam to the Horn of Africa. Some maintain that this is a vestige of an ancient worldwide culture, possibly advanced. Others claim it only proves that the Red Indians of the American frontier brought familiar symbols with them along with their families and flocks as they crossed the ancient polar land bridge. But the snaked omega was thought by these ancient peoples such an ill-favored design that they went out of their way to efface it wherever it was found, though its former presence can sometimes be ascertained by the designs around it. Only the most remote monuments still bear it. I have seen with my own eyes on the paradise-isle of Bali brave scouts turn pale and tribal elders grow taciturn when shown the design, the best rubbing of which was acquired from a half-sunken temple in the Selat Surabaya at the east end of Java . . .

Lara traced the sinuous design with her finger.

"I hate that thing," Borg said in her ear.

She looked up. "What's that?"

"That omega thing. Alison had an obsession with it."

"Obsession?"

"Is this the right word? Fixation. It reminded me of that

movie about the UFOs with Steven Spielberg's direction. The character who made the volcanic upthrust his idée fixe. He would create it out of mashed potatoes and mud and so on. Alison would do the same. One time I spilled sugar as we had coffee. I came back with a paper towel and found she'd etched it in the sugar. She hadn't even been aware of doing it."

"What did she say about it?"

Borg's eyes shifted to Mishez as she walked past, down the aisle. "She said she dreamed it."

"Was it like this?" She tapped the image in the book. "Or different?"

"I'm not sure." Borg used one of his artificial fingers to change the channel on his in-seat screen.

"Well, look at it more closely."

"I would rather not. It—it gives me nightmares."

"A symbol? You mean it's appeared in your nightmares?"

"No, Lara." He looked at her, and his eyes were deadly serious. "The symbol *gives* me nightmares. I see it, and then in the night I have nightmares. I dream of suffocating, of a mass pressing down on my chest. I wake and gasp for air. I do not like this nightmare. I am not looking forward to sleeping tonight."

Lara thought back to her own recently troubled sleep and dreams of suffocating. Could the symbol have given them both identical uncomfortable dreams? Could it be so deeply embedded in the collective human unconscious Jung had postulated?

Mishez replaced Lara's empty water bottle without being asked. Borg turned down the offer of a beverage and put his headphones back on.

Lara envied Mishez for a moment. No worries beyond her

career, dates, and how to spend a layover in Lima. The last time Lara had flown with Mishez, she'd been nursing bruises on both knees and her left elbow after her experiences in the Nevada desert.

Lara realized she was tired.

Strange . . . Usually at the start of a trip she was as antsy as a mongoose hearing a rustle in the grass. It was only after the battles against exhaustion and pain had been won, and the trip was over, that her mood sometimes darkened and she found herself wishing for a simpler life.

She closed Von Junst, took a swallow of the chilled water, and felt better immediately. No point letting that 19th century theosophist get the better of her. She lifted her eye mask and snapped the soothing gel pads over her face.

But she fell into a strange dream, where the omega design of the *Méne* grew and grew and expanded and expanded into an umbrella hovering over her until it dropped and engulfed her in its dark, smothering mouth.

After they arrived in Peru, there was a day's delay in Iquitos, with Borg fretting over his climbing equipment, which was supposed to have been shipped to him from the States but had yet to arrive.

"I've got plenty of gear," Lara said, fuming at the delay and keeping an eye on the bags with her guns and VADS gear. There were also parachutes. Her research into Ukju Pacha had mentioned that the ruins centered around a gigantic chasm called the Whispering Abyss. One legend said that sacrifices were thrown down it to prevent earthquakes, and priests descended an endless staircase to speak to gods who lived deep within the earth.

"This is . . . specialized. A different set of arms. I did not wish to haul them all over London; they're only useful for climbing. You never saw my TV program?"

"No. Television's just living vicariously. I'd rather have the real thing."

The courier arrived, sweat and apologies pouring out of him in equal quantities.

"There was some trouble at customs," the driver said. "The delivery fee will of course be refunded to you."

"Not me. My producer." Another man—and a certain Tomb Raider—might have bawled out the courier over something that wasn't his fault. Lara felt a tingle of admiration.

"Back in the good graces of your cable network?" Lara asked.

"Fortune turns again my way. The new host of my show is not working out, it seems. I have heard him called 'wannabe,' which, I understand, is bad. They want me to return."

Borg opened the cases, high-impact plastic equipment boxes with steel edges. Lara walked around behind him to look but only saw packing material before Borg closed them again.

"Now we are ready to find this boatman of yours," he said.

"Not mine. The young professor's."

They took a smaller plane, an old De Havilland floatplane, to the next stop. Their final flight destination was Puerto Maldonado, at the edge of the Madre de Dios rain forest.

"Ecologists?" the pilot asked.

"*Sí*. Photojournalist," Lara answered in Spanish.

"You travel with many cameras. All those boxes," the pilot said, referring to the cargo filling his bay and the third row of seats at the back of the plane.

"We brought our own darkroom," she said.

He landed the plane with the gentle touch Lara was used to in an aircraft owner-operator. Upriver she saw a catamaran-style barge, the *Tank Girl*, as the plane taxied across the water to the dock. Good; Williams was awaiting them, as planned.

A shirtless Peruvian native—a member of the *Machinguenga* tribe, to judge by his tattoos—looped lines around one of the plane's pontoons and secured it to one of several docks projecting from the riverfront. Lara and Borg climbed out of the plane, and the pilot opened the cargo doors. Lara gave the dockhand two dollars—she usually traveled with American currency—and he helped them unload.

Puerto Maldonado was one of those whitewashed South American towns where the age of a building could be determined by its distance from the stone mission church. It lived at the pace of an earlier century. Old men watched them from storefront benches; old women leaned on their elbows from wide-open windows. Children wore only underwear in the heat.

A vintage Chevy Blazer roared up to the dock in a blue haze of oily exhaust, just beating a tiny Volkswagen. The driver jumped out, landing on neon-colored athletic shoes endorsed by Michael Jordan. "Taxi? Taxi?"

The Volkswagen driver pounded his steering wheel in frustration, then frowned at the amount of gear coming out of the now-moored plane. He didn't bother to climb out of his cab.

"Taxi, sir?" he called to Borg out the window. "Very cheapest rates."

The Blazer's driver hurried over and grabbed one of Borg's cases. "Air-conditioned ride! Ten dollars American!"

Lara ignored him, pointed to a flat-bottomed canoe tied up at the dock. "Yours?" she asked the shirtless dockhand in Spanish.

"Yes."

"What is your name?"

"Julio, señorita."

She handed him a bill. "Take us out to that boat."

"Tank Girl, sí," the native said, smiling.

"We're going in the canoe," she told Borg, then turned to the driver of the Blazer. "Sorry, no taxi."

The man continued to pull at Borg's case, until the Norwegian put his weight into the tug-of-war. Then the driver shifted gear and began to help Julio load the long canoe with their gear. Lara handed a pair of dollars to the enterprising taxi driver. He accepted the money, then pressed a brochure into her hand in return. "Many good trips. Rain forest, bird-watching, Inca ruins. Air-conditioned ride." Then he was gone.

Borg wiped the sweat from his face with one sleeve. "I hope there is air-conditioning aboard the *Tank Girl*."

"I wouldn't count on it," Lara said.

They climbed down the short ladder into the canoe, and Lara helped Julio cast off.

A wide-eyed, mud-splattered boy watched them from the riverbank. Borg and the boy swapped silly faces. Lara gave in to a giggle. It occurred to her that she liked having Borg along; she seldom laughed when she was alone in the field.

Other boys in short smocks probed the muddy riverside with nets, occasionally lifting fish into tin buckets. Beyond them, the town slept in the afternoon sun, its structures hidden behind a hedge of balconies. Clouds were already piling up for the daily rainstorm. The sputtering sound of motorbikes carried from across the muddy riverside.

* * *

The *Tank Girl* was a river catamaran nearly twenty meters long with short deck space at the bow and stern. The rest was boxy superstructure in front and the silver fuel tanks at the stern that gave the boat her name. Atop the mobile-home-like superstructure was a flying bridge, protected from the sun by an awning stretched on squared loops of steel and accessible by ladders fore and aft.

Julio waved to another native on deck, who prodded a figure drowsing out the afternoon in a hammock slung across the back of the flying bridge.

Lara recognized Paulo Williams. He was two meters tall and thin. His collar bones showed at his crewneck T-shirt, and his legs were like bronze toothpicks, as though his NBA-sized body had shed every ounce of fat to protect itself from the heat.

"You must be Croft," he called as the canoe tied up. His was a strange accent, a combination of American drawl and Portuguese consonants.

Lara picked up her backpack and the duffel bag containing her guns and the VADS hardware. "And you're Paulo Williams. I'm sorry we're late."

"No complaints from me. A man can have a good time in Puerto Maldonado."

Lara didn't wait for him to elaborate, but pitched in to get the canoe unloaded. With Borg's assistance, the job went quickly.

"That's everything," she said at last, clapping her *Machinguenga* chauffeur on the shoulder. "Thank you, Julio."

Julio didn't say good-bye. Among his people farewells were only said to the dead. He shoved off and paddled away from the *Tank Girl*.

Lara heard the aft door to the main cabin open. A woman

in a sleeveless khaki vest, her red hair tied up off her shoulders in the heat, stepped out. "Glad you could join us, Lara."

Lara fought to hide her shock. *Heather Rourke*. The journalist she'd been avoiding. "What do you think you're doing here, Heather?"

"My job," the reporter said. "One way or another, Heather Rourke always gets her story."

Lara glanced at Borg. "Is this your doing, Borg? Did you tip her off?"

"I have never spoken to this woman before," he said somewhat stiffly.

"He's blameless," Heather interjected. "I called the publicist for his network. Asked a few questions. She was eager to inform me of where he was heading. Then it was just a matter of figuring out where a Tomb Raider might go after landing in this part of Peru. Ukju Pacha came up in my research. Short of parachuting into the jungle, this river is the only route to the ruins, so I took a chance on intercepting you here."

Lara turned to Williams. "Captain, I don't know what this woman may have told you, but she's no associate or friend of mine. I want her off the boat."

Williams shrugged. "Can't do that. She's already paid."

"You mean you *won't* do it."

"She's a paying customer, same as you two," Williams answered.

"You might as well accept it, Lara," Heather said. "I'm coming along for the ride."

Lara considered picking her up and throwing her bodily off the boat, but that would only be playing into the journalist's hands. Borg and she could hire a plane and get to Alex

Frys's camp by parachute drop, but for all she knew, it might take days to organize a plane trip, and Frys's message had stressed the need for haste.

The first few raindrops hit the deck of the boat. She could see the rain coming, a curtain masking the landscape.

"Suit yourself," Lara said. "But I'm warning you, Heather. It could get rough."

"Are you threatening me?"

"If I was, you wouldn't have to ask," Lara said. "I'm trying to put some sense into your thick head, that's all."

The reporter seemed offended. "I haven't spent my career at a computer, Ms. Croft. I've covered stories from Afghanistan to Zimbabwe. Dictators have threatened to have me shot. I can handle myself."

"She could help, Lara," Borg said. "The people upriver might fear the world press more than they fear the Peruvian government."

"Let's get inside," Lara said as the rain increased in intensity.

Lara looked around the box-shaped main cabin as they brought the gear in. The *Tank Girl* worked for a living. The barge carried no amenities for passengers. The cabin had scratched plastic windows and duct-taped cushions on the storage benches lining the walls. Cubbyholes filled with what looked like mail covered the stern side of the big room; forward was a dirty combination of galley, chartroom, and machine shop. Beyond a paneled partition festooned with lad-mag pinups, Lara could see the main bridge. A radio squawked within, broadcasting the chatter like a talkative parrot.

"Could I speak to you alone, Captain?" Lara asked. The rain hit with a roar. Water poured from the sky in torrents. A few drops found a way into the cabin.

Williams shrugged and led her forward to the main bridge. A young man whose tattoos marked him as another *Machinguenga* was lounging in a hammock chair.

"Francisco, take a hike." Williams flicked his thumb at a side door. Without a word, the man stepped into the rain and moved off along the narrow freeboard running along the side of the main cabin.

Lara decided to use her ass-kicking tone. The captain didn't look the type to fall for a bright smile and batted eyelashes. "What's the journalist doing here?"

"Like I said, she's paying her way, same as you. Fares are the next thing to pure profit for me." Williams took a milk jug half full of loose tobacco from a railed shelf. "Most places you keep your smoke where it won't dry out. In the Madre you have to fight to keep it dry."

"So you're bringing a journalist on a secret trip?"

"Nothing secret about the *Girl*'s route. Unclench those tight little cheeks; your friend upriver knows about it. When I told him who wanted to tag along, he about stroked out."

"Did he?" Perhaps Frys had been in the cloud forest too long.

"He wants a journalist around, especially one named Heather Rourke."

"Why's her name important?"

Williams rolled a cigarette with tobacco-stained fingers. "An old river turtle like me has to tell you who Heather Rourke is?"

"Apparently."

"She's got connections with SNN. You *have* heard of Satellite Network News?"

SNN was famous for providing free technology to developing nations. Internet access, dishes, fiber-optic networks even. She'd heard it lauded everywhere from *The Economist* to *The Wall Street Journal*. "Yes. I don't travel with a dish, though."

"There's even a little bar in Mal that has SNN."

Lara wondered why Heather had introduced herself as working for a magazine she'd never heard of. To get her off her guard? She'd certainly not recognized the face. Just her keeping a low profile was interesting, a rare thing for prestige journalists these days.

"Don't feel too bad about it," Williams said, lighting the cigarette. "I was funnin' you. Your friend Frys at the other end had to tell me who she was, too."

"You can get him on the radio?" She looked at the set, a military antique dating from the days of Che Guevara at least.

"If he's around."

She stepped away to give him room. "Do you mind?"

He went to the radio, twisted the dial. "Mynah, this is *Tank Girl*. You on this channel? Over?"

"English?" Lara asked.

"His Spanish isn't much. Makes him stand out more than his English does."

Williams tried again, and still didn't get an answer.

"What's 'Mynah' for?"

"He's not using his name in case the radio is being monitored. He's posing as a bird whachacallit."

"An ornithologist?"

"Bingo."

Not much of a cover. The mynah bird was famous for using its voice to fake its identity to fool predators. Plus, they weren't native to this part of the world. "And he trusts you because? . . ."

Williams took a contemplative puff. " 'Cause I showed him the old canopy tower when he first came upriver. Perfect for his purposes. Plus, I had it in for that expedition up at Ukju. The guy who runs their supplies is an old rival, you might say."

"How big a rival?"

"You know those movies where two sailing ships run out their guns and shoot at each other as they go past?" He gestured with his cigarette toward a scattering of bullet holes in the aluminum wall near the wheel. "Kind of like that."

"And are more bullets apt to fly on this trip?" Lara asked.

Williams grinned. "Hard to say. If they do, just keep your head down."

Lara smiled back. "That's not my style, Captain," she said.

It would be a two-day trip upriver. The passengers had a choice: they could either sleep in hammocks slung from the walls or on the narrow plastic cushions of the benches. The only privacy anyone would have on the catamaran would be in the washroom.

And it wasn't much of a washroom. The sink held the leavings of the captain and his mate's shaves, the floor of the tiny shower was black, and flies crawled on the rim of the toilet. Lara hardly had room to change into cargo shorts and a brief black tank top. She strapped on her pistols and felt much better.

The rain quit and a spectacular evening came on, the orange and purple of the sky turning the rain forest and the shadows it cast onto the river the deepest black. They didn't have dinner until they anchored for the night. The plastic windows and screens crawled with insects trying to get in at the cabin lights.

"Two questions answered already without me opening my mouth," Heather said over her plate of pork and beans.

"What's that?" Captain Williams asked, pouring a shot of gin into his water glass.

"The real Lara Croft. Question one: Why the skimpy outfits? Question two: Why the ponytail? The answers are the heat and the humidity." She lifted her own gorgeous ruin of a hairstyle from her damp neck and pulled her sweat-soaked shirt out from her chest.

Borg wouldn't fit at the table. He sat on one of the benches lining the cabin, next to Francisco the mate. Borg looked forward all the time, as if news of Ajay might come floating down the river.

"How many stops before our destination?" Lara asked.

"Three. Propane to the Macaw Lodge tomorrow, then more diesel for the Peruvian National Post at Delago. A diesel delivery to the Fitzcarraldo Gold Mine last. There's a couple Brazil nut farms and another mine I visit now and then, too, but they don't get anything but mail this trip. We won't even tie up, just toss the sacks onto their docks as we go by."

"They let you deliver mail?" Heather asked.

"I'm a private contractor, you might say. The police only care that I don't run coca or guns." He screwed the top back on his gin. "I make enough to support my lifestyle."

Heather looked at Lara's pistols. "Those don't squirt water. The police don't have a problem with your carrying them?"

"I've got a lawyer who knows how to get me the right paperwork. A kidnapping by local guerrillas would be a terrible inconvenience."

"I've been in the mountains of Iran and Afghanistan with nothing but a tape recorder and some cameras. Never felt the need for guns."

Lara knew a double bid when she heard one. She redoubled. "Did you have a guide?"

"Yes."

"He was armed."

"Yes. You know the men in that part of the world, I expect. Very attached to their rifles."

"Then the only difference between you and me is who would do the shooting."

"I didn't fly three thousand miles to make you an enemy, Lady Croft. But I want your story. The real story. I've heard some strange things in London and Washington."

"I can't remember the last time I heard something that wasn't strange coming out of those two places."

Heather Rourke snorted. "Point taken. But that's why I'm here. I came to get an accurate picture of your life."

"Why the interest? I'm not glamorous. I'm not political. I'm a scholar with a bent for adventure. You were at my lecture in London. You saw what I do."

The journalist picked up her plate and took it to the little sink. "My interest in you started in a house in Georgetown, of all places. A prominent senator was giving a party. The conversation got around to the most interesting man/most interesting woman you ever met. I listened to a Chinese businessman who'd served as an army officer in Tibet tell the most amazing story about you and some kind of underworld kingpin named Marco Bartoli. To hear him, you took down an entire syndicate single-handed."

"He exaggerated. I'd suspect anything a Chinese hatchet man has to say about Tibet."

Heather returned to the table. "It was an astonishing story, nonetheless. You made quite an impression on the local monks, apparently. One of them said something to this ex-army officer that he never forgot."

"And what might that be?"

"The monk said that you were a spirit warrior, strong as a mountain but supple as a river. He said that determination like yours could topple the throne of a kingdom. Well, after hearing that, I decided I had to meet you for myself."

"The Chinese do know how to tell a story to the credulous. I'm surprised you fell for it. Americans are paying tens of thousands of dollars to have their sofas rearranged by anyone who can properly pronounce 'feng shui.' Here are the facts, if you're interested. I was . . . involved with Bartoli. He was a thief and a smuggler, but it was the Chinese who smashed him. I just found the door, so to speak. I suspect the man you heard was Li Yuan, a Chinese Intelligence man who handled most of the arrests. I'd heard he'd gotten a private industry job in America as a reward."

Heather nodded. "That was his name."

"Li wouldn't admit to achievement without a set of thumbscrews. Even then you'd only get 'I was very fortunate to have arrested the criminal.' Confucianism."

"You impressed him enough that he told the story the way a military man might describe serving under Patton. What the monks had to say made a deep impression on him."

"Some monks who haven't seen a woman in twenty years have one drop in on a snowmobile, and you're shocked that I made an impression?"

Borg snorted.

"Call it a draw, ladies," Captain Williams cut in. "Let's have one more drink and get to bed."

"Water will do, thanks," Lara said.

"I don't like gin," the journalist said. "I don't suppose there's any wine on board?"

"This isn't a cruise ship, lady," Williams said.

Lara leaned across the table and caught the mate's eye. "Francisco, do you have any *masato*?"

"Yes, señorita. There is some on board."

Williams grunted.

"Then get it. Perhaps Heather would like to try a native drink."

Heather's left eyebrow almost met a bedraggled bang. "Native as in—"

"Local Indian. More of a beer. Very appropriate for an after-dinner drink."

"I'll try anything once," Heather said, emptying her water glass and pushing it toward Francisco, who was opening a jug.

Francisco poured some of the amber liquid for himself and a generous portion for the journalist. He offered it to Lara, but she shook her head.

Borg turned it down. "I've given up drinking for a while. I had a wonderful dinner ruined by too much wine."

He and Lara shared a sympathetic smile.

Heather sniffed the brew.

"You'll find it helps with digestion," Lara said, suppressing a smile with an effort.

Heather tasted it. "Not bad. Like a stout or a bock."

Francisco downed his and smacked his bare belly through his open shirt. Lara caught Heather stealing a glance at the tight stomach muscles. "What's that blue tattooing under your eye, Francisco?" Heather asked.

"I am of an ancient line. In my tribe, this means the blood

of Incan kings flows in my veins. In the days of the Sun Empire—"

"Cisco, give it a rest," Williams said, slamming down his glass. "That act is fine for some piece of tail working on her master's in environmental studies, but this woman's a respected journalist. Give her the story straight."

Francisco showed no sign of embarrassment. "The mark is from the days when my people were taken by the rubber slavers. Those who were the best gatherers were tattooed by the rubber men to show they had a good eye. It became a symbol of status, and from there became a tradition."

"Believe it or not, the truth makes you more interesting, Francisco." Heather took another swallow of the native beer. "What's this made of? Sweet potatoes? Plantains?"

Lara waited till Heather swallowed. "Manioc, fermented in women's saliva."

Heather still choked. "What?"

"Yes, the local women all use their saliva for fermentation," Francisco said. "My mother sends me what she makes."

Heather's eyes narrowed at Lara, but to her credit the journalist finished her glass. "Still tastes good on a hot night."

They awoke the next morning to a cacophony of screeches. Lara got out of her hammock and stretched as she went out by the tanks on the stern. Heather was atop the cabin, taking pictures of a sky full of birds.

Lara went back into the cabin, unzipped her pack, which hung at the head end of her hammock, and got out a tiny pair of lightweight binoculars. She went back outside and took in the breathtakingly colorful birds. They weren't really a flock, Lara noticed as she climbed the aft ladder to the top deck, just hundreds of groups of two and three and four birds rising and wheeling southeast.

"Red-bellied macaws," Captain Williams grunted. "Get under the awning unless you want to be dumped on."

Lara looked at the spotted deck and joined him at the wheel on the flying bridge. She saw Borg up forward with Francisco, gaping like the rest of them. Borg still wore a long-sleeved cotton shirt and gloves to cover his artificial arms.

"Macaws?" Heather said, joining them. "Those are three-thousand-dollar birds."

"Not down here," Lara said. "There must be a clay lick nearby."

"Yeah, in those hills there. We're going around a bend in the river today, then into the hills near the Macaw Lodge. They get a lot of bird-watchers." He inflated his lungs. "Cisco," he bellowed. "I'm not paying you to be a tour guide. Let's make some river."

The *Tank Girl* sputtered to life as the anchors came up. Borg helped with the lines in his own stiff way.

Lara enjoyed the clear-skied morning, and sat on the cool white propane fuel tanks with her research into Ukju Pacha. The others avoided the tanks as though they were live bombs, which, in a way, they were. If the tanks exploded, the whole boat would be reduced to matchsticks, but in the morning the metal was pleasantly cool against her skin. This time of year in the southern tropics, she would have to enjoy the air and the sun while she could before the inevitable afternoon rains came.

When Williams and Cisco made their deliveries, she retreated into the cabin; no point advertising her presence to the locals. Kunai knew who she was, but whether he was baiting her in some fashion through the kidnapping attempt, and perhaps the actions of the young Frys, remained to be seen. She'd been baited before. The would-be trappers always forgot that both prey and trapper had to meet at the bait and that when they did, the roles could be reversed. In any case, she could do little about it until she got to the headwaters of the Manu River.

Worrying about it wouldn't change the future. Verbally fencing with Heather about her background provided some mental diversion.

"What are you writing?" Lara asked from her perch, seeing Heather taking notes in a spiral notebook. It was the cheap sort of thing a student might carry, a strange accessory for a woman who could afford a tailored camel hair coat.

The journalist turned back a page. " 'As I watch Lara Croft read atop the riverboat tank, she puts to mind one of the jaguars lurking in the Peruvian jungle. In repose she sits perfectly still, save for a wiggling foot that betrays her working mind, the way that same cat might twitch his tail as he watches the game trail from a bough above. Her hair matches her brown eyes, her portrait-perfect skin goes with her swimsuit model's body, she might be reading *Vogue* while the photographer sets up his lights and equipment. But her military-cut shorts, hiking boots elaborately laced and tied, and black sleeveless top suggests she's prepared for a run to the heights of Machu Picchu instead of the makeup artist. Then there's her weapons—matched pistols in a two-gun rig of black canvas holsters—worn gunfighter style. Whatever mysteries of the past she might probe, she is ready to face danger in the present . . . ' Shall I go on? It's just impressions."

"Does it bother you that they're wrong?"

"What do you mean by that? You object to the cat metaphor? I thought I was being flattering."

Lara closed her book. "Flattery doesn't enter into it. You want to describe me to the world, right? Or I should say describe me to the world and get it right."

"Yes. Of course."

"It's impossible to depict reality."

"I do the best I can."

"This is why I don't like journalists. The act itself transforms."

Heather made a swishing sound and passed her hand over her head.

"Look, you've heard of those African natives who think taking a picture steals part of their soul."

"Yeah. Is it the Bushmen?"

"There are many different groups that feel that way. It doesn't matter. We laugh at it, but I've come to the conclusion they're right. Celebrity alters. It can't be helped. It's not your fault, of course. As soon as you write a sentence about me and someone reads it, that puts an image in the reader's head, an image that's nothing like me. I've been altered. A piece of my soul is gone."

"Why do you care what people think?"

"Why do you try to shape their thoughts?"

Heather tapped her pen against the wire spiral. "I don't."

"Strange thing for a journalist with your reputation to say."

"Why?"

"What you choose to make a story and what you choose to leave unexamined determines the political agenda. Is that journalism or advocacy?"

"I tell the truth."

Lara was tempted to tell her that there was no such thing. The fact that she didn't believe it kept her silent. "Find another subject."

"Like your friend with the artificial arms?"

"Your readers might like it better. Look at him with this boat. Determination. That's an example to write about. I'm not that interesting."

Heather cocked her head. "I've known you for all of a day, and I already think you're the most interesting woman I've met in years. Since you brought up determination . . ."

"Save the flattery for the next celeb you target."

"Small potatoes," Heather said quietly.

"What does that mean?" Lara asked.

"You want my cards on the table?"

Lara hopped down from the tank. "Absolutely. You'll find I respond to honesty."

She closed her notebook. "You won't think I'm mad? No matter what I say?"

Lara crossed her arms, waited as ten more meters of rain forest slid by.

"Ever since I 'made it' into big-league journalism, I've become part of those Washington clubs and circles that people like to call the elite. Some of the power-broker glitter disappointed; I learned that more public policy is created in corporate boardrooms than in congressional debates. Same story in London, and Beijing, for that matter. At the parties, at the meetings, at the conferences, I didn't talk much. I listened. Maybe it's part of being a woman, but when you're an outsider with your nose pressed up against the glass for most of your life, you get pretty good at reading lips and body language."

If you're waiting for an us-girls-against-the-world expression of sympathy, Lara thought, *you'll still be sitting there when we arrive upriver.*

Heather looked over her shoulder, then back at Lara. "I

started to wonder if I was really moving among the elite. I got the feeling that I was talking to middle managers and PR flacks. But every now and then, key people would just be gone for a week or two. And when they returned, it was like some decision had been made. A story changed, perhaps, or a policy dropped off the radar screen. I started looking into secret societies. I got an interview with a man. Even now I can't say his name—he's still in a hospital bed, dying—and he told me a story about his role in the Illuminati. And you."

"The Illuminati? He was hospitalized with senile dementia, I take it."

"He had captained a nuclear submarine before he ran one of the largest charitable foundations in the world. Straight and stable and sharp as a diamond drill bit."

"So you think I can give you insight into secret societies?"

"I'm pretty sure you work for one."

Lara laughed. "Despite my title, I'm too much the anarchist for oaths and countersigns and secret ceremonies."

"When the gentleman in the hospital dies, I'm going to tell his story. I'd like to tell yours. Call me an anarchist, too, but I don't like the idea of my life being influenced by twenty-one men meeting on some estate outside of Rome, or Sydney, or Denver."

"If that's what you want, I'll tell all, and then you can take this boat back to the airstrip at Puerto Maldonado."

Heather clicked her pen.

"There are secret societies. There are not-so-secret ones. Some have more money than they know what to do with. Others operate out of the back room of a Coventry laundry. People are social creatures. They work together to get things done. Most of these societies are just that: groups of men and women with an agenda. The world is full of powerful entities: corporations, government agencies, cartels, even the broadcasting network that I'm guessing is paying your expenses now. Once in a while it will seem that one rises to prominence, but none of them become predominant because there are so many other competing ideologies, religions, political movements, what-have-you. The world is a big, fractious place. Secret societies just sound scary because they're secret. There are a few that are malevolent, but then there are drug cartels and terrorist groups motivated by religion, too. But no one group runs everything."

"But you've fought them."

"I've defended myself. I've been shot at and chased by everything from poppy plantation guards to slavers."

"So you really just like archaeology? It's not a cover? I'll keep it off the record."

"Even if it were 'just a cover,' it wouldn't be very smart to mention that to the press, now would it? But, no, it's not a cover. It's a calling. Churchill said the further you can see into the past, the better you can predict the future, or words to that effect. Everything that's happened has happened before; we just keep remaking it with a different cast. Like all the film versions of *Dracula* floating around out there. Since nothing particularly new or interesting happens today, I try to learn more about how it fit together three thousand years ago."

Heather scrunched her eyebrows. "That simple? What about that 'spirit warrior' stuff the old monk said?"

Lara laughed. "Just because someone speaks with a bunch of incense burning in the background doesn't mean he knows what he's talking about."

"I promise you, off the record."

What could she tell her that wouldn't be a lie?

"Heather, I neither work for a secret society, nor am I Lady

Croft, cultbuster. I like to think of myself as a twenty-first-century version of Walter Raleigh. I like to explore. There are still many, many places on this planet where 'no man has gone before,' or at least not for a hatful of centuries. There have been times when I've learned that some icon, which perhaps possesses no more power than that which people choose to invest in it due to their own beliefs, is about to fall into the wrong hands—according to my judgment and sensibilities, anyway. I see to it that said object ends up where it won't be a harm to anyone."

"And you decide all this on your own?"

"No, the voices in my head get their say, too. I've been outvoted a few times." She drew her guns with a rip of Velcro, twirled them, and put them back in their holsters.

Heather blinked rapidly. She glanced over at Francisco, idling on the deck.

"That's a joke, Heather."

"You're very sure of yourself, aren't you?"

"I've learned there's precious little else I can be sure of."

"So what are you after on this trip? And why have you brought that giant along? You said you worked alone."

"Why don't you ask him?"

"I did."

"And?"

"He wouldn't say."

"Then it's not for me to say, either."

"Who can I ask then?"

"You'll meet him when I do. As to whether he'll be any more forthcoming with answers, your guess is as good as mine."

* * *

The next day the ship's whistle alerted Lara to trouble. It was just after the regular afternoon downpour, with the deck still awash in rainfall on its way over the side, that a second riverboat made its appearance.

It was long and narrow, and if it had had dragon heads fore and aft, Lara would have taken it for a screw-driven Viking longship. Instead, a long awning stretched from stem to stern, covering wheelhouse, cargo, and open deck space.

"That crazy bastard!" Williams shouted as Lara joined him at the wheel. "He's coming right for us. Outta the way, Dominguez!" Then quietly, "What's he playing at this time?"

"Trouble?" Lara asked.

"A new game."

"Your rival, I assume."

"Yes, the *Plato*."

Williams edged a little closer to the bank. Lara heard something scrape along the bottom of the pontoon. The *Plato* gave a derisive hoot of its air horn.

"Cisco!" Williams shouted. The *Tank Girl*'s captain opened a cabinet next to his knee. Lara spotted the red shape of a fire extinguisher. Williams pulled a shotgun out from behind it.

The mate hurried in, his hair slick from the rain.

"Take the wheel. Keep her straight."

She smelled the gun oil from the pump-action. Her hands went to her guns by themselves.

Williams dashed out onto the front of the catamaran. Lara followed him as far as the door. She leaned out and saw him put the shogun to his shoulder.

"Stay off, Dominguez!"

In the *Plato*'s wheelhouse, a pot-bellied man under a wide straw hat pinched thumb and finger.

"Bastard! Keep off!" Williams shouted.

The *Plato*'s captain edged his ship over as the two riverboats came alongside. Lara caught a flash of a wide-faced man in a camouflage-patterned T-shirt reclining against burlap bags with a book open on his lap, before another man, shirtless, stood up and flung a skin of something at the cabin of the *Tank Girl*.

"Go back to Dallas, gringo!"

Lara, again on instinct, drew, flicked off her safety, and fired her right hand pistol at the cartwheeling shape. Liquid sprayed. Her shots deflected the skin just enough so that, instead of crashing through the cabin window, it hit the pontoon with a wet slap before falling into the river.

The Tomb Raider half expected a Molotov cocktail. Instead, she caught the smell of something noxious, like American skunk.

The *Plato* passed with nothing more threatening than the sight of the shirtless man's buttocks pointed out over the side.

"You don't wear those just for show," Williams said as she lowered her gun. "I didn't know people could draw and shoot like that outside of a rodeo gun show."

Williams went to the pontoon, covered his nose and mouth.

"Animal entrails," he said from behind his hand. He grabbed a bucket from the side, dipped it in the river, and poured water over the deck and pontoon. Borg and Heather approached from the stern, smelled the splatter, and retreated to windward. "It's always something."

"So that's your rival for the river trade?" Lara asked, flicking the safety back on her gun and holstering it again. Monkeys hooted at them from the forest as Francisco turned the boat away from the riverbank and back into the channel.

"It's stupid. He's not even outfitted to haul fuel."

"Then why?"

"I forget. A woman. A case of bourbon. Maybe it was a song on the stereo in the cantina. He lost a tooth, and I detached a retina. Turns out men don't just shake hands and make up down here."

The *Tank Girl* changed directions with the river innumerable times as they moved between higher and higher hills, all coated with thick, multicanopied jungle. When they stopped for the night, they were in the cloud forest proper for the first time. Thick bands of white and gray hung about the hilltops like vaporous mushroom caps.

Monkeys and birds screeched and squawked and hollered, exchanging noises from riverbank to riverbank like opposing armies trading artillery shells.

"If man leaves the forest, does it still make a sound?" Lara asked.

"I like it," Borg said. "It is . . . it is untouched. No, what is the word? Like primitive?"

"Primeval," Lara said.

"I could take off my clothes and plunge into the water and cover myself with mud to keep off the insects. Become a wild man. Pound my chest when I find the right mate to keep the other males away."

She smiled at the image. Perhaps she'd slip into a leopard-skin bikini and a sloth-claw necklace and join him in howling at the moon.

He looked at the misty green hilltops. "What is she doing here, I wonder?"

Lara felt a twinge somewhere just behind her breastbone. There was only one "she" in Borg's life: Ajay. "I've wondered that myself. I've got a theory now. You want to hear it?"

"Anything."

"Some say the Inca weren't the first civilization here, but just built upon the foundations of an older one, one swallowed by the jungle but not quite digested."

"Older?"

"A theory. It's called proto-Ur, for lack of a better term. They crossed oceans; it's thought that they extended from the Mideast and then around the Pacific Rim. The protos worshipped gods, but they were strange sorts of gods, gods that dwelled here on earth, or perhaps beneath it, like the Polynesians with their volcanoes."

"Yes. They worshipped places?"

"No. Gods of places. Deep places, the bottom of caverns, the ocean. This religion was apparently ordered to an extent that wasn't seen again until the Confucians or the medieval Catholic church. Everyone in the faith was ranked by a number. They were called the *Méne*, the numbered. They had an important temple here, if I've done my research correctly. I think Ajay is after some kind of sacred *Méne* artifacts."

The ancient trees at the banks, weighed down with creeper, moss, and vine, black-trunked where the river touched them, extended sun-chasing boughs out over the river as though they were cupped ears listening to the conversation.

"In the ruins?"

"Below them. In a shaft, a deep pit. It translates as the 'Whispering Abyss.' That's why I brought the parachutes. At the bottom—"

"Uff, look at those," Borg exclaimed, lifting his mechanical arm. Something the size of a pointer trotted off a downed trunk and plunged into the river.

"Giant otters," Captain Williams called down from the flying bridge. "They're called river wolves in this part of the headwaters."

"Is everything around here of that size?" Borg asked.

Williams started counting on his fingers as he steered with his elbow. "Spiders that can cover a cantaloupe. River fish weighing hundreds of pounds. Snakes about as long as this boat. Funny thing, though: It's the small stuff that'll kill you out here. Bugs and fevers and intestinal parasites and so on. Snakes got nothing on them."

"Do you think she is all right, Lara?" Borg's voice wasn't any louder than the sound of the river passing over the catamaran's pontoons.

Lara put her hand on his bowling-ball-like shoulder. There was nothing to regret; he was never hers to begin with. "We'll know in a day or two."

Green, cloud-cloaked mountains filled the eastern horizon. A stream joined the river at a stretch of grassland, and behind the grassland a small mountain of a thousand meters or so rose above the adjoining hills.

"End of the line," Williams said. "Old *Girl* can't navigate much further upstream. Rapids."

"Where are we?" Borg asked as Lara checked the gear.

"An old coffee plantation," Williams said. "The would-be coffee man who built the place went out of business decades ago. The Peruvian government seized the property over taxes and decided to try to cater to the eco-tourist trade. They built a canopy observation tower and ranger station in the old plantation house. But there were plenty of birds and animals to see in easier-to-reach areas of the Madre de Dios preserve where the guerrillas didn't operate."

Lara could make out moss-covered pilings where the dock had once stood. Now only a series of rocks jutted out from them, with a cable to use as a handrail.

Francisco threw a lasso over one of the pilings and pulled the boat to the rocks. "There is the canopy tower on that mountain; you can just see it above the trees. See the wood?" Lara followed Francisco's pointing finger and saw it, a rounded hut colored to blend in with the treetops.

"What happened to this place?" Heather asked.

At the bow, Williams dropped an anchor.

"Guerrillas," Francisco explained. "They burned the dock and the old house that was being used as a ranger station. They have been driven away, but there is no money to rebuild. What would be the point? Few want to come here except those interested in the ruins." He opened the gate at the ship's rail and dropped a gangplank. "Hurry."

"Why hurry?"

"This part of the mountains. No good. The forest people do not hunt here."

To Lara it looked no different than any other stretch of river, save that the channel had grown rockier and the hills crowded closer.

"Is it the ruins?"

"I don't know. Even the Shining Path never stayed here long, just passed through."

Lara threw the pack with her VADS gear over her shoulder. "Thanks for the warning."

Heather navigated the gangplank first. Borg and Lara, with Francisco's help, got the gear to the grassy riverside. There was a path, flanked by tree trunks pitched the color of railroad ties.

Lara pressed a booted foot outside the path. The ground

was spongy and wet but firm. A helicopter might be able to get in here, provided the pilot was sharp enough to perform a hover pickup.

"You're not going on vacation anytime soon?" she called to Williams.

He laughed. "Lady, my whole life's a vacation."

"Keep your radio on," she said.

"You call anytime, I'll come get you. But allow for a couple days' notice if I'm at the other end of the route. The *Tank Girl* isn't an airport cab service."

"He's got that right," Heather said, quietly enough that it wouldn't carry out to the barge. "New York taxis are cleaner."

Lara inventoried the luggage. Something was bothering her, but she couldn't put her finger on it yet. She gave Francisco a hundred American dollars as he handed her the bag with the jump gear. "Extra danger wages."

He pocketed the bills smoothly. "Thank you, beautiful lady. Sleep light."

"I will."

"You deserting or what, Cisco?" Williams bawled. "Daylight's wasting!"

Francisco nodded at Lara. He ran down the rock-drift, lifted the tether line, and trotted up the plank just before it fell. No good-byes, just like the man with the canoe.

Heather swatted at her exposed arm. "Damn bugs!"

Lara tossed her a bottle of DEET. "Use it. A little does a lot. Careful; it can melt plastic."

Lara and Borg found a pole and began to put together a hammock gear-tote when they caught sight of a broad-brimmed sulfur-colored hat bobbing swiftly through the brush from the treeline, as if whoever was wearing it was jogging.

"We are being welcomed after all," she said, touching Borg's elbow and pointing.

Borg craned his neck. "A man, I think."

A figure that looked more like a beekeeper than a park ranger emerged from the tall grass. His broad felt hat had netting fixed over his face and bound at the neck, and he'd tied his sleeves and pants at the cuffs. He wore thick work gloves over his hands. All in all, Lara thought that he resembled the Scarecrow from *The Wizard of Oz*.

"*Whoo*—that was a run," he huffed. "I dressed and left as soon as I caught sight of the boat. Captain Williams wastes no time. Sorry about the outfit. Ran out of repellent. I'm Alex Frys."

Lara suddenly realized what had been bothering her. Williams had left no supplies, no mail, for Frys or for the Peruvian ranger, Fermi.

Frys extended a gloved hand. "Lady Croft, I presume?"

A nervous little laugh at the end of his question—along with his glittering eyes and the sweat on his face behind the netting that dangled like a veil from his hat—made Lara wonder if he'd been in the jungle too long. Malaria? His skin clung tight across his cheekbones.

Perhaps just a man in the throes of an obsession. She shook his hand.

Frys turned to the others. "Heather Rourke. Pleased to meet you. The press could be helpful to me in unmasking these murderers. And who is this strong-looking gentleman? A bodyguard?"

"Nils Bjorkstrom," Borg said. He gave a short bow rather than shaking hands. Frys kept his eyes fixed on Borg's and away from the artificial limbs. "Not a bodyguard. I am here out of concern for someone thought to be in the ruins on that mountain you watch."

"A woman?"

"How do you know?"

"I know they have a woman working with them."

"Then she is still alive, at least. Thank God."

"Won't you follow me?" Frys said. Borg picked up his pack, and he and Lara took the pole bearing the rest of their gear.

A poison dart frog, impossibly green against the pathway log it clung to, jumped out of the way as they started up the trail. Lara caught a serpentine flash of mottled coral in the stalks as a deadly fer-de-lance went after the frog's movement. Biting flies tried to get at her scalp through her hair. She dabbed repellent across her tightly bound mane.

"The heat's bad down here, I know," said Frys. "Once we're in the canopy tower, you'll be more comfortable. Welcome to paradise!"

10

Thanks to the supplies and gear, the trek up the small mountain took the better part of the afternoon. Even Borg began asking for breaks—he had the heavy end of the pole going uphill—as they reached the halfway mark.

Lara arrived at the canopy tower wet and enervated. The afternoon rain found its way through the canopy via a million cascades, turning the hike into an uphill slog under a series of shower heads. Once thoroughly soaked, though, with the greasy layers of sweat and insect repellent washed away, she felt cooler and clean . . . for about five seconds. The footing on the path had been poor. They'd slipped many times, and each fall required a break while they got set to lift the equipment again. While the way had been cleared by machetes, undergrowth, decomposition, and mudslides had broken down or covered the wood-chip path. Here in the rain forest, paths did not last long.

Lara looked up at the platform, almost eight stories high. Supported both by the three-meter-thick Samauma tree in which it sat and and a long spiral staircase paralleling the smooth-sided trunk like another tree, it looked to be about the size of a modest one-bedroom flat. She was happy to see a cargo net and winch for hauling up their gear.

"Not powered by anything but muscle, sorry," Frys said. "Where is your police friend?"

"Fermi? Back in Puerto Maldonado. I was worried something would hold you up, so he went down to expedite things. Naturally, you showed up right after he left. Serves me right for getting anxious."

"He didn't take a little launch called the *Plato* downriver, did he?"

"I think so. Sergeant Fermi knows all the captains. The *Plato* can make it upriver, to some of the mines in the mountains; it happened to be passing, and he hailed it over the radio. Why?"

"We met her on the river. The captains of our boat and the *Plato* had a minor altercation."

Frys chuckled behind his veil of mosquito netting. "That's how it is down here. Everyone is either crawl-over-broken-glass friends or enemies, it seems. Care to come up? It's dry."

Luckily the stairs had a rail. Lara lost count of the tightly turning steps after seventy-two, when Heather sat down and moaned: "That's it. Between the slope and these steps, I need a rest."

Frys offered her his arm, and the party continued their slow, clockwise climb.

The canopy tower had been built to last. Thick hardwood beams, fixed to the tree with steel cable, made a platform for a one-room house with wide windows under a sloping overhang. Lara marked a trapdoor allowing access to the underside of the house where it joined the top branches of the tree, presumably for repairs.

At the top, their host stripped off his hat and, with it, the netting, and wiped his high forehead with a towel. He still looked a little like Shakespeare, but she'd never pictured the Bard with a suntan and graying facial hair. "No mosquitoes up here."

Frys's camp gear lay scattered around the inside of the house. Above the windows, lines of hooks for equipment or hammocks or perhaps even weather curtains extended around all four walls. A tiny toilet room filled the northeast corner, with a spigot mounted above a stainless steel basin next to the WC's door. A pipe fixed to the wall ran up from the spigot to what Lara assumed to be a rain catcher on the roof. On the other side of the toilet room, a case on the wall—she saw a fringe of broken glass—held a newly tacked up map.

The western viewing window, the one facing the ruins of Ukju Pacha, had a portable telescope with University of Dublin stenciled on its barrel. The university's telescope rested on its own tripod, with a camera mount attached to the eyepiece.

"The ruins are about eight kilometers away on that mountain that's a little higher than this one," Frys said, standing next to the telescope. Butterflies the size of dinner plates fluttered among the treetops. "Where you landed is opposite. The river goes on a southern hairpin turn here. It actually comes up against the ruins, but I understand there's a good deal of white water in between."

A clipboard hung next to the field telescope, filled with notes. Lara had a quick look. Frys had been marking how many people he observed on any given day, along with the equipment they brought into the ruins. "It's a splendid view if there's no rain or fog," Frys continued. "When the sun goes down and the granite of the mountaintops goes red . . . spectacular."

"How many people working the ruins, on average?" she asked Frys.

"Usually around ten or so. The most I've ever seen is fifteen, but there may very well be more. Hard to tell exactly at this distance, even with the telescope. I think some may be underground, out of view."

"But no tourists?" Heather said, rubbing her right and then her left quadriceps.

"Shining Path scared them away. It's tough to get even the *Machinguenga* into this part of the cloud forest. No guide business to speak of. Which is too bad; this is a biologist's paradise. I should know: I am one." He giggled again.

Lara redirected the rain catcher to refill her canteen. She took a mouthful and spat it out the window, then drank. Delicious. If blue sky could be bottled, it would taste like Andean rainwater. "None of Kunai's people know you're here?"

"The roof is green shingle, and there's camouflage-pattern paint on the walls for the bird-watchers. It doesn't stand out against the rest of the jungle. Besides, even if they see the platform, there's no reason for them to think it's inhabited now. I've been keeping a low profile."

Lara leaned out the window and looked at the exterior. Forest lichens and bromeliads living on the canopy tower added their own natural coloration.

"Have you taken any pictures?" Borg asked, noticing a camera mount on the telescope.

"Just a few. So far it looks like a minor archaeological survey. I just get a few figures at this distance. Can't tell male from female half the time. Tea? It's one of the few things I'm not out of."

Over tea, held like a children's party on the floor with water heated on a small gas camp stove, Frys told them more about his father's research, how, in recent years, his father had become more guarded and reclusive, taking some of his papers out of the college library. "I thought he was just slipping," Frys said. "Being alone, after cancer took Mum, hit him hard. In the last year, after he retired, he went on and on about the *Méne*. If only I'd paid attention."

Heather looked over her notes. "Cults, ancient markings, secret societies. Murder. Now mysterious goings-on at a mountaintop."

"Welcome to my world," Lara said from the telescope. The sun began to break the rain clouds up. With better light, the ruins stood out against the green mountaintop. They did not look like much: just some rings of stones crowning the hilltop.

"You suspect this Kunai in your father's death?" Borg asked.

"My father feared him," Frys said.

"He's the Prime, isn't he?" Lara put in.

"The what?" asked Heather.

"The leader of the *Méne* cult," Lara said.

"Yes, I heard my dad mention that term," Frys said. "And I came across it in that paper he wrote with Von Croy. I read it before coming out here, thought I might find a clue. A lot of mumbo jumbo, if you ask me."

"Mumbo jumbo?" Lara shook her head. "Hardly. Some of the Frys–Von Croy paper was guesswork, but it was pretty good guesswork, as far as I can make out. Von Junst actually spoke to some alleged members of the cult back in the 1840s, in Finland, of all places. There have been attempts to resurrect the *Méne* over the centuries, some more successful than others. What they said matched another account from the other side of the world."

Lara spoke as though addressing a room full of students. She gave an overview of what she'd discovered about the *Méne*, their gods from the deep places of the earth, and the Prime, the man who spoke to and for the Deep Gods. "Their leader, the Prime, cannot lie, or so it is said. He can shape the thoughts of others, give men strength and courage in battle through special gifts brought from meads made from the berries of sacred flowers.

"I believe that's how Kunai first happened upon the *Méne* cult. It was an accident. He made a study of native medicines in Peru. Sold a few to a German pharmaceutical firm and became rich. There's a blossom in this cloud forest called the Orouboran water hyacinth . . . at least, that's what it's called now. But back in the days of the *Méne*, it was called the Dreamflower."

"But I thought the Mene were a protoculture, before all civilization and writing. How do we know what they called anything?" asked Borg.

"That's correct, of course," Lara said. "What I should say is that those who came after the *Méne*, who preserved fragments of the old knowledge, the old ways, into civilized time, called it the Dreamflower, at least according to a translation of Babylonian laws I obtained from a rather unpleasant colleague."

"That sounds interesting," said Heather. "Who is this unpleasant colleague?"

"He'd be worth a story, but I don't think he's involved with this."

Lara looked through the telescope again. Her vision momentarily blurred. She was dead tired from the long, hot trip. *Better to go tomorrow night.* "The police, the government, can't arrest Kunai?" she asked Frys.

"Not enough evidence in Scotland. No sign that he's been in the UK in years, but he may be traveling with a false passport. Down here, he's untouchable. According to Fermi, the Peruvians will only act if we get evidence that he's taking artifacts out of the country. Then the law will step in."

Lara slowly shifted the telescope, traversing the extensive site. She could make out a line of overgrown ruins, not nearly as well-preserved as some others she'd seen in Peru, and therefore possibly older, running around the distant rounded mountaintop like a king's crown. She smelled an old secret over there the way a hunter felt game on the trail ahead: tiny impressions, each unimportant in itself but together a red flag, what another, less attuned to the little signals, might call instinct or even precognition.

"We'll make the Peruvians listen," she said. "But anything can happen out here. That's the challenge to those who go into the jungle. It's got its own law."

11

After a night wrapped in hammocks they breakfasted on tinned meat and cereal-like breakfast bars.

After breakfast, with the sun now well up from the horizon thanks to their tropical latitude, Borg showed Lara his specialized climbing limbs. Still experimental, they fitted onto his stumps better than his everyday arms.

It was Lara's first good look at his stumps. Metal capped the limbs just below the shoulder, complete with stout, knoblike fixtures for locking on his arms. A short wire, tipped with what looked like a USB plug, dangled from each metal cap.

"I had a second surgery in Japan. There are computer chips implanted in the stumps," Borg explained. "They read tension put on them by different muscle fibers from my shoulders. My everyday arms only use it to open and close the working fingers. The climbing arms can do much more.

"A German engineering firm for climbing equipment and a Japanese robotics company worked together to make them."

Borg knelt over the open case. The mechanical arms resembled props from a *Terminator* movie. Each appeared to be specialized.

"The left is really a piton gun. It works on the same principle as a nail gun, only it takes a slightly larger spike. I place a magazine of five pitons in the forearm, here." He showed Lara the flattened, nail-like climbing anchors with their eyeholes for rope, linked together like a line of nails for a nail gun. "The right one, the 'claw,' has a grapnel that also works as an anchor."

Lara found a moment to admire the four-fingered hand as Borg worked it. The talonlike fingers spread like flower petals, and could reverse themselves. "I have ten meters of cable I can play out, attached to a power winch. Takes me up or down."

"Must have cost a great deal."

"The idea was for me to make climbs no other single man could. So far all I have done with them is promotional videos and some easy climbs. Perhaps someday. For now, it will get us back up the Abyss."

"There's that boat again," Heather said from the window. Her hair was bound up at the back of her head in a pair of thick rubber bands.

"The *Tank Girl*?" Lara asked.

"No, the other one. The boat with the yahoos that threw the dead animal."

She left Borg and rushed to the window. The *Plato* waited on the banks of the river, only its bow visible among the trees.

Lara looked back to the landing, three kilometers away, but motion on the trail halfway up their mountain caught her eye. A dozen or more men in khaki pants and black T-shirts, gripping an assortment of assault weapons, rushed out of the forest. Some gestured to guide the others.

"We've got callers," Lara said grimly. She went to her VADS pack.

"Perhaps Fermi has returned," Frys said, a quaver in his voice. He went to the window, then ducked back. "Those are men from the ruins!"

"Not such a secret hideout after all," the Tomb Raider said, mentally kicking herself for not going to the ruins the previous evening despite her fatigue. Or setting a watch. *Sloppy, Croft.* She closed the VADS belt around her waist and slipped on the headset. The belt-box computer winked green at her, and her headset gave a confirmation tone.

"Are you going to fight them?" Frys asked.

"Got a problem with that?" Lara asked in turn.

"Well," said Frys, "there are an awful lot of them. Maybe we should just surrender."

"They didn't let your father surrender," Lara said. "And they won't let us surrender, either."

From far below came the sound of boots clattering up the stairs.

Lara looked at the staircase again. The tight spiral would provide ample cover for the men until they were almost at the top. The attackers would be able to use tear gas, shotguns . . . If only she could get at the stairway from the side . . .

The hammocks caught her eye, especially Alex Frys's. It was huge, with elastic cording at either end.

She took it off the wall and hurried over to the little hatch in the center of the hut that allowed access to the underside, presumably to trim branches and repair the network of cables securing the platform to the treetop.

"Lara, what are you doing?" demanded Heather. "There's got to be fifteen or twenty men out there!"

Lara pulled open the hatch and looked for footholds, a way down below the platform. "They're not professional soldiers, Heather," she said meanwhile. "Professionals wouldn't have run in a mob, all bunched up like that." Nor would they have run pell-mell for the stairs as though in a race to be first to the top, but she didn't have time to explain everything.

The voices of Borg, Heather, and Frys, all offering conflicting advice, blended into a babble. Lara shut them out. She dropped through the hatch, crouched on a branch, and threw one end of the hammock around the three-meter-wide trunk. Catching it, she fashioned the hammock into a lumberman's belt.

The Tomb Raider needed her hands free.

Borg's face appeared above the open hatch. "What can I do to help?"

"Close the hatch and pray," Lara said.

Then, trusting her life to something designed for a summer afternoon, she leaned back against the nylon and elastic of the hammock. It held. She gripped the smooth gray bark between her knees and lowered the belt, then her knees, then her belt again, being careful to stay opposite the spiral stairs.

She risked a peek around the tree trunk.

The black-and-tans pounded up the stairs, some carrying assault rifles with bayonets fixed, others with Taser guns mounted under the barrels.

The Tasers looked like flashlights with pistol grips; they fired a pair of needles with wires leading back to a capacitor in the handle. Upon impact, a 50,000-volt charge, enough to incapacitate anyone, completed the circuit.

She'd been hit by a Taser once. It felt like being struck between the shoulder blades with a mallet. Her heart hadn't settled down for fifteen minutes afterwards.

The man first in line on the stairs carried an assault shotgun. He could kill everyone in the canopy tower by just sticking the muzzle over the lip of the floor and sweeping the room. The question was, were they here to kill or to capture?

"VADS: right rubber."

A clip appeared at her right hip point. She slammed her gun down on it, leaned around the tree using the elastic lumberman's belt, aimed, and fired.

The Tomb Raider bounced a rubber bullet off the lead man's stomach. He dropped his shotgun, gasping. The man behind him crashed into him, and both sprawled on the narrow staircase.

"Turn around, boys," she shouted in English. "Trespassers will be punished. Severely."

Her second rubber bullet caught the third man in the temple.

Muzzle flashes against the green canopy and the angry chatter of automatic weapons fire sounded across the treetops. She heard bullets *thunk* into tree trunks behind her and punch through branches with cracking sounds. She supposed that answered her "kill or capture" question. Back behind the tree, she used VADS to load fléchettes into both her pistols. "Not easily discouraged, don't want to play nice," she said to herself.

Swinging on the pivot of her hammock, she popped out from the other side of the tree and opened fire. The brass cartridge cases tumbled far, far down to the forest floor. Blood spray from the stairway followed the cartridge cases down, and she hid behind the bole again to the sound of curses, screams, and moans.

Bullets whizzed through airspace she'd occupied a moment before, ripping the skinlike bark off the three-meter-thick Samauma.

She scooted out and dropped two more of the men on the stairs. This time she felt the bullets hit the tree near her feet. She drew them back, relying on the hammock to hold her up. They shot at the hammock, but the web of nylon cording couldn't easily be cut by gunfire.

A pair of hissing grenades—she caught a whiff of tear gas—flew past her before spinning downward.

Not overly bright, or perhaps just overexcited.

The Tomb Raider heard footfalls between the gunshots at the tree. The black-and-tans were rushing the platform despite her. She swung out again and cut three more down.

A whistle sounded. "Back to the boat!" someone shouted in Spanish.

On her next swing outward, Lara saw that it wasn't a trick. The black-and-tans were hurrying back down the circular steps, carrying or dragging their wounded.

The Tomb Raider could have put more bullets between the retreating pairs of shoulderblades, but there were already four dead on the staircase. The hot USP Matches went back into their holsters.

Lara Croft worked legs and hammock to get back to the treetop before one of the black-and-tans reached the bottom of the stairs and took advantage of the better shooting position.

"Are they gone?" Frys asked as he extended a hand to help her through the trapdoor.

The look she gave him made him pull it back.

"They're running. Leaving dead on the stairs, too." She hauled herself up through the hatch.

"Are you okay?" Borg asked.

"It was like hitting targets on a range. They were totally exposed from the side on those stairs. Slaughter."

"How terrible," Heather said.

"I like my fights as one-sided as possible," Lara said. She went to the window and gazed down at the fleeing men. One turned and ran backwards down the trail, emptying his magazine at the canopy tower until he tripped and flipped over. Not a single one of his bullets hit the structure, though it was nearly as wide as the broad side of a barn.

"Let's see that map." Lara strode over to the east-facing wall, which had a smaller window than the others. She traced the river, looked at the elevation marks.

"Think they'll take the river all the way back?" she asked Frys.

"The hike would be formidable. Solid forest between here and the ruins, and there's no trail that I know of."

"That's what I thought." Lara smiled grimly. "Borg, you up for a run? This might be our chance. We could get in ahead of them."

"Help me with my arms, please."

Another time she would have been interested to learn more about the elaborate connections between Borg's stumps and the mechanical arms. But with time an issue, she just followed his directions. Attaching the arms was no more difficult than putting a lens on a camera body: All she had to do was line up a red triangle and a red square, then turn, and the arm clicked into place. Then she plugged in the USB cables.

Lara and Borg helped each other into the special packs they'd brought, and slung water-carrying camel packs over those. The packs came equipped with straws to make for convenient rehydrating on the move.

"Are those parachutes?" Heather asked, indicating the closure on the larger packs Lara and Borg wore beneath the camels.

"They are," Lara replied.

"Umm, so where's the plane?" Heather continued.

"There isn't one," Borg said. "It will be a base jump, from the edge of the Whispering Abyss."

Heather blinked her eyes.

Lara adjusted the straps on her lucky pack so that it would sit nestled atop the parachute. "Don't let me forget to change this before we jump."

Borg nodded. "Of course."

She went to the window. The healthy survivors of the attack on the canopy tower were splashing into the river, to be hauled up on board the *Plato*.

"Bring the telescope over here."

It took her a moment to get it aligned. She looked through the eyepiece, searching for the face she'd seen on the back of the book jacket, that of Tejo Kunai. Instead, she saw someone else.

Ajay.

Her old schoolmate stood at the front of the boat, one booted foot on the rail. She had machine pistols strapped in holsters on either thigh, a tank top, and wraparound blue sunglasses. Her hair hung from the back of her head in a single braid.

Perhaps Ajay saw the distant flash of telescope glass in the morning sun. She stared straight at the canopy tower, slapped her pistol butts.

Then Lara recognized another face. Fermi, the Peruvian park ranger, was helping the wounded to board the boat.

She turned away from the window, addressed Heather and Frys: "There are bodies on the stairs. You two can bury them while we're gone."

"Shouldn't we put them somewhere for the police?" Frys asked.

"Leave them out, then. Just make sure it's downwind. The

ants and the flies will leave less for the Peruvians than if you just buried them."

"I'll radio Fermi," Frys decided. "He can bring the police back with him."

"I doubt it," Lara said. "He's already back, aboard the *Plato*."

"No!"

"I just got a good look at him through the telescope. It's him, all right."

"But that means . . ."

"Right. They've known you were here the whole time. You can't trust Fermi, and that means you can't trust the park service, either. Radio Williams. Get him to call in the police. Whatever's going on at Ukju Pacha, the *Méne* are willing to kill to keep it secret."

12

Lara Croft ignored the bodies on the stairs, but not the blood. This wasn't the time for a slip: It was a long way down.

At the bottom, Lara and Borg dashed for cover in the great roots of the tree. Lara listened for a few minutes for footfalls, conversation, any sign that the black-and-tans had left a team behind. Nothing. She pulled out her global positioning system, a handheld device about the size and shape of a pocket PC, and checked the location of the first waypoint on the route to the ruins.

Then they ran.

After the first sprint, they settled down into a jog. Only a few broad-leafed shade plants and spiky ferns thrived beneath the thick canopy. The spongy footing endangered them only on the slopes.

Dead branches lay on a carpet of dead leaves, and fallen trees were being slowly consumed by moss and lichen. Lara had been in enough rain forests to know that it took only a year or two, if that, for even the biggest deadfall to become nothing more than a fern-nursing clump of compost on the forest floor.

They jogged for thirty minutes, stopped for five, then jogged for thirty minutes more, sucking water from their camel packs. The run became more difficult as they headed uphill. She spotted a familiar looking plant, and stopped to gather its plump leaves. Borg asked to be shown her GPS.

"I thought so," he said. "Why this course? The ground isn't much easier, and we're taking the long way to the ruins."

"But it's the short way to the river gorge. I want to go to the cliff here." She tapped the waypoint on the green screen.

"Why? To see how far upriver the *Plato* has gotten?"

"We'd win the race to the ruins, but only by an hour at most. I want to try to slow them up a little more."

"There's water at the ruins, I hope," Borg said.

"I can't see them making the climb down to the river every time someone needs to brew coffee."

"Coffee. That sounds good right now."

She extracted the leaves she'd gathered. "Try this. It's *muna*, a native remedy for headaches and fatigue."

"What's in it?"

"Don't worry, it's not a local methamphetamine. The biochemistry, as I understand it, just helps your body move oxygen around more efficiently. Salicylic acid, too, for the pain, probably."

They both chewed the slightly bitter leaves. She felt her batteries recharge.

Borg looked over his shoulder at a sudden crunching noise. A furry face blinked out at them from behind a fallen trunk, its jaws working on a tuber of some sort. The animal squeaked, turned tail, and disappeared beneath two roots of an upright tree.

"A sloth?" Borg asked.

"No. It looked like a guinea pig."

"I have never heard of a guinea pig of that size."

"They grow them big around here, I guess. Perhaps Frys

can explain . . . if we ever see him again, that is. I've never tried a BASE jump like this."

Borg lifted his classic chin, and his seafarer's eyes met hers. "I have much experience with such jumps, Lara. We can do it, as long as the legend of the Whispering Abyss hasn't grown in the telling. All it takes is nerve and skill, and you have no shortage of either."

How could Ajay have left this man? Every time he spoke, Lara had a hard time not daydreaming about climbing into a seagoing yacht with him and sailing up a fjord.

The *Plato* hadn't rounded the southern hairpin turn before the gorge when Lara and Borg reached the cliff. They were on the shoulder of the mountain holding the ruins of Ukju Pacha, but those ruins were still a few kilometers away, at the narrowest point of the river. Lara placed her feet carefully at the edge of the cliff and looked down six hundred meters of sheer rock, thankful that she didn't suffer from vertigo. Pure whitewater flowed beneath, with a tow path running along their side of the cliff.

The river made two turns here, like the letter zed with a short middle line. At the top corner of the zed was the ruins, and another cliff. She and Borg stood downriver at the bottom corner of the zed. She picked up a rock, tossed it underhand, and then watched, timing its descent into the foaming water far below.

A moment later, the *Plato* came into sight, pulling up the rapids at the end of the zed. A team of horses or, more likely, mules—she couldn't tell at this distance—had a line out to the *Plato*, hauling it up through the spots of rushing water too swift for the boat's engines.

"Like shooting fish in a barrel," Lara observed.

Borg adjusted the straps over his beefy shoulders with his claw hand. No wonder he had a frame like that, if he spent much time with those heavy arms attached. "And how will you shoot? You have perhaps a rifle in sections packed away?"

"I don't need a rifle." Lara picked up a cricket-ball-sized rock she'd spotted earlier. "Find a few about this size, would you?"

"You will stop them with rocks?"

"I will stop them with physics. Force equals mass times velocity squared."

"Meaning what?"

"You'll see."

Borg searched the cliff's edge for rocks as Lara planted herself on a prominence. She threw her stone cricket-bowler style. She watched it fall as Borg handed her another stone of similar size.

The pop-pop-pop of small-arms fire aimed back up at her echoed in the canyon above the rush of water, but the bullets fired straight up at the cliff top were no more of a threat at this distance than the hummingbirds that flitted among the blossoms at the cliff's edge.

It took her three tries before she hit. The fourth rock went through the canopy and out the boat's bottom, judging from the frantic bailing that commenced. She threw two more rocks. She saw one splash beyond the boat, but the other hit dead center.

The black-and-tans fled the filling center of the boat, shouting at the man with the mules in harness. She saw water come in over the boat's side, dusted her palms off, and pulled her minibinoculars out of her pack.

The black-and-tans worked like demons to save their

wounded. She watched a man, helped by Ajay, pulling another through the water using the towline to get to the shore. If nothing else, the *Méne* were loyal to one another.

Borg gasped. "Give me those glasses."

"Yes, Ajay is down there. She's a strong swimmer. The current is quick, but it's not that dangerous. All the white water is at the turns in the river."

"I want it anyway."

Lara adjusted the straps on her pack. "There's no time, Borg. We have to get to the ruins."

"We are here for Ajay."

"Yes, but she's down there, and we're up here. Unless you're Superman, there's nothing you can do from this distance. Besides, it's more than Alison now. Haven't you been paying attention? We're going to get Ajay out, yes, but the *Méne* are up to work I haven't quite fathomed yet. Murder, attempted murder—I don't like anything I've learned about them. We need to find out more, and the ruins are the best place to do that."

Borg nodded. "All right. I will wait. I know one thing, though. The *Méne* have brainwashed her. Alison would never be with such people, a murderer like this Kunai, willingly. I'm sure of it."

Lara wasn't so sure, but Borg was already running toward the ruins. The sight of Ajay had renewed his energy even more than the *muna* leaves.

Far above Ukju Pacha, condors circled on their spread wings, tiny black crosses against a blue sky. Crouched out of sight behind a fallen tree, Lara examined the *Méne* camp through her minibinoculars, but saw no one moving either among the tents or within the ruins.

The "expedition" had camped under the three-meter-tall walls of Ukju Pacha. Their garbage was bagged according to customary practice, but rain forest raiders had torn open the sacks to get at the refuse within. Lara nodded at Borg, and they rose from concealment and approached the seemingly deserted camp from downwind, masking their scent with the odor of the garbage in case the *Méne* used dogs to guard their enclave. But there was no barking, no sound or movement at all from within the camp.

The ruins—above ground anyway, the Tomb Raider corrected herself—were not as extensive as Machu Picchu, nor did they have the horizon-changing outline of Mexico's Mayan step pyramids. But the blocks of stone that made up the walls still stood flush, to the ancient engineers' credit, though root and vine covered the quarried granite.

They searched the camp. The tents were deserted. Lara found a flowerlike rain catcher with several white plastic water jugs set beneath. They refilled their camel packs from one.

The *Méne* had guns enough for a military camp, as Lara learned when Borg lifted the lid of a crate and found weapons and ammunition stacked inside. She lifted a shotgun by its sling, smelled the residue in its lethal muzzle. What had they been shooting at?

A path descended to the cliff. She turned down it.

"I thought you wanted to go into the ruins," Borg said.

"Not just yet. We need to slow up our friends a little further." They trotted down to the cliff. It was not as sheer as the one from which she'd given the *Plato* its physics lesson, but it was still a precipitous drop. A series of wooden steps snaked its way up the side of the cliff from the river, with platforms placed every ten meters or so for tourists to rest and look down the picturesque gorge.

The wood was old and gray, sagging in some parts. Until recently, the Peruvian rain forest had owned it. But the stairs had been cut clear, and recent repairs with rope and rough-hewn logs had made the rickety structure serviceable again.

Lara hurled a rock at a pair of scarlet macaws perched on the handrail halfway down.

"What did you do that for?" Borg asked.

"I didn't want to hurt them. VADS: right nitro, left pyro."

"What's that you said?"

Lara loaded her guns and took aim at the platforms hugging the vertical part of the cliff.

She aimed, first right, then left, then two more rights, then another left . . .

"Good God!" Borg exclaimed as the bullets reduced the stairway to burning kindling.

She reloaded, selected a new section of the stairway.

"The Peruvians aren't going to like this."

"If we live, I'll write them a check. Back up."

A third load destroyed the top landing. The wood gave off a wispy white smoke as it crackled and burned.

"Now they'll have to take the long way around. With any luck, we'll be long gone by then."

Borg stepped back as the staircase shrieked and collapsed with a crash. "What do you expect to find here?"

The Tomb Raider slid the hot guns back into their holsters. "I'm not sure. There's something at the bottom of the Whispering Abyss that they need. If we can't steal it somehow—"

"You'll destroy it just like the staircase."

"Only as a last resort."

Borg shook his head. "You're some archaeologist."

"I never claimed that title," Lara said. "Once, long ago, a

man called me a Tomb Raider. Started off as a radio call sign. I didn't like him much, but I liked the name. I get in, I get what I want, and I leave again before matters get complicated."

"So now we walk all the way back up to the ruins."

"Not exactly," she said, checking her laces.

"How's that?"

"Haven't you been around me long enough? We run, of course."

13

Whatever Ukju Pacha had been, it wasn't a city. There were no dwellings or aqueduct-fed plots, as at Machu Picchu. Occasional towering stones jutted out of the ground next to smaller markers. A few post-and-lintel structures remained, roughly the size of the triptychs at Stonehenge, though the posts were built from many smaller stones and only the lintels were a single block.

Lara and Borg found no depressions of any kind, no staircases leading to any kind of abyss, whispering or otherwise.

"What did your books say about this place?" Borg asked. He stood on his tiptoes to touch a lintel.

"Not enough. 'Unidentified pre-Columbian,' which is archaeologist-speak for 'not a clue, sorry.' "

"It reminds me of a cemetery. Grave markers."

Lara touched an ivylike plant growing up a mound of markers. Closed buds about the size of pea pods indicated it was getting ready to flower. She tore one open, pulled out the white petals. They began to turn brown in the warm air and sunlight.

"That's an odd reaction," she said.

Borg grunted. "Perhaps they are night-blooming flowers."

Lara nodded. "The *Méne* worshipped the deep places of

the earth. It makes sense that they might have worshipped flowers that bloomed in darkness. I wish I could see the ruins from the point of view of those condors! Perhaps a pattern would emerge . . ."

She broke off.

"What?" asked Borg, looking around. "Did you hear something?"

"No, I just realized something." She scrambled up the marker, using narrow cracks in the stone as hand- and footholds.

"There's an opening up here," she called down to Borg. "Like a chimney."

"Can you get in?"

Lara felt a mild breeze of cool air wafting from the opening. Taking her battered MagLite 6 cell from her pack, she had a look inside. The passage extended beyond the beam. "It's too narrow," she called back. "But at least now we know what to look for."

Borg hunted amongst the markers for a wider passage.

Meanwhile, Lara returned to the strange vines with the closed buds. She felt that she was missing something, something about how they were growing . . .

Cultivated, that was it. No weeds grew where the flowering vines thrived, unlike the riotous chaos at the walls and gardens and outer markers.

The plants circled an area of three rounded chimneys. In the center of these, three slabs of stone leaned together, like drunks hanging on to each other around a bottle. A spill of budded vines fell from the top and grew thick all about the four-meter-high blocks.

The Tomb Raider tried beneath, but old masonry filled in the arches between the stones.

Nothing to do but go up again.

She grabbed a vine and used it to haul herself up the smooth, sloping granite. She made it to the top, stood triumphantly astride a triangular shaft leading into darkness. All around her other little chimneys of stone conducted air, and possibly light, into the earth. She marked a circle of them sixty meters away. A very wide circle. Could that be the cap of the Whispering Abyss?

Big enough for her. And Borg.

The *Méne* had even left a ladder within.

"Borg, get up here. I've found the way in."

Borg made a motion with his right arm like a fisherman casting. Metal flashed as it fell. It took Lara's eyes a second to recognize what they'd seen. Borg's claw hand, at the end of a cable, landed in the hole. Borg reeled the cable back into his arm, and the grapnel-fingers fixed at the edge.

The Tomb Raider stood on the claw for good measure as Borg climbed—or rather winched himself up, using a pinch-hook he extended from the left piton arm for assistance at the top of the slab. The climb done, he folded the hook back into the piton arm as a man might close a Swiss Army knife.

"Does it have a magnifying glass for starting fires?"

Borg laughed. He pointed to a jawlike protrusion near the piton-firing muzzle with one of the grapnel-fingers. "No. It does have a pincer, so I can grip a stick." He worked the grapnel-fingers. "Then I can rub it with another stick here. But I find it's easier to just hold a butane candlelighter."

His shaggy hair was like a golden halo in the sun. Lara wanted to kiss him, but she held back. His heart still belonged to Ajay, and it wasn't for her to judge whether Ajay was brainwashed or not. At least, not without meeting her first.

Lara stuck her head in the triangular gap, shifted her body so that it blocked the sun, and let her eyes adjust. The ladder had duct tape running down one side of it. How odd. She followed the tape up and down with her eyes.

One of the rungs had what could be a pressure switch. The wires ran down to what looked like a plastic canteen.

Booby trap. Not powerful enough to damage the giant blocks, but anyone at the top of the ladder would be launched out the entrance like a circus performer shot from a cannon.

Cute.

It wasn't that far down. She let herself fall through the hole headfirst, somersaulted as she dropped, and landed on her toes next to the ladder. A red switch at the side of the canteen glowed beside a small antenna. So they turned it on and off by radio.

Best not to touch.

She stood in a plain chamber, triangular, with an arched tunnel about a meter and three quarters high leading from each wall. They would have to crouch.

"Can you jump down?" she called up to Borg. "The ladder is dangerous."

"Move the ladder, please."

"I can't. It's wired to explosives."

"I thought you meant it wouldn't hold my weight. Just a moment."

He blocked the sun, then descended at the end of his cable, his arm humming.

"How long are those batteries good for?" she asked, vexed for not thinking to ask sooner.

"Four days of use. A little less in extreme cold, or if I use the winch to pull my weight up a great deal. I climbed the

Cordier Pillar of the Grands Charmoz with what is in the batteries and had power for thirty-six more hours."

"We should be all right then. That's some feat of engineering."

"They made a video. The Japanese say I will be in the commercial once they go to market: 'Extraordinary gear for extraordinary people.' But they're still having trouble with the artificial legs they're working on. They want to bring out the arms and legs as a set. We shall see."

She searched the floor. Footprints went into and came out of each arch. Beams of light from above illuminated all three dark tunnels at irregular distances. But only one had brown stains about the size of a euro coin.

"Looking for bread crumbs?" Borg asked.

"Bloodstains. Let's start there." It also went in the direction of the circle of air shafts she'd seen.

The tunnel was a tight fit. Lara had to crouch, and Borg had to duckwalk, through the tunnel for about thirty meters before it widened out into a long chamber, pyramid shaped, that just gave her room to stand up. Borg still had to crouch. The limited light from the air shafts in the tunnel didn't allow them to view this new chamber, so they turned on their torches.

Dead end. Something glittered at the far wall.

"The builders weren't very tall," Borg grumbled.

The bloodstains ended abruptly in the middle of the floor, clustered a little more thickly near, but not at, the end of the chamber.

Near a gap in the floor.

Lara followed the gap; it ran along to the join at the bottom of the sloping walls at the edge of the room and turned back the way they'd come in. She had to go on hands and knees to explore thanks to the sloping roof. "This whole part of the floor is separate."

"Same on this side," Borg said, sniffing. "Do you smell oil?"

"Yes. Like a garage."

She went to the far end of the pyramid chamber. It dead-ended at what turned out to be a mosaic, the first decoration they'd seen. Green glass, recently cleaned, formed the omega sign she'd seen before, though this one was more oval shaped than the others, almost skull-like.

"Never seen this variant," she said, letting the light play in the reflections.

"I wouldn't mind never having seen it in the first place."

Was the bloodstain a false lead to another trap, perhaps? But her instincts gained over years of tomb raiding told her she'd gone in the right direction.

She saw a shadow on the other side of the glass.

"Borg, get your light closer, please."

A bar, placed horizontally, descended from the center of the omega-skull, just as the spinal cord did from the human brain.

The Tomb Raider searched above and below the glass, pressed here and there and—

A matched pair of stone panels below the omega-skull swung inward. She checked the space with her flashlight. Not wide enough to crawl through, but she could easily reach the bar.

"Careful, Lara!" said Borg, looking over her shoulder. "It might be another booby trap."

"What religion are you, Borg?"

"Roman Catholic. I'm not observant, really."

"Even though you're not observant, would you booby-trap a cross at the front of a church?"

"Of course not."

"Neither would the *Méne*. The bar is in a groove. I think it's a lever of some kind."

She tried moving it to the left.

The floor vibrated, and both Lara and Borg started at a deep rumble. A section of floor at the entrance to the pyramid chamber rose and rotated as it came up, turning into a shark-tooth of stone moving to block their entrance as the floor with the mass of bloodstains dropped.

"Run," she called, jumping to her feet and hurrying to the gap. Borg was a step behind. Both jumped and landed on the descending square of stone.

She hadn't noticed the gap bisecting the first section of floor.

The platform descended about three meters, into cooler, damper air, then stopped. The lubricant smell filled their nostrils.

They stood next to a pillar of salt. Or so it looked.

Lara wondered about the column. It was some kind of whitish crystal, slick with fluid, rising to a hole in the roof where the section of floor that had risen would be. It was the width of a mechanic's lift and came out of a crystal ring set in the floor.

"Hydraulics," she said. She wondered if the mechanism had survived the millennia intact, or if these new *Méne* had somehow brought it back into repair.

They stood at the edge of a cave—or, rather, a tunnel, now. It had a disturbing uniformity to it; it was about the diameter of one of the older London tubes.

Only one direction to go.

If time weren't an issue, she would have taken measurements, photographed the sides of the cave for tool marks, chipped off a sample of the rock face, even taken a vial of the water trickling from cracks here and there before it disappeared into fissures in the floor. As it was, she just searched the cave ceiling long enough to find another bar like the one she'd found above. It shone faintly silver in the beam of her flashlight. She hopped up on a small ledge to better examine it.

The Tomb Raider tapped it with a fingernail. It looked like solid platinum, but it was harder than the precious kind. Perhaps it was the industrial kind with iridium mixed in to harden it.

Platinum existed in the Andes, along with richer deposits of silver and gold. But industrial platinum? Man-made, that—for in nature it was usually found mixed with baser metals—and only very recently, in archaeological terms, at that.

Unless this was an entirely new kind of metal.

They followed the tunnel, using their lights. It sloped down gently beneath them.

"It is a relief to be cool again," said Borg after a moment.

"Yes. Almost pleasant down here." Lara caught the sparkle of foil in her flashlight, lifted up a breakfast bar wrapper. "Garbage: the archaeologist's friend."

"What does it tell you?"

Lara pocketed the wrapper. She hated litter. "Our society values speed and convenience over taste."

"So we're still far from the Abyss?"

"No. And if I'm not mistaken, this may be it."

They turned off their torches. Their eyes adjusted, picked up a faint glow.

"Hell?" Borg joked.

"Maybe just a doorway to it."

"I don't see a sign reading, 'Abandon hope all ye who enter here.' "

"Wouldn't keep me out anyway," Lara said.

She gazed in wonder as they entered the domed chamber, which was perhaps a little bigger than the forty-three-meter circumference of the Pantheon in Rome, if not as high. Around the edges of the dome, narrow, triangular-shaped shafts brought in light and fresh air. Modern lighting and power equipment waited, deactivated. A gaping hole in the center echoed with the faint sound of moving air. Kunai and his *Méne* had made improvements to the old stonework in the form of a girder, winches, and lines. A gigantic spool of cable rested at the end of the winch. Other cables went down the edge of the Abyss, some electrical, others climbing line.

Lara looked up a light shaft. It looked large enough to wiggle up, and at about head height the surface became rougher, though it appeared to narrow near the top, as a chimney does to better draw up air. Polished surfaces lined the back and sides of the shaft, helping the light down. Platinum again? The *Méne* used the stuff like pig iron. At the bottom of the shafts, where the light fell, little plots of earth supported slimelike lichens. She checked another shaft, found similar shining plate. This one had brown residue on it. Dried blood.

"The Whispering Abyss," she said. The currents came up the shaft.

Borg crouched next to the generator. "Do you want this on?"

"No. I'm not trusting anything of theirs that's electrical after seeing that bomb on the ladder. But we could use a bunch of these." She tapped a box with her toe. Row upon row of chemical lights lay within, cylinders about the size of a small cigar, along with neatly wound lengths of cording. She cracked one and shook it until it glowed green, then picked up a lanyard and attached the chemical light to it with a small hook at the end of the lanyard. She hung it around her neck.

"Fill your pockets," she said. She put another lighted lanyard around his neck.

She cracked another and shook it until it glowed green. Then walked to the center of the room.

The Whispering Abyss yawned beneath them. She measured the diameter of the sound with her eye. It was perhaps a little smaller than legend had it. It would make the jump difficult.

Some might say suicidal.

14

Borg joined her at the edge of the pit.

She dropped the chemical light in her hand, watched it fall past the stone stairs, past their crumbled end, become a dot, then a wink, then a nothing.

"Bottomless?" Borg asked.

"They built a staircase leading nowhere, just for show?"

"Then to what purpose?"

"The priests would go down and return with revelations. Their gods spoke to them from the depths. Another legend says that sacred etchings are down there. All this gear makes me think the second. Think we can do a BASE jump?"

Borg got down on one knee to look at the side of the sound. "A climb would be safer."

"Time, Borg. We may only have hours."

"Too bad the film crew isn't here."

They laid out their parachutes, put on the harnesses. Lara took extra care with Borg's.

"Did we ever decide who would go first?" Borg asked.

"I will," Lara said.

"How many BASE jumps have you done?"

"A dozen or so. I jumped off a skyscraper in Hong Kong once."

"I've done over a hundred, including a cavern jump in Mexico. The cavern was much bigger than this, of course."

"The air currents will help. We don't know what we're going to land on. I'll go first."

"Very well. Tight spirals, Lara. Very tight."

He helped her place her specially designed chute on the floor. It spread out behind her like a huge wedding train.

They put on light-intensifying goggles. Lara shook a chemical light to life.

Borg gave her a nod. "Good luck, Tomb Raider."

"See you in hell."

She ran so that the chute could partially fill. Behind her, Borg gave her chute a fluff.

The Tomb Raider jumped into darkness, felt a reassuring jerk as the stunt chute opened fully with a whipcrack sound. She grabbed her right toggle, tried to get into a spiral—

Chute and parachutist hit the wall. Her canopy collapsed. She fell in a tangle of lines, righted herself, and her chute opened again. Pulled on the right toggle again, tried to get herself into a spin . . . but hit the wall again, the breath rushing out of her at the impact, and pushed herself away by instinct before the chute collapsed further.

Lara Croft felt like a pebble falling down a drain.

She tried the left toggle. *Méne* mysticism or no, the left toggle worked better for her, and her breathing returned to normal as she descended in a smooth, tight spiral.

Even so, each turn swung her farther outward, forcing her to kick against the wall whenever it got too close. The chute required constant adjustments; she performed them with precision and skill.

Then the shaft widened. She found herself able to drift. The stairs clung intact here.

She looked down, saw a ledge. She caught a glint of shining metal beneath it.

Her heart sped up, as it always did when she was in sight of an objective. The walls sloped inward again—like a bowl's—around the ledge, almost a mirror image of the chamber above. The shaft continued down beyond the ledge. She turned so she'd hit the walkway lengthwise.

The wind flowing up from the Abyss caught her chute oddly. She ran into the wall again, slipped, and tumbled—rolled off the ledge in the tangle of her harness.

She grabbed as she fell, caught the ledge with her left hand, then got her right up, too. The chute hung beneath her. Lara managed to wedge one foot into a crack, but the other leg was tangled up in her lines.

She pulled herself up, caught her legs in the chute again, and slipped back.

Something struck the wall next to her with enough force for the impact to transmit through the wall. She turned her head and saw Borg land on the ledge, cleaner than she had. The chemical light stick around his neck filled his face with shadows. He looked like a child holding a torch under his chin while telling a ghost story.

He pulled in his chute. "The piton, by your left knee."

Eight centimeters of steel stuck out from the wall. She swung her left foot up, got it on the piton.

Accurate with that cannon of his.

With the leverage from her leg, it was easy to get back on the ledge. The Tomb Raider sat for a moment, legs dangling over the edge of the walkway, gathering in her chute and getting her bearings. She looked up at the circle of light far above. They'd come down perhaps the height of New York's Empire State Building.

She noticed something on the wall between her legs.

"Borg—," she began.

A buzzing sound rising from below cut her comment off.

An impossibility flew straight for Borg. Occupied with drawing up his chute, he didn't see it until it was on him.

Lara caught a flash of yellow chitin, trailing legs, the hum of wings.

The flier was the size of an eagle, but far more agile. It looked like a gigantic bee. It changed course without banking, like a helicopter. She swept her guns up.

But before she could fire, another yellow-armored flier erupted from the darkness and flew at her face. She knocked it away; her forearm felt like it had struck a glass vase.

Borg yelped. One of the things had landed on his metal claw arm, where it pumped frantically with its abdomen, trying to sting.

Now there were two more darting around the Tomb Raider. She crouched, fired. The explosive and incendiary shells turned the insects into burning goo. Chunks fell away into darkness.

Borg swung his arm, smashed the thing clutching at his cybernetic limb against the wall. Another came up at him, and she shot it on the wing; it described one neat loop and dropped back into the Abyss.

More came up, and she shot them, and then still more came up, and she reloaded and shot again. She had VADS switch to explosive bullets, and the bugs exploded like fireworks all around them.

Then they were gone, as quickly as they'd come. Bits of insect, bulbous-eyed heads and crablike legs mostly, lay scattered about the ledge.

Borg was looking at his piton arm. A broken-off stinger was lodged in the joint. It was the size of a switchblade.

"Nils, are you stung?" No answer. "Borg, are you stung?"

Borg shook his head as though awakening from a dream. He used the digits of his other arm to pull the stinger free. "Where were those things?"

"I don't know. Remember the oversized butterflies and other creatures we've seen? I'm beginning to think that something in the ecosystem here is creating mutations."

"They are deadly, whatever they are."

"Keep your voice down," Lara cautioned. "Maybe the noise drew them."

Borg nodded. "What do we do now?" he asked in a whisper.

Lara knelt at the edge and and ran her hands across the side of the shaft beneath the ledge. It was pebbled; she held her light up close to see better. The Abyss wall was encrusted with masses of tiny shells, long dead, empty and dry.

And something else. The same things she'd seen glinting beneath the ledge before the insects came.

Borg gasped, seeing them, too.

They were panels, the now-usual platinum color. Dirt-covered but legible, each about the size of the *Mona Lisa* in its frame and covered with fine engraving, close-placed, the lines orderly and regular, not quite letters and not quite hieroglyphs. Lara counted nine of them, just beneath the base of the stairs where the ledge was a little thicker. Netting and lines lay here, placed by the cultists in readiness for drawing up the plates if they could ever be detached.

A strange place to put holy texts, the Tomb Raider thought. It would be like putting artwork around the wainscoting rather than at eye level.

She saw a roll of cargo netting, a crowbar, and a hammer

left on the ledge. She'd bet the contents of the Croft bank account that Ajay's fingerprints could be lifted off those tools.

"Is this what they are looking for?" Borg asked.

"I think so."

"You mean to take them?"

"If I can get them off the wall without making a racket and bringing those bugs back up—yes, I mean to take them."

"Let's have a look." Borg bent and shook another chemical light, put it in his mouth, and hung over the ledge. Lara imitated him, her ponytail dangling down the Whispering Abyss.

The Tomb Raider could detect no fitting. Not so much as a fingernail's gap could be found between the plates and the wall behind. Each one was infinitesimally curved to match the shape of the wall. It was as though the platinum alloy had grown from the cave wall, etching and all.

The edges of the plates were scored with fresh chisel marks.

Why didn't they just do rubbings? Take photographs that could be examined at leisure?

Lara tried pushing on a plate, hard. She searched the rim with her fingernails. Nothing. No, judging from the marks, Ajay had already tried forcing the plates in all sorts of different ways.

But only from the outside?

"Borg, check the ledge. There's got to be something."

She examined the stairs, the wall next to them, then the wall beneath them, holding her green chemical light, trying to detect any—

What have we here?

A thumbprint-sized triangular stone was recessed into the rough cave wall so it could only be seen if you held your light close and at a certain angle. She pressed it, and heard a distinctive click.

Nothing more.

"Borg, the wall here, start pushing."

They both did so, huffing and puffing as they tried the side of the wall beneath the stairs. Lara got on her knees at the base of the stairs, shoved, and was rewarded by the feel of the bottom three stairs disappearing into the wall.

A meter-wide chamber ran in a ring around the Abyss.

"I'll have to go in. You're too big."

She lit another chemical light and tossed it in. The backs of the panels could be seen, all secured at top and bottom by a long, curved platinum rod passing through triangular loops at the edges of the plates. The rod was also etched with tiny lines. Why decorate this concealed space?

She crawled inside.

The bars had an obvious handle, and showed no signs of corrosion after all the millennia they had sat there. She pushed the top handle to the left. It wouldn't move. She tried moving it to the right, and it slid with only the faintest of grinding sounds.

"You got it," Borg whispered loudly.

The bottom slide moved identically to the top. She tried a plate, experimented with pulling and pushing, careful to keep a finger in the triangular securing loop so it wouldn't fall away into the Whispering Abyss.

The plate came free when she pushed down.

The plates were thin, perhaps five millimeters thick, and flanged so that the interior side was slightly larger than the exterior side. Each weighed a few kilos.

Borg's upside-down head suddenly appeared at the hole, a chemical light clutched between his teeth. She let out a frightened gasp.

He spat out the light. "Got you!" he chuckled.

You've got me all right, Nils. Too bad you want someone else.

"Fine time for jokes," she said, moving to the access-chamber entrance at the base of the stairs and placing the panel up on the ledge. "Get the netting ready."

Soon eight more plates joined the first. They stacked them each atop the other. Slightly curved, they fitted together perfectly, and heavily.

"Those will be hard to climb with."

"We'll use the *Méne* lines, just tie them into the netting down here and haul them up once we've made it back to the top. They've got strong enough rope. I think I saw a muscle-powered winch."

"Let us hope these stairs last for a while," Borg said, looking at the lighted exit far above, seemingly as distant as Mars.

Lara secured the netting shut with D-rings, standard climbing gear that they both carried. She looped a length of *Méne* mountain line through the rings and tested the weight. Sixty kilos or so. The line would hold easily.

They repacked their chutes carefully. This way, in case of a fall during the climb, there was at least a chance for survival.

"Let's try the stairs," she said.

"Just like Ajay. Go, go, go. It will be a difficult climb, Lara. Let us sit for a moment and eat so we have strength when we need it. Five minutes, okay?"

Without waiting for her to agree, he sat and opened a meal bar, washed his mouth out with water from his camel pack, and began to eat.

Lara looked at her watch. The smell of the food bar made her stomach growl. Perhaps he was right.

A little worried that the smell of the fruit bar might bring back the flying whatever-they-weres, Lara dropped down next to him at the base of the stairs. The chemical lights gave their faces strange green mottles as they ate and drank in silence; easily portable food kept the body going, but it didn't inspire dinnertime conversation.

When they finished, they started up the stairs.

"What is the plan to get Alison out?" Borg asked.

"My plan is to have a bunch of helicopters filled with Peruvian soldiers show up and arrest the whole lot of them for attempted kidnapping and murder. Ajay will have sense enough to surrender. We can sort everything out after that."

"Sense? She is brainwashed."

"Not necessarily, Borg. She may have seen the *Méne* as her ticket to a lot of money, enough to restore her family fortune. That's always been her goal."

"She would never willingly join such killers."

"Maybe she didn't know they were killers until it was too late. For all we know, she's playing a game of her own, going along with the cult until she can get away with the platinum."

Borg took a deep breath, let it out slowly. "Perhaps. She could be impetuous. And the lure of riches would be strong, as you say. But I still believe she has been brainwashed. This Kunai has her under some kind of spell."

"Is there something you're not telling me, Borg? What makes you insist on that as the only explanation?"

"Her attitude, everything. It all changed while I was in the hospital. I saw a different person when I got out. I can understand some strangeness at first. The arms. I was not used to them. The limbs disgusted even me at first. But she could hardly stand to look at me with the arms off."

The hurt in his voice put a knot in her stomach. How well had Borg really known Ajay? She was a woman of dreams and passions and single-minded, even obsessive, drive. In her quest for an El Dorado to restore her family's wealth and name, would she ride an injured horse, no matter how much she loved him?

After all, Lara hadn't. When Ajay had proved herself unfit for the Tomb Raider's fieldwork, endangering both herself and Lara, Lara had ended their brief partnership without hesitation, even though she'd known it might cost their friendship as well, which it had. Ever since, she'd worked alone. Attachments slowed you up. Feelings got in the way. How long had she waited next to the body of Oliver, or Von Croy?

Stop it, Croft. You're in the field, not your bed. This is one of the mind trips that brings tears, and tears are the last thing you need right now.

"We'll get it sorted, Borg. One of us is wrong about her. I'm hoping it's me."

"But what if I am the one who is wrong? What will you do then? Shoot her?"

"I can't imagine it coming to that."

Borg stopped climbing the stairs. "I won't let you hurt her, Lara."

"Is that a threat?"

"A promise."

"Borg, this is no time to argue. We've got to work together so everyone comes out of this alive. I have to trust you, and you have to trust me."

He said nothing, just turned and resumed climbing the stairs.

15

Usually vertical climbs meant screaming winds that brought freezing mountain temperatures and ice crystals, numbness and joint pain from the cold and altitude. But the climb back up the Whispering Abyss had none of these.

A trail of pitons commenced once the stairs gave out. All Lara and Borg had to do was grasp piton after piton in the inchworm progress of climbers and continue to feed line back to the panels sitting on the ledge below.

Lara let Borg lead. Whatever awkwardness he had displayed in getting on and off jets, or shaking hands, or eating was gone now. For the first time in her life, Lara found herself wondering if she was slowing a man down. Borg climbed, rested, climbed again, never wasting a motion or a chance to give his body a break from the strain if the placement of the pitons allowed, then after a moment continuing up with faint clicks and snicks as his arms hooked pitons and tested them. At times he improved the vertical path, using his piton arm to drive new holds.

Behind him, Lara yanked out some of the pitons as she climbed, sending them spinning down the shaft. She wanted delay, to keep the *Méne* in the ruins of Ukju Pacha long enough for the Peruvian army to arrive, and putting gaps in their path down might prevent them from discovering that the plates were missing until it was too late.

"It is too bad we did not know the way was so well prepared before we made our jump," said Borg. "We could have climbed down."

"We still would have had to jump," said Lara. "It would have taken us too long to get down and back. Besides, I saw the look on your face as you landed. You wouldn't have missed that jump for the world."

"It was . . . invigorating," Borg admitted.

That was not exactly the word that Lara would have chosen.

When they reached the lines left by the *Méne*, Lara spliced one to the rope at the other end of which was the plates. Despite the cool of the underground, her back was a sheet of sweat under her parachute and packs. Her guns and VADS gear seemed an unbearable weight at times, and she fought the temptation to just unbuckle and fling them the way of the pitons.

Lara took the lead when they reached the spot where the stairs resumed. At last, muscles shaking and sparking, she put a hand up over the lip of the Whispering Abyss and followed the muzzle of her gun into the domed chamber. It was deserted. She holstered her pistol and glanced at her watch.

They'd been in the Abyss for more than three hours. That was cutting it close. The crew of the *Plato* could arrive at any moment. They had to hurry.

She helped Borg up. Quickly, the two of them fixed the smaller line leading back to the platinum plates to the hand winch. Lara bent to operate it, then paused. Something nagged at her, but she couldn't quite put a finger on it.

"What is it, Lara?" Borg asked.

She looked carefully about the chamber. Then she saw it. There were nine shafts cut into the top of the dome, so closely placed that the amount of sunlight streaming down each one should have been the same. Except it wasn't.

Something—or someone—was blocking four of the shafts.

She drew her pistols.

Too late. Half a dozen men dropped down from the shafts, armed with shotguns and assault rifles.

"Drop your guns," came a voice that sounded somehow familiar.

The Tomb Raider looked for its source, but saw only the men who were training their weapons on her and Borg. With a curse, she dropped her guns. The USPs clattered to the floor, now just so much impotent metal.

"Lie down," said the voice. "Face down, arms out."

Lara complied. Through the corner of her eye, she saw Borg obeying as well.

Méne came and stood with pistols to their heads while others handcuffed both of them. With Borg, the black-and-tans were forced to attach the cuffs to metal fittings intended for other uses. . .

"Clever trick with the boat," the man with his gun to Lara's head said in an Irish accent. "The Prime figured you'd shoot the donkeys."

"The only asses I wanted to hurt were aboard the *Plato*," she said.

She got a pistol-smack on the side of the head for that.

Footsteps entered the domed chamber from the tunnel. Lara raised her head from the ancient floor. She saw three people. She knew them all.

Heather Rourke, her arms behind her back, perhaps handcuffed . . . perhaps not.

Alison Harfleur, her left hand on Heather's elbow, her right on the butt of a machine pistol dangling from a strap about her shoulders.

And Alex Frys.

He smiled at her. "Thank you for fetching the Prophecy Panels, Lady Croft."

Now she recognized the voice she'd heard earlier, but she said nothing.

Ajay, meanwhile, let go of Heather and walked over to where Lara's guns lay on the floor. She looked older than when Lara had last seen her, eight years ago. A bit more muscular. A lot more tan. Was she savoring the moment? Her expression was that of a student with the highest grades posted after an exam.

Ajay stooped and picked up Lara's guns. "Very nice." She extended the pistol, sighting between Lara's eyes. "You always did insist on the best accessories, Lara. The best guns. The best friends. But why not? You could afford it, couldn't you? Money was never a problem for Lady Croft."

Frys glared at her. "Give me those, Alison. We don't want any accidents."

Alison thrust out her jaw, her eyes clear and hard as diamonds. "Croft is dangerous. She should be killed."

"That is my decision, not yours. Give me the guns. Now."

For an instant, the two locked eyes, and Lara wondered who would prevail. But then Ajay held out her hands, and Frys took the pistols from her. He examined them for a second, then walked casually to the edge of the Abyss and tossed them over. "You won't be needing these anymore," he said.

Lara felt as if she'd just lost a favorite pet. Two of them.

Borg chose this moment to speak. "It is me, Alison. Nils. Don't you know me?"

"I'm not likely to forget a freak like you," Ajay sneered.

"That's a fine way to talk to your fiancé," Lara said, still stung by the loss of her custom pistols.

"Fiancé? He told you we were engaged?" She seemed uncertain whether to be insulted or amused.

"We'd spoken of marriage several times," Borg said defensively.

"Before your accident," Ajay said. "And I never accepted your proposals."

"I'm still the same man I was then."

"Not from where I'm standing."

Despite the millennia-old rocks beneath her body, Lara felt the world shift. She'd trusted Borg . . . and he'd lied to her. He and Ajay had never been engaged. She wondered what else he'd lied about.

Frys, meanwhile, turned to one of his men. "What are you waiting for, Sixty-one? Winch up the panels!"

He looked back at Lara. "Don't pretend that you saw through my little charade," he said. "Admit it: I had you fooled completely, didn't I?"

"Where's Kunai?" Lara asked in turn.

Frys smiled. "Many creatures in nature survive by imitating another. I used the name of a dead man, a ghost for you and others, like the police in Glasgow, to chase."

"You murdered Kunai, took his identity. Is that it?"

"Tejo Kunai put the pieces of the *Méne* faith back together, and he'll always be honored for it. But like John the Baptist, he was but a meteor presaging a greater light."

Megalomania, even good-natured megalomania, gave

Lara the creeps. Nor had it escaped her notice that Frys hadn't answered her question. He seemed decidedly reticent on the subject of Kunai. She decided to change the subject. "What about the panels? What do they do?"

"You'll find out soon enough. The whole world will find out."

"You are crazy. Insane." It was Borg. "Listen to him, Alison. Can't you see that he's done something to you? Brainwashed you in some way?"

"Nobody has brainwashed me," Ajay said. "You're an idiot, Nils. You always were."

"You loved me. I know you did."

"I needed you. There's a difference."

Frys approached, his hiking boots expanding to fill Lara's vision. "Our guests look uncomfortable there on the ground. Two-twenty-one, Forty, help them up, would you?"

Strong hands hooked Lara under the armpits and pulled her to her feet. Borg was likewise hauled erect. Alison's cruel words seemed to have hit him hard. He looked as though he'd been physically beaten.

Frys checked the fit of Lara's handcuffs, then returned to where Heather and Ajay stood. The journalist seemed dazed. She showed no awareness of her surroundings.

"What have you done to Heather?" Lara asked.

"Ms. Rourke has decided to join us," Frys said.

"Is that true, Heather?"

No answer.

"You've drugged her," Lara said accusingly. "Are you going to brainwash her like you did Alison?"

"I told you," Ajay said. "Nobody brainwashed me."

"I never figured you for the cult-joining type, Ajay," Lara said.

"If your wit were as quick as your mouth, LC, you'd see the big picture."

"And what's that?"

"Alison," Frys said. "Enough. We've got what we want. The panels are ours!"

The netting containing the panels had finally been winched to the edge of the Abyss. Two of the *Méne* maneuvered the netting onto solid ground and cut it open. Frys and Ajay knelt to examine them.

"Beautiful," Ajay breathed. She turned to Lara. "How did you get them loose, Lara? I tried everything!"

"Obviously not everything."

Frys gave each panel a loving polish with a piece of chamois before slipping it into in an empty crate produced by another of his minions.

Lara glimpsed motion behind Borg. He had extended his claw hand fractionally and was working to get the fingers into the links of his handcuffs. She had to cover the noise, provide a distraction. "Alex, was it worth killing your father over those?"

The leader of the *Méne* stiffened. "I didn't kill him. He panicked and drove his car off a cliff. I would rather have waited until he died of natural causes . . . but the stars were coming round right, you see, and would not do so again in my lifetime. Sixty-one, Forty, the crate is ready."

Lara didn't want the subject changed. "The stars will be right for what?"

"To learn that now, you would have to join us," Frys said.

"I might," she said, "if I knew more."

"Give it a rest, LC," Ajay said. "You're not fooling anybody."

Borg quit working his mechanical hand, waggled the fingers at Lara. "Alison, you don't belong with this circus," he said. He took a step toward Ajay, but men with guns shoved him back . . . and into Lara. She moved to block their view as his claw hand began to explore her wrists.

At a signal from Frys, the men started filing out of the tunnel.

"Now what?" Lara asked. "Are you going to kill us?"

Before Frys could reply, the *ting* of Lara's handcuff link parting echoed off the dome. Borg lifted his arms—

Ajay reacted faster than Lara would have given her credit for. She pivoted, extended her leg in a classic Tae Kwon Do kick, and connected with Borg's chest.

Borg stumbled backward, his prosthetic arms windmilling. Then he cried out as the floor dropped away beneath him, and he vanished into the Whispering Abyss.

"Nils!" Lara hurled herself backward, twisting as she dove after Borg. She saw him falling beneath her, clutching at his chest, tumbling as he fell. By clasping her hands to her sides, turning her body into an arrow, she caught up to him, grabbed a strap of his harness just as they struck the wall. They bounced off, but Lara kept her grip. Borg seemed to have been knocked unconscious by the impact.

Biting back the pain, Lara pulled Borg's chute open from the back, then let go so her shoulder wouldn't be dislocated when it opened. She heard it flutter open with a crack. Then she bounced off the wall again. Somehow, despite the blinding pain, she got her own chute open.

God, she hurt.

This descent made the last one seem like a picnic. She bounced off the wall again, and her chute folded and seemed unlikely to open again properly; perhaps part of it had caught a piton and ripped. She fell fast, but in a tight spiral. Too dark to see the walls . . . like falling in a nightmare.

The nightmare ended with a painful jar when she struck bottom. She fell onto something that felt like a soggy mattress. She untangled from her chute, found one of the stolen chemical lights in her pocket, lit it, held it up as she stood shakily. Her left leg was stiff and wobbly, but it held her up. At least nothing seemed to be broken.

Bulbous structures, each with a single round entrance, clung to the walls. She saw one of the huge beelike insects emerge from one opening, and instinctively reached for her empty holster.

Then she saw her guns. They lay one beside the other near a mound of insect debris. She took a step toward them, and the flying thing launched itself at her with an angry buzz.

P-kooof!

From above, a metal spike drove through the huge insect, carrying parts of arthropod with it as it plunged into the litter-covered ground. Lara looked up to see Borg drifting down, an avenging cybernetic angel on nylon wings.

He landed and came out of his chute with the facility of a commando.

Lara, meanwhile, made it to her guns. They were both in one piece, a testament to H&K's rugged engineering.

"Nice shot," she said.

"Nice save," he complimented her in turn.

An angry humming from all around quieted them. Lara stood with pistols ready, but nothing emerged from the hive to attack.

They stood in a trash pit: pieces of broken nest mostly, pressed material that looked like attic insulation. Among the nest fragments were bones and parts of animal carcasses, old and desiccated. Above the garbage layer, whole nests ringed the bottom of the Abyss. The noises of insects moving about in them, like the scratchings of a thousand mice behind the wainscoting of a decrepit old house, made Lara eager to get away before more killer insects emerged.

"Is your VADS system still operational?" Borg asked in a whisper.

Lara checked the inventory screen on the tiny hard drive that controlled the device; fortunately, it too had survived the fall. "I think so. But I'd rather not have to shoot our way out. I used most of my fancy shells on that wooden staircase. As for what's left, the illumination rounds might not penetrate their chitin, and the rubber bullets might just bounce off. That leaves armor piercing, and I've only got twenty-four of those, plus a couple of reserve clips in my holsters. I never entirely trust technology."

Borg looked back up the shaft of the Abyss. "I do not think I could climb out of here again."

Lara shook her head. "Me, either. But there may be another way out. Do you feel that?"

"A breeze!"

It flowed past them as steadily as though it came from a ventilation duct. Holding up her chemical light, Lara followed it. The floor of the Abyss sloped away under an overhang. The breeze was strongest here. She crouched, took a look under.

Another rounded tunnel, silted up with the dirt and dust of ages, sloped down. The wall was covered with fossilized barnacles and mussel shells. Had some long arm of the Pacific once extended this far beneath the Andes? "Looks like this is our best bet," Lara said.

"Do we have enough light?" Borg asked.

"Don't like full-dark spelunking? Don't worry. I have lots of these glo-sticks. We'll die of thirst before we run out of light."

"I don't want either to happen. I will trust you to get us out of here alive."

"Then you're going to tell me what really happened between you and Alison. We might not be down here if you'd told me the truth to begin with."

"I know. I am ashamed." His expression took on a hang-dog look in the light of Lara's glo-stick. "But I thought of Alison as my fiancée, please know that. I loved her very much."

"How do you feel now?"

"I . . . don't know. But I still believe she is in this man's power somehow."

Lara remembered Ajay's intent face, her cold blue eyes, as she delivered the kick that sent Borg over the edge. "Nils, you have a lot to learn about women."

16

As he waited in the sun atop Ukju Pacha for the helicopter to arrive, Alex Frys, the Prime, reflected on his triumph. Words that had not been spoken since men hunted mastodons would soon be chanted. Rites performed, offerings made.

The world transformed.

It bothered him that Croft and the Norwegian were dead. Croft, anyway. The Norwegian was worth more as spare parts, as an auto broker might say. But the deaths were his responsibility, and though he did not shirk at killing, the Prime preferred live converts to dead heroes.

Tejo, dear Tejo, if only you'd not insisted . . .

If the Prime stood up and walked about thirty meters farther into the ruins, he'd be at the spot where he first met Professor Tejo Kunai. He'd been, what was it, sixteen? Doing college work already on the Amazon headwaters ecosystem, thanks to his father, who was doing fieldwork that summer here at the Ukju Pacha ruins. Kunai had been setting up a clinic on the river and had taken a few days off to visit the ruins and gather botanical samples. The professor had been darkly handsome, with bright, intense eyes that blazed out like Rasputin's from his thickly bearded face.

His father had been lonely. In those days, the Peruvian archaeologists were busy preserving the tourist mecca of Machu Picchu, and his father's friend and sometime collaborator Von Croy was somewhere in Southeast Asia. Alex had introduced the Old Man to Dr. Kunai, something his father forgot in his later years, and they had formed a strangely complementary triumvirate. Kunai spoke of flowers and native medicines handed down for generations, the Old Man gabbled on and on about a lost civilization that might explain everything from the legend of Atlantis to Noah's flood, and he, with schoolboy enthusiasm, couldn't wait to put in a word about the strange animal species found in this isolated reach of the Andes eastern slope.

When Professor Frys spoke to Kunai of some translations of ancient texts from Egypt and the Arabian Peninsula that mentioned a holy plant bestowed on the *Méne* by forgotten gods, Kunai could hardly contain himself. He'd heard native legends about a plant granting immortality. They rushed out and gathered specimens by lantern light.

Thus the first domino that would lead to the Old Man's death had gone down on the table.

At the end of the summer, Alex had gone back to school. He kept in loose contact with Kunai, swapping occasional postcards. It was gratifying to know a celebrity, even if Kunai's name was only recognized in humanitarian circles. They did not meet again for a decade.

The Old Man had retired from fieldwork by then, and Alex was a doctoral candidate in biology.

Kunai, who had taken a long-distance avuncular interest in Alex's schooling, came to England for a conference, and after a courtesy visit to the Old Man, invited Alex to join him for dinner one night. There, over bottles of sherry—the surgeon's sole remaining Portuguese affectation—Kunai related a fantastic story.

Over the past decade, he'd devoted every spare minute to running down legends about the *Méne*. He'd learned a great deal and was on the verge of acquiring far more knowledge. He'd finally tracked down the family of a gentleman who had sailed with Captain Cook to the South Seas. On Easter Island, this sailor had acquired—some said stolen—a curious clear crystal from a native priest. Six months ago, Kunai had tried to purchase the crystal, sight unseen, but the family, suspicious, had refused to sell it, or even to show Kunai their ancestor's collection of South Seas artifacts. Apparently, there had been an ugly scene, one that made it impossible for Kunai to approach them openly again. But Alex could do it. Would he, as a favor to his old friend, use his university credentials to pose as a researcher seeking to examine the old artifacts for a scholarly article?

Kunai's eyes blazed across the dinner table; it was impossible to resist such passion. If Alex had asked any questions about the ultimate objective of the visit, he'd since forgotten. But he did consult his father. After a roundabout conversation, making up a story about a possible trip back to Peru, Alex asked him about the *Méne*.

"The *Méne* shouldn't be spoken of," his father said. "It's too dangerous."

"Dad, your whole career as a scientist has been about bringing forgotten cultures and religions back into the light. You've rejected ignorance and superstition!"

"You have much to learn," the elder Frys said. "When Von Croy and I started researching the *Méne*, we thought as you do now. But we concluded that there are some things that should remain cloaked in ignorance. Not all knowledge is a good thing, Son. And not all myth is mere superstition."

"What is it you're so afraid of?"

"I've said too much already. And why are you so curious after all these years? Has Kunai been expounding his theories to you?"

"No, of course not," Alex lied.

Frys shook his head. "He was a good man, once. Now . . . His search for old secrets has warped him, I'm afraid. He worries me. I know that the two of you have kept in touch. I can't forbid you to see him. But be careful, Son. Not everything he says can be believed."

But his father's warning had only made Kunai seem more interesting to Alex, a figure of mystery and ancient wisdom possessing a courage his father lacked.

Alex and Kunai traveled to the country house in Cornwall after making suitable arrangements with the elderly couple. Kunai did not go to the door, but waited in the lane in a rented car.

The couple lived the sort of life the newspapers always called "quiet." They offered Alex tea and took him up to a study. Alex found it difficult to believe that this polite and friendly old couple had nearly come to blows with Kunai. Surely it had all been a misunderstanding.

The proud gentleman turned off a burglar alarm, opened a wall safe, and took out his seafaring ancestor's souvenirs one by one, explaining their provenance to Alex as he did so. Alex examined an old spyglass frozen open, a sextant, some maps and buttons, leather-bound journals, and a triangular piece of clear crystal mounted at the end of an ivory and brass handle.

"We're not sure what this is," the old man said. "At first we thought it was a sort of monocle, but it doesn't appear to alter an image for the better. A doctor told us that surgeons used to put a mirror under a man's nose to see if he still lived—it would fog if he breathed, you see—and thought it might be a unique tool for that purpose. The glass in it is most smooth, you see."

The old man held it under Alex's nose and showed him the telltale moisture.

Alex sat down and made a show of taking notes from one of the journals. The couple retired from the upstairs, leaving the door open and saying he should just call out if he needed anything.

Once alone, Alex went to the double-glazed window and waved to Kunai, sitting in the car below, out of sight from the ground floor of the house but visible from this height, parked on the other side of a hedge. He returned to the table, looked through the strange glass. The old couple were right; it didn't appear to refract light, or magnify. If anything, objects seen through it looked a little cloudier. Not knowing what else to do, he traced its shape in his notebook.

The doorbell rang downstairs.

Alex heard the door open, then a startled cry, then a crash, a shout, and another breaking crash. He rushed down the stairs.

Kunai stood, a blood-splattered pipe in his gloved hand, over the bodies of the old couple. "They put up a struggle! Can you believe it? The crazy old bitch picked up a poker from the fire!" He laughed and tossed the pipe aside.

A frightened family cat hissed from beneath the television carriage.

Alex might have said, "Good Lord, man," or something even more ineffectual. He couldn't remember very well. He leaned against the wall, his legs threatening to buckle. Kunai dashed upstairs, squeezing past Alex on the stairs and giving his shoulder a reassuring squeeze as he went by.

When Kunai returned moments later, he held the strange triangular glass in one hand. "Well, I've got it," he said happily. "At last, I've got it!"

Alex could only stare at the mess in the parlor.

Kunai squeezed his shoulder again. "Never mind them, lad. They're dead, and overdue for it, too. Natural life span should never have risen much above fifty. Causes difficulties the world over. We'll set that right."

Kunai went into the kitchen. Alex followed listlessly, as in a dream. The older man rummaged around, found cooking oil, and dumped it into a deep pan. He poured the cooking oil all over the stovetop, the wooden cabinets, and the floor. Then he placed the pan on the kitchen floor and turned on the burner full blast. The oil on the stove top began to flame and stink immediately.

"That'll do." Taking Alex by the arm, Kunai led him out of the house and put him into the car. He went around the front of the car and climbed into the driver's seat, then calmly stripped off his blood-spattered gloves and stuffed them into a plastic bag, which he slid beneath the seat.

"You're a murderer," Alex managed to say once the engine started.

"Great men have great responsibilities, Alex. These responsibilities require them to do unpleasant things at times. I'm the leader of a movement that's one day going to make a new world."

"You're a mad murderer, then."

"Let's have dinner, Alex. Chinese food is conducive to—"

Suddenly Alex's strength and will came roaring back, as if he had just awakened from a dream. Except it had been no dream. "I'm getting out of here! I'm going to the police!" He pulled at the door handle; he would jump, though the car was moving swiftly now.

"Look at me, Alex."

Such was the commanding tone of Kunai's voice that Alex did look. Sparkling and shining between them was the piece of triangular glass on its ivory and brass handle.

"It's quite reasonable, really," said Kunai, glancing at him through the glittering glass. "A bargain, when you think about it. Why, a whole civilization perished once, warring over possession of this thing. The death of two old codgers is a small price to pay."

"A small price." Yes, when you put it that way, Alex thought, it was a bargain. Suddenly he felt much better about everything. He even had a bit of an appetite.

They talked it out over noodles and plum wine. Alex found himself in the mood to listen, in the mood for anything Dr. Kunai suggested.

Kunai told him that humanity, from time immemorial, could be divided into three groups. Ninety percent of the run of mankind weren't much more than cattle. Stolid, unimaginative, easily led as long as everyone else in the herd moved in the same direction around them. Of the remaining 10 percent, 90 percent of them were useful enough thanks to charisma or skill to serve as guides and overseers of the herd, setting the standards for culture, thought, behavior. From policeman to pulpit-pounder, politician to professor, this middle order could be counted on to move the herd without even realizing they were part of it.

Then there was the third group. Kunai thought it numbered less than the traditional one out of a hundred, but the ancient texts, added to by ages of secret learning, quoted that figure, so he accepted it. Visionaries who could keep their light a little ahead of the rest. Some became madmen or artists or prophets, unable to channel what burned within but desperate to relay it to the world somehow. A few more, unable to bear seeing the human world for what it was, committed spiritual suicide and fell back into the herd by adopting conventional religion or politics or commerce, drugs, or sex. A very few were suited by temperament to take on real responsibility for the control of the beautiful, terrible virus that was mankind. Stalin. Mao. Hitler.

History called these men monsters. And perhaps they were. But they had at least risen above the common herd and dared to stamp their dreams into flesh and blood.

"You admire Hitler?" Alex was aghast.

"Admire? No. One does not admire failure." The glass twinkled again in Kunai's hand, and Alex realized how reasonable the older man was being. How wise. Of course one did not admire failure. But to succeed in such a world-shaping dream . . . that would be worthy of admiration. He heard himself saying as much to Kunai, and Kunai nodded his head in agreement.

"But there's one thing I don't understand," Alex said. "Why didn't you kill me with those two in the house?"

"Why do you think?"

"Is . . . is it because I'm one of the one in a hundred? The third group?"

Kunai laughed, the crystal winking in his hand. "Perhaps . . . someday. I think you have a destiny, lad. I've had the most brilliant dreams of late. Every now and then your face appears in them."

Kunai then told him of the *Méne* and the Forgotten Gods.

They dwelled in the deep places of the world, mostly sleeping, awaking only now and again to glance at how the world had grown. Long ago they'd channeled some small part of their formidable mental energies into a dexterous life-form on the African savannah that showed an aptitude for tool use, intending to fashion living tools of their own to gather information on the constantly changing, and therefore inhospitable, surface of the world. The Deep Gods selected the *Méne* to act as conduits to this new race so that the work might be performed efficiently.

The *Méne*, exalted among men and humble before the Deep Gods, carried out their duties. Their labors done, the Gods charged the *Méne* with the ordering of men on the surface of the world and returned to their slumbers. They wished to wait for the day when their servants might carry them to other worlds.

Alex still remembered that wondrous conversation over packets of sweet-and-sour sauce and placemats covered with trite explanations of Chinese astrology. Everything seemed so clear after that, the details of the world so bright and sharp they almost hurt his eyes, like the light bouncing off the crystal that Kunai had taken from the foolish old couple. It was like that picture in the Gestalt psychology textbooks of the old woman with the gnarled, hawklike nose, and babushka, her neck buried deep in her fur collar. Tejo Kunai told him to look again at the woman's nose, and suddenly the profile of a beautiful young woman in a feathered hat appeared, her graceful neck plunging into an elegant dress.

Kunai went on to tell him that it was the *Méne*'s responsibility to weigh men, judge them, and place them in their proper category. The Deep Gods bestowed gifts to further set the *Méne* priests above the ordinary run of men. For the faithful, there was even a "final conversion" that guaranteed immortality on earth. Unfortunately, at some point in the mists of history, the *Méne* had lost control of their charges, and mankind had escaped the tyranny of the ruling *Méne* caste. They bred and spread and bred still further, covering and dirtying the earth as flies will a slice of fruit, fighting and ultimately hunting the *Méne* who tried to keep them in line.

They even revolted against the Deep Gods, exposed and killed those that could be found near the surface. Consciousnesses that had watched the birth of stars and pondered the expansion of the universe winked out.

The Deep Gods had made their tool too keen. They woke and reacted, turned the Earth on its head and covered the surface in water and ice. Old mountain ranges sank and new ones rose. Whole continents broke up.

But man survived.

Over the millennia, man grew again while the Deep Gods slept. Only now, said Kunai, the technology of man disturbs the Deep Gods' dreams, interferes with their sight, blots out the calls from others of their kind among the stars. The Deep Gods are waking. Man must again be hushed and organized and put under the control of a firm hand.

"They told you this?" Alex asked.

"Not in so many words. It's still an incomplete puzzle, but I can see what the picture is supposed to be. They send dreams on certain nights to those of the right temper, loyal through prayer and deed, saying that the time is coming, the stars are moving, and soon it will be the hour for the Deep Gods to wake."

"You are one of these priests?"

"I've learned much. The *Méne* were all but dead. Much of the religion had fallen back into ritual, without understanding what the ritual meant. Even more was mere superstition, grafted on over thousands of years by the credulous, the stupid. I've begun to piece the true faith back together. There are more of us now. I helped get a Dutch madman out of a sanitarium in Switzerland, made contact with an owner of a Buenos Aires shipping firm who is a devout believer, recruited an excommunicated Kenyan bishop now living in South Africa. There is much yet to do, but time is running out. You've seen how things are going in the world. If we don't blow ourselves up, it'll be a slow death from poisoned air and water. The extinctions have already begun. You're a biologist, Alex. Surely you've seen it coming."

"And you want to preserve the environment? Protect life on Earth?"

"It's what the Deep Ones want. What they've always wanted. The greatest danger to life on this planet is humanity itself. That's why they must be kept under strict control."

Kunai stayed with him for a few weeks. The bodies in Cornwall made the papers, described, of course, as a "quiet couple." The police traced phone records and visited Alex, but by then Kunai had coached him on the story. He told the police he'd visited the couple two days before the fire. Shocking. Showed them the receipts from hiring the car and a petrol station purchase. Asked if the journal of their seafaring ancestor had survived the fire.

"It's cooked. You open the pages and it crumbles," the detective said.

"They should have donated it to a library," Alex said, shaking his head sadly.

All the while Kunai, described as a "flatmate," sat in front of the television, the bit of crystal in his hand along with the television clicker.

The crystal worked exactly as Kunai had promised it would. The detective looked at the receipt printed May 29 and read it as printed May 27. Alex had the feeling he could have told the detectives he'd flown down to Cornwall on Icarus's old wings and they'd have smiled and nodded and taken his word for it as long as Kunai was there, gazing through the crystal, making it glitter and sparkle in his fingers.

He heard no more of the case or the CID men.

Alex asked about the crystal. Kunai explained that it allowed him to put whatever he desired into another person's mind: belief, fear, hope.

"How did you find out about it?"

"It was from your father, many years ago. I asked him about the paper he was writing with Von Croy. He mentioned legendary crystals that allowed the priests to influence others. He even hinted that there might be one still in existence. I got a little more out of him, but then he became suspicious and would say no more."

"Yes, once Dad clams up about something, that's the end of it. But how do you operate the crystal?"

Kunai answered, "It's a little like acting. First I summon up in myself the state I wish to induce in another: in the case of our friends from the constabulary, simple credulity. Then I put it into the subject's head by looking at him or her through the crystal. By the time that sailor with Cook discovered it, some fat old Easter Islander was using it to seduce the neighbor's daughters and then get a feast thrown in his name when the inevitable pregnancy was announced. There was a murder, but such things weren't closely investigated back then. Anyway, the chief died, and the sailor took the crystal away with him. The secret of its power was passed from father to son, and then from father to son again. Then some pious son suspected it to be Satanic and stole it away from his father after a wild night's carousing, which led to the death of both father and son in a struggle over its possession. The crystal's purpose and powers were forgotten by the family after that."

"Can you use it to control anyone?" Alex asked.

"Some people are more easily influenced than others. Indeed, some seem to be immune altogether. Either I'm not able to summon up a strong enough feeling to overcome their will, or their brain is wired in such a way that it has no effect. Magic and technology become one and the same at a high enough level, as that writer Clarke pointed out, and this thing didn't exactly come with an instruction manual."

Alex began to secretly read his father's research, at least the parts of it that weren't under lock and key, and he and Kunai traveled to an ancient temple near Rangoon and spoke with the priests there. Shortly afterward, Alex had an omega-like symbol that Kunai told him was the oldest known sign of the *Méne* tattooed on the back of his head, then let his hair grow back over it. At the same time, he received his first number in the old *Méne* tradition. That number was four hundred and ninety-one. As the newest was always the lowest, that meant there were at least four hundred and ninety other people in Kunai's network.

The *Méne* hierarchy reordered each supplicant's number yearly to reflect his or her standing in the cult. Always it was divided into the same 90 percent, 10 percent, 1 percent ratio. The

10 percent decided the order of the lowest 90 percent, while the top 1 percent decided the order of the top 10 percent.

Only Tejo Kunai's number didn't change. He was number one.

The Prime.

Alex's number grew steadily lower, until, after only seven years, he made it into the top 10 percent. At that point, he gave up all but a small portion of his university duties and devoted himself full-time to the business of the *Méne*. With his higher position, he learned more and more about the nature of his responsibilities, which were not always pleasant. And he began to have dreams.

Sometimes he flew in his dreams, but more often he dove into deep, cool waters. Voices would whisper phrases to him, and dates. They promised him power, foretold that he would rise above all other men to a universal throne that none had ever sat upon, although many had tried. He saw Kunai's face, still and peaceful and as composed as a death mask. He saw faces at a conference table, nodding as he spoke. He saw a beautiful woman with sharp blue eyes. He beheld himself seated upon a golden throne that shone like the sun . . .

He hadn't seen Kunai for four years when the old man showed up bedraggled on his doorstep during a spring storm. Kunai had lost weight, a little of the fire was out of his eyes, and his hair was gone.

"Leukemia. It's in remission. The doctors tell me to rest, but what is that against the Awakening?"

With that, dripping first in the hall and then on the kitchen floor and table, Kunai told Alex that he'd dreamed that the Deep Gods were beginning to rouse themselves. One or two had awakened, a vanguard of the consciousnesses to come.

Alex made him a cup of coffee, forced him to eat some

buttered toast. Kunai tore into the bread like a starved man and then went on with his tale.

"Meet, yes, we're going to meet. I've been to Capricorn Atoll to prepare for instructions. Detailed instructions, not just impressions from dreams. I need to get the nine plates, the Prophecy Panels used to communicate with the Deep Ones. The ones originally at the atoll were destroyed long ago. But I know where there is another set."

"Not another cottage in Cornwall, I hope," Alex joked.

Kunai did not smile. "They're in the Whispering Abyss, or so it's written on an Ethiopian monolith. Whispering Abyss. You know from whom I first heard those words?"

"No."

"Your father. Where I first met you, in Peru. I saw some bits of an article he was doing when I first became involved in the Truth and the Old Order. All this time, right under my nose."

"He's quit all his research into us, you know that. Warned me a dozen times not to have anything to do with you."

Kunai's eyes lit up as he smiled. "Now you understand why I told you to keep your membership a secret from even your father."

"I'll call him and ask for a visit. You can use the crystal on him before the door's half open and—"

"I've already been to Scotland, Eighteen. The crystal didn't even make him blink. Tough-minded old bird!"

The Old Man was that.

"What do you need of me?" Alex always had that phrase ready on his lips when conversing with someone ranked seventeen or higher.

"Visit your father. Any pretense will do. We need those old papers of his on the *Méne*. The precise location of the

Abyss is recorded there, I'm sure of it. Someone's killed Von Croy, so the only other copies are buried somewhere in Lara Croft's vault, and I'm content that they remain there. I don't want her to get even a whiff of our interest. If half of what I've heard about her is true, she could spell trouble for us. Meanwhile, I've put together a team that can go anywhere in the world on three days' notice and retrieve the plates as soon as you get the information."

"It shouldn't be a problem," Alex said.

"Wait. Your task is greater than mere theft. It won't be enough for us to possess your father's papers. He, more than anyone now living, will know the danger we pose. He will alert the world."

"No one would believe him."

"Perhaps not. But we can't afford to take that chance. You're going to have to eliminate him, Alex."

"K-kill him, you mean? My own father?"

"Eighteen, I've been waiting for some time to make you my direct subordinate. As number two, your power would be second only to my own. But there's one final trial before you join the elite. One last test to pass. To show your devotion, you must sacrifice someone near to you. It's something that all of us 1-percenters have done to reach our positions."

"I thought the text read 'sacrifice that which is dearest.' I was going to give up my college chair."

Kunai chuckled. "Like a Catholic might give up chocolate for Lent? No, Alex. A blood sacrifice is necessary." Kunai produced a revolver from his jacket pocket and pushed it across the kitchen table. "Wipe it off carefully and then wear gloves."

Alex ate dinner with the Old Man—well, the Old Man ate, and Alex made enough of a hash of his broiled meat to make it look as if he'd eaten—then left. After a visit to the hardware store and two strong cups of coffee laced with equally strong whiskey, he hurried back for the ferry across the Irish Sea to Dublin.

He bought a ticket but never boarded.

He went back to the Old Man's house, wearing a cheap woolen cap with oversized earflaps.

The glass cutter hadn't even touched the window when he saw the Old Man standing in the doorway of the kitchen, carrying a Clint Eastwood–sized pistol. He almost ruptured himself in his haste to get away, leaping the hedge and cutting through backyards to a chorus of barking dogs.

"I'm sorry, but I couldn't do it," he confessed to Kunai later. They sat in his tiny kitchen. Alex poured himself a hot cup of coffee and spiked it with scotch.

There were dark circles under Kunai's eyes, his skin had thinned against the bones of his face. "You disappoint me. I fear you won't keep your number very long."

"No!" Alex protested. "I've given my life to this."

"But you can't give your father's? Getting those papers was your responsibility. You've failed."

"I've had dreams too of late. Very specific ones." Alex felt as light as air. When he walked to the counter, it seemed as though his feet didn't touch the kitchen tiles.

"Specific how?" Kunai coughed.

"You can't keep up the pace anymore. You're making bad decisions."

"What are you saying?" Kunai fumbled at his shirt pocket, going for the crystal that he always carried.

"Responsibility flows up, as well as down," Alex said. He grabbed the scotch bottle and smashed Kunai across the face with it. The blow sent the older man spilling from the chair, and Alex dropped down on him, driving his knee against Kunai's throat. Cartilage crackled under his knee, sounding like bubble wrap being popped.

Alex prized open Kunai's weakening fingers and grasped the crystal on its ivory handle. He looked at the distorted image of his mentor, tried to funnel his own sense of exhilaration and peace to Kunai.

But the image in the glass shrank to a tiny point, black and dead.

The Prime is dead, Alex thought as he knelt above the body, gasping for breath.

Long live the Prime.

But Tejo Kunai still had work to do. Alex called a meeting of the top 1 percent, in this case numbers two through eight; he had spoken in Kunai's name often enough before that no one was suspicious. All knew of the man's health problems. At the meeting, Alex entered with the crystal in hand and announced that Kunai had died and appointed him successor. For men and women who claimed to be an intellectual, spiritual, and moral elite, they became convinced of his inheritance of the mantle of leadership astonishingly easily. Not one of them proved able to resist the suggestive power of the crystal. He asked for detailed, written status reports of their current projects and the responsibilities of the 10 percent under them, especially those of the team selected to recover the plates.

Among those reports, he first saw Alison's picture. She'd been hired through lower-numbered functionaries as an archaeologist willing to work for money. He recognized her beautiful blue eyes from his dreams.

He used the substantial funds now at the *Méne*'s disposal to have Alison visit him in Lisbon, then Buenos Aires, then

India, as he became familiar with the global organization that before he'd only known from having his strings pulled. Now he pulled the strings. She needed only the tiniest nudge of the crystal to be convinced to join. He fell in love with the brilliant mind first, then the young, strong body. They first made love the night she got her tattoo.

The Prime looked across the ruins of Ukju Pacha, brought back to the present by the sound of helicopter blades in the distance. Ajay hung about one of the vents to the Whispering Abyss as though listening for clues to the fate of Lara Croft and her ex-lover, Borg. His Tomb Raider swayed on her feet; the effects of the *avitos* bulbs she'd crushed between her teeth before entering the chamber, which had allowed her to kick the Norwegian with enough strength to send him flying into the Abyss, were ebbing, leaving her sapped and moody.

He didn't want to think about Alison anymore. He was getting tired of her anyway. He resolved to look to the future.

And there she was, sitting on the grass, waiting for her next set of instructions: Heather Rourke. Bright, pretty, mature, and plugged into the Washington, D.C., power network, where journalists often wielded as much or more influence than the politicians they covered. The time for globe-trotting and obelisk-rubbing was just about over. Once the Prophecy Panels were in place and had served their purpose, it would be useful to have someone with the keys to the global telecommunications kingdom among the chosen *Méne*.

17

The wasps chased Lara and Borg.

At least, that was how she thought of the giant insects that had been attacking them for what seemed like hours now. The other bugs had resembled fat bumblebees, but these were waspish, their thin black bodies splashed with bright yellow; their long legs dangled limply as they flew.

The Tomb Raider backpedaled, a necklace of chemical lights strung across her chest, guns out, protecting Borg as he picked their path through the tunnel. The buzzing suddenly grew louder, indicating that the wasps were coming again.

"Incoming!" she cried, and dropped to the ground.

Tight streams of sticky tobacco-juice-like liquid flashed out of the dark, passing over her head. Lara fired back, lighting the twisting tunnel with muzzle flashes. Her VADS system had run dry awhile ago, and she was down to reserve ammunition now. But again the wasps retreated.

Borg cried out in Norwegian as a parting salvo of wasp spit struck his neck. As they had discovered, the liquid was a powerful acid; Lara had taken some across the back of her hand in an earlier assault and it still burned. Thankfully, neither of them had been hit in the eyes, ears, or mouth yet. Now Borg dropped his chemical light and clawed at his already-blistering skin.

Lara slung her camel pack under her arm and squeezed it like a bagpipe, directing the spray across Borg's neck. When it was washed clear of the poison, she helped him to his feet. "Still with me, Borg?"

"For now," Borg said. "But I do not think we can hold them off much longer."

"With any luck, we won't need to. The breeze is stronger than ever. We're going to make it."

Water was flowing somewhere ahead of them, and together they hurried toward the sound. Behind them, the buzzing began to grow louder again.

At a Y-intersection in the tunnel, they came to an underground river. Lara knelt and put her hand into the swift-moving flow.

Cold. Not quite ice-cold, but cold enough for hypothermia to set in within twenty minutes or so.

Lara ignored the buzzing as best as she could and looked around.

They stood in a much rougher underground chamber. They'd traveled west, or perhaps southwest, some distance—GPS didn't work deep underground, so she'd navigated on instinct and air currents, following the breeze.

The river plunged into the rock wall of the chamber a stone's throw away. The breeze was coming from a narrow space between the river and the wall.

"I hope you are not thinking what I think you are thinking," Borg said.

"How are you at swimming with those arms, Nils?" Lara asked.

"I am an excellent sinker," he replied.

"We have two choices," she said. "Either we take a deep breath and jump in this river and hope it comes out into the open before we run out of air, or we try to fight our way back past the wasps with the twelve bullets I've got left."

Borg knelt and peered down the river, just as she had.

"Cover up your light," he said.

She pocketed her chemical stick, placed a hand over the glow that made its way through the cotton canvas.

After a moment in the coal-mine dark of the cave, they both saw a faint smear of light in the river.

"Sunlight," Lara breathed.

"It seems a long way off," Borg said. "But it's there."

The buzzing behind them grew louder again. The wasps were coming back, with fresh poison to spit.

"It looks like the river is our best chance," Borg said, glancing nervously behind them.

"I agree." Lara turned off the VADS gear. According to Djbril, water wouldn't harm the system, but there was no point taking unnecessary risks. "Were you serious about not being able to swim?"

"My arms are functional underwater, but their weight drags me down. I can fight against it for a time, using my legs, but not for very long."

"You'll have to hold on to me. I won't let you sink."

"I hate this," he said.

"Just think of it as another BASE jump. A really wet one."

"It is not the wet that I mind. It is the cold."

"When we get back to civilization, I'll put us up in a Jacuzzi suite."

"The current is swift," Borg observed. "It's going to be quite a ride." He lit a chemical light and tossed it into the river. The light disappeared into the cavern mouth. "Hopefully, that will show us any rocks in our path."

"Good thinking, Nils." She lit one of hers and tossed it in for good measure.

"Here come the wasps!" cried Borg as the first stream of spit splattered off the rocks beside him.

"Hang on to my backpack with that claw of yours," Lara said, then rolled into the river with a splash. Borg was right behind her.

The chilled water stuck its knives everywhere in Lara's body. Diamond-pointed filaments of shock ran up her limbs. Right after her dip in the Jacuzzi suite, she'd write a check to a university to come up with a microthin survival wetsuit that she could fit into her lucky pack.

As she rode the swift current, trying to keep her toes pointed downstream, Borg's kicks struck her own quickly fluttering calves.

"You managing?" Borg sputtered.

The Tomb Raider's eyes didn't leave the bobbing glow of the chemical lights ahead. "It's okay. We're in the tunnel."

Blast, a rock.

She bounced off it sideways. Ahead loomed an overhanging bulge—

"Duck!" she croaked. There was just enough time to submerge. She hoped Borg would sink as well as he'd promised. A sharp tug at her backpack, and Borg no longer kicked. He'd struck the rock, perhaps been knocked unconscious.

The mechanical hand kept its grip where a human hand would have let go. Lara fought the deadweight, broke the surface as the water plunged down a short drop. She managed to get a breath before being sucked under again.

The deadly cold flow, indifferent to the humans fighting in

its grip, worked for them for a change and pushed them to the surface.

Lara turned so she could sidestroke and pull Borg along. Her chemical necklace revealed a larger cavern. They came up and out of the water, followed by her head. The channel widened, slowed. She could see the lights they'd thrown floating ahead, hardly bobbing at all.

Borg, a hundred-plus kilos of deadweight, twitched, started kicking and thrashing. Lara risked not looking ahead and shifted herself so she could support his head.

"Borg! Borg!"

"Ja, ja!" he sputtered, but calmed down a moment later.

The Tomb Raider turned and swam on, holding the light up as much as possible. She caught up to her thrown light, bobbing gently in the cold, dark water; the current had slowed with the widening of the tunnel. The pain in her limbs ebbed, replaced by a warm feeling.

Alarm bells went off somewhere, but her brain was muzzy. In Russia she'd had a wetsuit . . . Where was Michelov? The Spear . . .

The next thing she knew, she was being dragged out of the water and onto a smooth-pebbled shore. Borg was pulling her, but whether he was even aware of doing so, she couldn't tell. Once out of the water, he collapsed, holding his head. A distant roar filled the cavern, and a stronger light shone from further downstream. Their two thrown chemical lights floated past, heading toward the light. The breeze here was warmer, and smelled of green, growing life, though the rocks were still cave cold.

The Tomb Raider stripped off her backpack with numb fingers, took out her shiny silver survival blanket. She threw it around Borg and herself, then pulled him up and off the cave floor. She wrapped herself around his back, put her legs around his stomach, and searched his wet hair for the cut that was the source of the blood running down his face. She lifted a flap of skin and saw pink-tinged skull beneath.

"You're cut. Not too bad," she lied. A dressing from her lucky pack helped. When she had better light she'd have to do stitches.

"C-c-cold."

"I know. It hurts the worst once you're out of it."

Lara clung to him, feeding off his warmth, hoping that her body was feeding the warmth back into him and not just draining his life away. His hard, warm body and the masculine scent trapped under the survival sheet stirred her . . .

"Where did you grow up, Borg?"

"Tretten in the Gudbrandsdalen, near Lillehammer."

"Did you see the Olympics?"

"I was seventeen. Of course. We went into town every night to see what was going on, ten of us in a van."

"Which country had the sexiest women?"

"Norway, of course."

Lara squeezed him. "A true patriot. How about second sexiest?"

"Hmmm . . ." Borg pursed his lips. Lara felt his heart beat a little stronger. "The Italians dressed very well. The Americans went to the most parties, or that is what I was told by the Norwegians. I had a crush on a Chinese skater, but though I tried many times, I never saw her in person. The Chinese women were guarded like a harem. But I think I will have to say the Czech women came in second. They were proud to be led by a poet and flirted with everyone. Worse than the French girls, even."

"Did you kiss any Olympians?"

"Ha!"

"And that's Norwegian for?"

" 'None of your business.' "

It had grown warm under the blanket. She looked at his dressing. It seemed to have stanched the worst of the bleeding.

"Borg, do you think you can stand?"

"Yes. Let's find the sun. But first, some food, Lara, to keep us on our legs."

They lit chemical lights and gasped.

All around them, half submerged in stone, crystal arcs like great pieces of clamshell stuck up. In the cavern, which stretched far beyond the range of their lights. In the water. There were some even in the ceiling.

The Tomb Raider got out her MagLite, probed the shadows.

"It is like . . ." Borg gasped. "It is like Krypton."

"Like what?"

"From the Superman stories. The planet where he was born . . ."

Lara had spent much of her childhood reading Aristotle and Cicero—with a dash of Sappho or Ovid when she felt in the mood for something spicy—rather than comics. But she understood what he meant. "You're right; it is like another world. But we need our strength, and we can't afford to waste it on exploration. Let's eat."

They sat next to one of the crystal outcroppings, an arc of mineral as clear as a pane of glass. Did the creatures that lived in the Whispering Abyss, presumably Von Junst's Elder Gods, shape this crystal in some way? What had lived among these sloping old pieces of dome?

There were bits of shell among the ruins. More sea bottom, thrust up into the Andes?

Once they had eaten, they felt stronger. They rose and left

the strangely beautiful crystal city, splashing through ankle-deep water at times as they followed the channel and the now-fading light.

"It's light outside," Lara said, checking her watch.

"Let's run," Borg said. "I thought I'd never see another sunrise." He hurried toward the familiar surface world.

"Just don't hit your head again!"

Later, she berated herself for not noticing that the cavern wasn't inhabited by bats. They could see sunlight now, so bright to their dark-inured senses that they had to wince.

That's when they hit the web.

It stretched, two volleyball nets across, over the cavern mouth, partially supported by a couple of roots descending from above. Borg hit it and stopped. Lara, partially blinded by the bright light, tried to pull up to keep from running into him and lost her footing in the loose riverside pebbles. She fell headfirst into the strands.

They were as thick as heavyweight fishing wire and as sticky as superglue.

Out of the corner of her eye she saw something dance down the web on horribly hairy legs, its body about the size of a snapping turtle's.

Not counting the swollen abdomen and long, hairy, frantically working legs.

Her eyes adjusted, and she saw cocoons with a few parrot feathers sticking out, and something that looked like a monkey's tail.

"Lara, shoot!" Borg shouted as the spider alighted on his piton arm.

"Hands . . . stuck!"

His claw arm was free. He reached for the sheathed survival knife at his belt, pulled it out, dropped it next to her hand.

She grasped the hilt, got a rush of strength from it, enough to pull the web far enough so she could saw at it.

Borg fired a piton. He didn't have a hope of hitting the spider, but the recoil startled it. It ran up the web.

"Hurry, Lara," Borg said.

"I am!"

It was hard to cut with the blade held so it faced back along her forearm.

"Hurry very much!" Borg insisted.

"Why?"

"You don't want to know."

At the elbow, her arm was almost free!

"I do want to know."

"It's above you and coming down on a line NOW!"

She took a chance, dropped the knife, and reached for her holster, not wanting to think about what would happen if the gun were tangled as well—

The butt in her hand, safety flicked off, she pointed it upwards, unable to see.

BLAM! BLAM! BLAM!

The hot cartridge cases landed on her uncovered thighs, burning, but she didn't care.

She felt wet goo strike her back.

"It's going back up!" Borg said.

She fired twice more for good measure. Spiders were sensitive to vibrations, and she hoped it wouldn't stop fleeing until it hit the Brazilian border.

The hot gun went back in its holster, and she retrieved Borg's knife, cut away the web from her face so she could better see what she was doing, and freed the rest of her. She drew her other gun, searched the roof with flashlight and eye.

The wounded spider didn't return. Just a thousand tiny ones, each with eight eyes glittering in the light. Babies.

Hungry babies.

She tore Borg loose, and they fled.

The river spilled out into twilight. Lara and Borg stood on a precipice overlooking another stretch of river, westward flowing and therefore not the same one they'd followed to the canopy tower and ruins. The humidity felt like an old friend welcoming them. Squawks and howls of perfectly normal jungle life were like applause.

They'd come out of the Whispering Abyss.

"Not this time!" the Tomb Raider shouted at the heavens.

"You are crazy, Lara."

She loved how he said crazy. Hell, she was one wet ponytail hair from loving him, period. Alison or no Alison. A kick about a meter below the teeth sends a clear message about a girl's commitment to a relationship.

18

"That's quite a story," Heather said, looking out over Lima's white rooftops from the plushly fitted top-floor El Condado hotel suite. She'd just heard an outline of the history of the *Méne*. She didn't have to fake her interest in the story, just in Frys.

Frys lounged in a gold-and-beige upholstered armchair, playing with his odd bit of glass on a handle. The affectation struck her as cute, like Leslie Howard's Scarlet Pimpernel with his monocle examining the prince regent's waistcoat and cuffs and criticizing His Royal Highness's tailors. She felt a little better disposed toward him now that he'd revealed the reasons behind her kidnapping, although she had a strange feeling that he hadn't told her the whole truth about what had happened to Lara Croft and Borg. He'd told her that they'd been tied up and left for the park rangers to find, but every so often, images returned to Heather as if out of a half-forgotten dream, images that told a very different story.

Alison Harfleur, that Lara Croft wannabe, reclined on one of the king-sized beds, supported by a small mountain of fringed pillows, reading *The Economist*.

"It's the story of a lifetime," Frys assured her. "And it can be yours to tell."

"Wouldn't be the first time the human race has had what it thought was the history of the world rewritten."

The blond version of Lara Croft threw down the magazine and punched her pillow. "You don't mean to take her to Capricorn Atoll?"

"Ms. Rourke, won't you excuse us," Frys said, escorting Alison to the connecting door between suites.

"So it's 'Ms. Rourke' now, is it?" said Alison bitterly.

But Frys leaned close and whispered something, holding the crystal up to his eye, and Alison exited without further complaint, though she left the door open.

Heather was intrigued by Frys, but she didn't trust him, not for a second. She'd seen how he'd used Alison, then cast her aside. Now it was her turn. But nobody used Heather Rourke. And nobody, but nobody, cast her aside. "Can I go down to the café and get something to eat?" she asked when Frys returned.

Frys shook his head. "There's room service."

"I need to go to the pharmacy in the lobby. Splitting headache."

"Alison will go for you. Just tell her what you—"

"Let her get her own damn Tylenol!" Ajay's voice interrupted from the other room.

"I'd like to stretch my legs anyway," Heather said. "Besides, we have to trust each other if we're going to work together."

Frys smiled. "Yes, of course." He opened the door, and six feet six inches of muscle looked up from a magazine. "Thirty-two, would you take Heather down to the chemist in the lobby and bring her straight back up?"

"Yes, sir," the cultist said.

Heather followed the meaty guard down the elegantly wallpapered hall.

He pressed the button on the elevator. The doors slid closed.

"Do you have a name to go with that number?" she asked him.

"I am Boris," he replied expressionlessly.

The elevator slid to a halt. The door opened, and Boris stood half in and half out until she exited into the lobby. Then he conducted her past a women's restroom and into the chemist's.

There Heather picked out a suitable assortment of aspirin and travel necessities and a new lipstick, then tapped her foot as Boris paid. As they walked back to the elevator, she snatched the bag out of his hand and ducked into the restroom.

"I have to pee," she said, jumping through the door before he could interpose his bulk.

Boris actually came in behind her, then blanched and withdrew at a glare from the Peruvian matron working on her eyes at the bulb-lined vanity mirror. Heather felt like a runaway heiress in a Depression-era screwball comedy as he pounded on the door and demanded that she come out.

"Can you help me?" she whispered in Spanish. At first she'd just planned to leave a note in lipstick on one of the stall doors, but the woman might be a better choice.

"*Siiiii?*" the woman said disapprovingly, one painted eyebrow rising almost to her widow's peak.

"Do you have a piece of paper and a pen? It is a crisis."

The one-woman-to-another, this-is-really-serious urgency in her voice brought a quick response. The matron produced a pen and a slip of notebook paper from her purse, suddenly eager to help.

Heather wrote her name, a pair of phone numbers, and the words CAPRICORN ATOLL—BIG MEETING on the paper. "Please go somewhere with a . . . with a . . . fax." She had to use the English word. "You know, fax?"

"*Sí*, fax, my office has one," the woman said.

"Fax this to both these numbers. Right away, please. Right away."

"What is this?"

"I'm sorry, I don't have time to explain. Please help me."

"If there is danger, I can call the police."

"They have friends in the police."

To her credit, the unknown woman didn't look frightened. She glanced toward the door, against which Boris was still hammering. "I will do it. Don't let a doubt enter your thoughts."

Relief flooded through Heather. "Thank you. If you give me your name and phone number, I'll make sure you are paid for your trouble."

"No, no, please. I am happy to help." A smile, not a bright one, not a charming one, but a reassuringly small one, appeared on the woman's face. She squeezed Heather's hand and walked out of the bathroom.

Heather heard a growl, cracked open the door.

Boris had grabbed the woman by the upper arm.

"Wait, you," he said in very thick Spanish. "Come with me."

The Peruvian matron, the top of her hairstyle not even reaching Boris's shoulder, spun her head like a wolf snapping at a challenger. "Unhand me this instant!" she said through bared teeth. The opera diva Troyanos as Carmen couldn't have put any more fire in her voice.

Boris shrunk away from the matron, who walked off with what Heather could only describe as imperious dignity.

Then Boris grabbed Heather by the arm—the thug had a thing for grabbing women, evidently—and walked her back to the elevator.

Borg hardly flinched as the curved needle passed through his skin one more time.

He looked a little like a lobotomy patient with the side of his head freshly, if poorly, knife-shaved. They were two kilometers from the cave, on the unfamiliar riverbank.

"Last stitch is done," she said. "I just have to tie it."

Six granny knots, stained with iodine, now held Borg's scalp on. She dabbed up the blood. "It's not a bad look, really. I can see it catching on with the soccer rowdies."

"I need another Tylenol," Borg said.

She handed him a tablet.

"Strange. You'd think after what happened to my arms, such a minor pain would be nothing."

"Pain doesn't work that way, unfortunately. It always finds a way to come back as strong as ever."

Lara knew a lot about pain. She'd been in a codependent relationship with it for most of her adult life. And on those occasions when she wasn't bruised and bloody from one of her overseas challenges, she pushed her body to its limits with athletics or making a hundred round-trips through her assault course, feeling the burn of hot pistols through thin leather gloves, paying for her achievements with coins of freshly minted pain.

She kept Borg talking as she put together a tent out of a parachute, her concerns about a possible concussion or him slipping into a coma fading.

"Where is she, I wonder?" Borg asked in the middle of the chitchat.

Lara knew whom he was talking about. "We can't worry about Ajay now. We have to think about where we are."

She had her answer, calculated to within a meter, of course, thanks to the GPS, which had begun working again once they'd emerged from underground. The problem wasn't that: It was that their location was a long, long hike from the nearest airport. The river they camped next to flowed west, toward the Pacific Ocean, but a mass of mountains were in the way. She looked at the stands of Peruvian hardwoods all around. Among them stood balsa trees: easily shaped and more buoyant than cork.

"Borg, how much do you know about dugout canoes?"

"The front provides power, the rear steers," Lara said. Working with fire, Neolithic tools improvised from river rocks, and their knives, they'd managed to fell and then hollow out a balsa trunk. It looked like a conveyance from *The Flintstones*, but it would float and carry them.

"I'll take the front," Borg offered.

Lara added an outrigger, weighted with pitons, and fixed it to the body of their canoe with cording and parachute harness. Their biggest danger with such a makeshift float was tipping over.

The oars looked like broken tennis rackets, built of bundles of trimmed branches roughly tied together and covered with parachute nylon. It would take days to whittle proper oars with knives, and they didn't have days. Borg attached his to his piton arm with a D-ring and gripped it in the claw arm.

Using their parachute packs as seat cushions, they got out on the river. They experimented with their canoe, tried some turns. Draft was the canoe's only asset. Balsa would float on heavy dew; as long as there was a river, and no rapids, they wouldn't need to portage. With a little luck, within a few hours they'd run into some natives, hopefully before white-water wrecked their canoe. It wouldn't be the first time Lara had traded a cheap watch and expensive sunglasses for transportation out of the bush.

They heard the rapids before they saw them, which was always a bad sign.

Whitewater appeared beneath them. It happened too fast to react. One second they hung at the top of a forty-degree slope of solid white froth descending into a gorge, the next they were plunging down into the wash.

The balsa-wood canoe tore down the incline like an out-of-control Alpine schusser on one ski. You can't fight white water, but you can control what it does to you by using your momentum. Lara paddled like a fury—if the canoe turned sideways in the flow, the outrigger would be ripped away, and then the canoe would turn over, and the river would win against them.

Too busy trying to steer to even know if her voice carried above the roaring water, she shouted instructions to Borg.

Then a rock—and ruin. She didn't even see it until it was too late.

It ripped away the outrigger; hours of labor turning raw materials into a careful balance of wood and lashing were destroyed with a single sharp blow. The impact tore the paddle from Lara's hands and set the canoe on its side. Lara and Borg plunged into the river.

But they hung on.

They rode the cool water, submerging and coming up for a breath, then plunging in again. Borg locked on to her and the canoe in a mechanical death grip. A rock struck her in the hip; the blow stunned her into letting go of the canoe.

But Borg's claw held.

Somehow he hauled her back to the canoe, somehow pushed her atop it so she rode it like a lizard hugging a tree. Borg hung off the end, preventing it from rolling, performing the function the outrigger had. Then she discovered she could hear Borg panting and sputtering.

And so they came through the rapids.

The gorge opened into steep mountains at the base of the rapids; a little ways downstream a few huts on stilts fought against river, mountainside, and forest for a place on the bank. Dogs barked at the drenched pair and chickens flapped at the commotion.

A single log fishing dock-cum-bridge, sort of a split rail fence for access to the river and its banks, projected out and across the river. No doubt it was torn away and rebuilt several times a year thanks to floods. She slipped off the canoe, and together they kicked toward the dwellings.

"Boating never was my calling," Borg said.

Alex Frys got the call on the charter jet, an airbus, somewhere over Pitcairn Island in the South Pacific.

"Lady Croft is in Lima, making a stink at the Tourism Bureau," the voice said.

"The Tourism Bureau? Not the Interior Department?" Frys wasn't sure he'd heard right; the airplane phone had a good deal of static.

Well, he hadn't wanted her dead, after all. She'd been of service to the *Méne* Restoration. Shooting her and throwing her into the Abyss just hadn't seemed—cricket. Killing unnecessarily was a failing of Kunai's, not his. Not that he'd been too disappointed when she'd jumped. But not half as disappointed as he was now to learn that she had somehow survived.

"Tourism Bureau," his contact confirmed. "Talking about guerrillas and gunfights and getting stranded thanks to corrupt park officials. She's threatening to write an article for the *Times* Sunday color supplement: *Peru, a Journey Into Hell and Back*. Needless to say, the men at Tourism are not amused."

"You don't say," Frys said, making conversation while his mind worked.

"I understand this has gone all the way to the president. He's put them up in a hotel on the seashore south of Lima, sent a doctor and two nurses down to tend to them, even ordered one of the state-dinner chefs to supervise their meals. Questions are being asked. I fear your friend Fermi will not be in uniform much longer."

The Prime smiled. One day, perhaps soon, Fermi would be able to laugh in the face of the president. "Anything else, Thirty-three?"

"Lara Croft knows you have left the country."

Too late, Lara Croft.

Perhaps he shouldn't have hurried out of Peru, but it had been necessary to gather the fourteen others of the 1 percent to witness what was being prepared at Capricorn Atoll. He had thought it would be jolly for them to travel together. But that wasn't thinking like the Prime, now, was it? He had responsibilities.

"You know the name of the hotel where she is staying?"

"Of course," the voice at the other end crackled.

"Contact Don Sabato. He owes Tejo Kunai a favor for improving the potency of his coca crop. Tell him Kunai is calling that favor in. Croft needs to be killed. He might use La Raza again. La Raza arranged the disappearance of that troublesome lawyer last year."

"The president will go mad!"

"Let him. The time is coming when presidents will not matter."

"I heard that from Kunai. Now from you?"

The Prime sighed. "With such questions, you wonder why you remain Thirty-three year after year?"

"Sorry, sir. I will call Don Sabato at once."

"Thank you, Thirty-three. Tell him to hurry. This opportunity moves quickly." He turned the phone off.

Alison had an I-told-you-so look on her face that he longed to wipe off. Perhaps she needed words. "You were right," he said. "I was wrong. We should have not left loose ends."

"We'll hear from her shortly, I'm sure," Alison said.

"I doubt it. Don Sabato has killed an American ambassador and three Peruvian generals. I believe his men can handle one woman. And if not, the Pacific is a very big place in which to hide."

19

Peru did not have the world's best beaches, but where the dramatic Pacific shoreline met the desert beauty of Andean mountains, one did without beaches and just drank in the beauty.

Lara didn't have time for scenery, however. She read the confirmation from her favorite Pacific Air pilot, a New Zealander called "Shanks," and snapped shut the laptop on loan to Lady Croft from the Ministry of Tourism. Ever since reading Heather's fax, scanned and put into her priority e-mail box by Gwenn back at the Croft Foundation offices, she'd been making travel arrangements.

It had been a rough pair of days getting to Lima, then a rough three hours alternately kicking butt and dropping names in government offices. When it was done, she had a car at their disposal, a hotel suite, and round-the-clock medical care.

But Borg still didn't have arms. His prosthetics had a new kind of mount, quite experimental, and the technology had hardly made it out of the labs yet, let alone to the otherwise adequate Peruvian hospitals. So Borg still wore his climbing arms, which he hid beneath an extra-long coat to avoid looking like a half-exposed *Terminator* cyborg while in public.

Lara nodded at the private-duty nurse in the anteroom of

the suite and looked in on Borg. He lay with his feet propped up on the hotel bed's headboard, snoring deep in his chest like a largish dog.

The first morning flight to Hawaii would carry them out of Peru, and from there they would travel south to Fiji. Djbril would have a fresh lot of VADS ammunition for her .45s waiting there in forty-eight hours thanks to overnight mail by a security service courier. Then Shanks would get them to Capricorn Atoll.

She'd considered trying to make a few calls to London and Washington to see if she couldn't get the Special Boat Service or a SEAL team on board. But having friends in high places didn't always translate into action, and she knew she didn't have enough hard evidence to persuade reluctant governments to act. Plus, their special forces were otherwise engaged at the moment.

So it was up to her.

Again.

A hunch told her that whatever was going to happen would happen on the twenty-first of December. While the world was Christmas shopping, in the Southern Hemisphere they would be celebrating the first day of summer. Von Junst had mentioned ceremonies celebrating the Deep Ones taking place at the summer and winter solstices.

She left Borg a note to meet her at the hotel pool cabana, mentioned it to the nurse, and changed into a just-purchased black bikini, flip-flops, and new sunglasses. Air and sun poolside would recharge batteries drained by her week in the Amazon headwaters and escape from the Whispering Abyss.

The hotel, a beautiful colonial style with colonnades both facing the city and the sea, stood atop the sandy cliffs of the Costa Verde. She'd never been to this part of Lima before, the

Barranco district, full of old trees and older homes, and found it utterly charming. Too bad she didn't have time to explore.

Most months this part of the coast lay under blankets of fog, but for a few glorious months around Christmas, the sun turned Lima into paradise. She watched Peruvian penguins and Inca terns search the breakwaters below the cliffs, then found an unoccupied chaise.

Bikini: fitting nicely. Sunglasses: on. Sunscreen: slathered. Bruises: healed or covered by towel.

She'd better carbon copy her diving inventory to Shanks so he could check it over before she arrived. She didn't sleep, but fell into something that wasn't quite a nap, but just as relaxing. Feisty salsa music from the cabana bar forced her to tap her fingers, keeping time. She rolled over.

American and European tourists yakked with the cabana bartender about pizza, and she opened her eyes.

"What kind of cheese do they use? Do you know what deep dish is? No, not peppers, pepperoni."

The sun turned orange as it approached the horizon. She felt rubbery; the sun had performed its usual gentle, warm massage.

She swung her legs off the chaise, saw Borg circumnavigating the pool, looking out of place in his long coat.

At the hotel's rear colonnade, a sun-dried Peruvian who looked as though he was dressed for a golf game lowered a pair of microbinoculars and spoke into a cell phone. The phone was the kind that could take and send pictures. He snapped two shots of Lara Croft wrapping a towel about her waist, chose one, and hit "send."

* * *

Borg spoke first. "We leave again tomorrow?"

"I want to see what they're going to try to do with those plates. Unfortunately, anyone who might know is either dead or working for them, and I don't think my only other source is in the mood for a third talk. How's the head?"

He tapped the stitches. "I have an appointment with the hotel stylist. I will ask her to shorten the rest."

"Hmmm . . . from the right angle, you look like Brad Pitt with bed hair. Could be worse."

"Brad Pitt has metal arms?"

She sensed an uneasiness behind his joke. "What's wrong, Nils?"

"I had a strange dream. It made me think of something." They walked out to the rail looking out over the sand cliffs and the water below.

"About the *Méne* glyph?"

"No. No, not that dream. About Alison. You, too."

"Men and their fantasies," she joked.

"No, not that. I was thinking . . . It went bad with Alison after my accident. She hated when I touched her with the arms. The touch made her wince. She said she did not mind them, but preferred the old me."

"Yes?" Lara asked, wondering what he was getting at.

" 'The old me.' You never knew the old me."

"I wish I'd known you when you were chasing Chinese figure skaters in Lillehammer. I was a pretty fair gymnast at that age, and only a couple of years behind you. Maybe I'd have put English girls on your list."

"You don't mean—"

She took a step closer. "Nils, put your arms around me."

Borg smiled, moved his arms.

Whirs and a click signaled that his hands had joined behind her. To Lara, they were not artificial, just the strong limbs of a strong man.

Lara patted the hair at the back of his head. "There. Your arms are around me. *Your* arms. You're an incredible man, Nils."

"But not a whole one."

"Whole where it counts. Determination. Kindness. Courage."

His eyebrows knitted. "You would have such a man in your life?"

"Most men can't keep up with me. Back in the Abyss, I had a hard time keeping up with you. You saved my life after the canoe tipped."

"Perhaps. You saved mine first."

"I think convention demands a kiss. If not convention, then this sunset." Lara tipped her head.

He kissed her, a little tentatively. It made her think of his reluctance to shake her hand back in London.

"You call that a kiss?" she said. "This is a kiss."

But before their lips could touch again, Lara heard a metallic thunk behind her. At first she feared that some piece of Borg's arm had fallen off. But then Borg shoved her roughly to the ground.

In a flash, she saw the grenade, a lethal cylinder spinning where it had landed.

Borg plunged down on it without a word, without an instant's hesitation, covering it with his metallic, multimillion-dollar limbs.

Lara ripped her towel off and threw it over his hands just as the grenade went off. Borg flew back, hit the rail.

Gunfire ripped across the pool patio, followed by screams. Lara flattened at the sound, hands going to her thighs where her holsters usually rested. But not, unfortunately, at the moment.

Her ears searched for the source of the gunfire. She heard only screams from behind and in the cabana and a shout from the greenery bordering the pool.

Borg moved, his limbs blackened and badly scratched but still intact.

Lara rolled into the pool as more shots struck the pool patio near her, sending chips flying. Blood from a cut on her side—either a bullet or a ceramic chip had grazed her; she hadn't felt the impact in the heat of the action—dissolved in the blue pool water.

A woman under a tipped-over chaise longue shrieked horribly. Children were screaming in terror.

If flesh were a conductor of emotion, Lara's anger would have set the pool to bubbling. Grenades and machine guns near a pool filled with children! She saw a linen jacket and a tropical shirt fleeing through the shrubbery and disappearing around the side of the hotel.

Lara kicked off her flip-flops as she swam, clambered up the pool ladder, and dashed, dripping, across the patio. She hurdled a line of chaises, then a hedge, and turned the corner of the hotel in time to see the man she was pursuing disappear into a silver sedan in the hotel turnaround. The car—as she ran across the decorative stone at the edge of the pavement, she saw it was a Volvo—raced up the tree-lined hotel lane in a haze of diesel smoke, just missing a teenager driving a small motorcycle with a red plastic bin attached to the back.

The lad pulled up to the front of the hotel. As he got off the motorcycle, Lara read the white letters on the back of his red vest: CHICAGO'S HOT PIZZA and a Lima phone number.

Just a dirt bike. My kingdom for more horsepower!

No time for explanations. She snatched his helmet out of his hands as he fiddled with the box on the back of his motorcycle—it was a tiny starter Kawasaki, great gasoline mileage but woefully underpowered—and jumped into the saddle, feeling the engine's heat on her bare legs.

"Señorita!" the astonished teen said.

"I'll fill it up before I return it," she said, putting on the helmet. The inside smelled of onions and Calvin Klein cologne.

She gunned it off the kickstand and changed up two gears in as many seconds. By the time she turned onto the Avenida Arequipa, she had a feel for the nimble bike, which thankfully had fairly new tires.

The Tomb Raider would need the tread.

La Raza, in the passenger seat of the Volvo, slapped the leather upholstery in disgust. "What do you mean you're not sure?"

"We threw the grenade—"

"You were supposed to shoot her!" he shouted angrily at the two men in the back seat. "Walk up to the pool, pull out your guns, and shoot her. The grenades were only if she hid behind the bar or what-have-you. Don't you hear a word said to you?"

The Volvo's driver held down the horn and screamed obscenities at the car ahead, which was creeping past a truck.

"Calm, Jorge, no need to get us in an accident," La Raza said. Turnip heads! But one made soup with whatever ingredients were handy.

"Now, tell me again. You shot her, and she fell into the pool."

"Most definitely." The machine gun man sitting directly behind La Raza searched the pockets of his linen sport coat, came up with a packet of cigarillos with a book of matches strapped to it with a rubber band. "Now, after the shooting, the smoke! It settles the blood again." He had two red tears tattooed at the edge of his eye. In the language of prison, it meant he'd killed two men. La Raza wondered if he'd bull-shitted them to death.

The man in the tropical shirt behind the driver just looked at his feet, passing his pistol from hand to hand.

"Did you see her die?" he asked Tropical Shirt.

"I saw her fall in the pool."

"I saw her blood. I know I saw blood!" Sport Coat insisted.

"Jefe," Jorge said. "We are being followed. A motorbike is coming up fast."

La Raza tried to see around the truck behind him. He took Jorge's word for it. "Police?"

"A woman in a bikini. A young woman, athletic. Very attractive. Perhaps a ponytail."

Sport Coat took the cigarillo out of his mouth. "No! She was wounded by the grenade, killed by the bullets. I saw her fall!"

"Get in the other lane!" La Raza ordered.

It was the target, the same woman as the one in the phone picture. Though she had a helmet on, there could be no mistake with such a figure. La Raza watched the girl, half mesmerized, and thought for a moment of his wife as she'd been on their honeymoon in Aruba fifteen years ago.

"Hurry, you fool, she's gaining on us."

Lara gunned the Kawasaki down the Avenida Arequipa, fearing that the Volvo would turn at Surquillo and get on the Pan-American Highway. She doubted the little Kawasaki could keep up with the Volvo there. Only her ability to nip between cars was allowing her to keep up with the car in the evening after-work traffic.

The Volvo passed Surquillo without turning. It shot along the parkland and golf courses of San Isidro, heading for central Lima. They would probably dump the car somewhere in the poorer northern sections of town and change vehicles.

The traffic dissolved into a mass of taillights as the sun continued to set.

"Jefe, I do not mean to tell you your business," Jorge began, looking in the rearview mirror. "But we are four men, armed, in a car. She is one woman on a motorbike. *We* were supposed to kill *her*. Why is she chasing us?"

The fixer felt his cheeks burn. Old habits died hard; the instinct to flee a crime scene and be home in time to listen to the first reports over the radio had clouded his judgment as much as his anger toward the two third-class gunmen the Don had fobbed off on him. His wife, who thought him a security expert specializing in protecting visiting executives, always wondered why he laughed so heartily when a movie mentioned "professional killers."

La Raza tightened his seat belt. "You are right. Perhaps a traffic accident, Jorge . . ."

The brake lights exploded in her face and the back of the Volvo rose. The analytical part of Lara Croft's mind listened to the squealing tires: The aged Volvo diesel was either pre-antilock brakes or they'd been replaced by conventional ones. Her eyes and hands and body, connected in a loop that didn't go through the conscious part of her brain that was now occupied with brake technology, leaned left, and the bike jumped onto the grassy median.

Her rear wheel kicked up a rooster tail of dirt, and she shot ahead of the Volvo, now skidding a little left, starting a scherzo of squealing tires and horns behind.

The Volvo accelerated out of the skid, followed her as she turned into Lima Centro.

The chase turned into a classic duel between power and agility. After each corner, the Volvo gained on her a bit more, until at last she could make out the Mars symbol in the Kawasaki's compact-sized mirror. Gunfire chased her up the street and around corners. A department store window fell in a shower of shards as she turned into the heart of the old city.

Where were the Peruvian police? The chase blew through more lights than she could count, swerved into and out of oncoming traffic, and was causing a fender bender every thirty seconds or so.

.She turned into the Plaza Mayor and forced the issue. She swung around a horse and carriage in front of the two yellow towers of the cathedral and rode up onto the square of crisscrossing sidewalks that filled two city blocks at the center of town.

Evening strollers scattered.

The Volvo followed. Lara turned the headlight on and off and shouted, not having a horn to blow. In the distance, she saw police lights flashing.

Finally!

She shot across traffic, foot and vehicle, and up the Jirón de la Unión. The glowing decorations and window displays of the stores and boutiques, filled with Christmas shoppers, cast a colorful patina on the avenue. The Volvo followed, weaving around cabs, and she exited the Plaza San Martin, a square not quite as big as the one she'd crossed at the other end of the crowded connecting street.

She saw a red and white flag ahead, before an imposing building. She drove up on the sidewalk next to the flag and forced a controlled skid to turn around, leaving a crescent tire mark. She straightened her motorcycle, faced the oncoming Volvo.

Her six-cylinder nemesis charged, its dazzling headlights stabbing out toward her like horns. Lara loosed the bike. The Kawasaki jumped forward.

The opposing vehicles closed the gap in a flash. Lara downshifted and lifted her front wheel off the pavement just in time for it to hit the oncoming car. She threw her weight forward, and the driving rear wheel climbed the bumper and grille. She launched the bike off the windshield, straightened the Kawasaki in midair by throwing her weight, and landed with a knee-popping bounce of tires.

The Volvo tried to turn but struck the curb and slid into the building instead. Before the occupants could fight their way past the air bags and out the doors, they were looking at a dozen pistols and shotguns. Lara marked the approach of sirens from both directions.

The Volvo, one axle broken, leaked oil onto the sidewalk in front of the Ministry of Justice. Uniformed Peruvians ordered the four men to lie down. Other officers approached her, guns drawn.

Smoothly, Lara retrieved the red plastic case from the back of the bike and turned to meet the arriving officers.

"*Señores*," she said in Spanish as they lowered their guns and their faces broke into disbelieving grins, "I believe someone has ordered a pizza."

PART THREE

20

The gull white seaplane skimmed the choppy South Pacific waters at thirty feet, Capricorn Atoll a blue smudge on the horizon ahead.

From above, Capricorn Atoll looked like a shark rising out of the depths. One side of the atoll was made up of a conical mountain, sheer where it faced the ocean and sloping off to the lagoon in the center. The mountain ridge fell off into two arms embracing the lagoon at the center, which was partially open to the sea on the west side, where just a series of rocky shards, the teeth at the bottom of the shark's open maw, protected a deep harbor.

The circle of land surrounding the lagoon gave the island its topographic designation: atoll. Its position, precisely on the tropic of Capricorn, gave it its name.

It was dusk on December 21, the summer solstice south of the equator.

The man at the controls, a sun-streaked island-hopper named Shanks, kept checking the sea. His right eye would wince, then his left cheek would twitch, causing his eye to wince again, as though the two sides of his visage were fighting for control of the whole. Shanks was a ragged bundle of nerves everywhere but his hands.

From his forearms down, Shanks was the coldest dead-stick pilot that Lara had ever known.

"Sea's a little better now that we're away from the storm," Shanks said in his rasping New Zealand drawl. They all wore headsets and microphones plugged into the plane so that they could hear each other over the engine noise. "Should be fine in the lagoon. You know about this island, right?"

"I've learned about it only recently," Lara said.

"What about the island?" Borg asked. Like Lara, Borg wore a wet suit and surf shoes.

Lara launched into lecture mode. "Capricorn Atoll used to be the home of a tribe the Fiji Islanders to the north called *Muwati*. In 1863, investigating the disappearance of the whaler *Giron*, the French frigate *Loire* stopped at the island after sighting a set of masts in the lagoon. No one knows what happened during the visit. The emperor Louis Napoleon put all records pertaining to the *Loire*'s investigation of the *Giron* and the island under government seal, but when the *Loire* turned north again, the atoll was uninhabited and the lagoon at the center had been named Blood Bay. Upon the frigate's return to Fiji, the natives feted the first officer—the captain had died during events on the island—and his crew with such enthusiasm that the French-Fijian babies born nine months later were given noble names and wanted for nothing over the course of their lives."

"Were they cultists?" Borg asked.

"We'll never know. Then, in 1926, the National Geographic Society sent an expedition to explore the island over the objections of the French Republic. The explorers, photographers, and naturalists spent only one night at the atoll and returned one man short. According to a couple of lines in *National Geographic*, they'd picked up a quick-presenting fever on arrival and spent a delirious night before quitting the atoll for a Fiji hospital. The missing naturalist, a Canadian named DuBois, had evidently wandered into the lagoon in his illness and drowned. It wasn't the sort of article that inspired tourism to the atoll."

"Enough history," Shanks said. "You know how to creep a guy out, Lara."

"We need you to set us down well away from the island," Lara told him through the headset.

"Here?" Shanks' voice crackled back. "I thought we'd set down inside the atoll."

"Sorry, we don't want our presence announced."

Shanks tipped the wing and circled. "I don't like the looks of that chop, Lara. Won't be an easy landing. Or takeoff, for that matter. And we've got typhoons brewing east and west of the Fiji chain. Ocean's getting all stirred up."

She knew all that, but none of it made a difference. "You can do it," she said into the mike.

Her long-haired pilot looked at his controls. "Yeah. Every time I hear from you, Lara, I think, 'Finally. An easy trip. She'll just need a shuttle to Raiatéa.' But it never is. I've always got to punch a hurricane and land in the eye of the storm, pick you up, and take off again before my ship gets tossed, or get you off a volcano before the bugger goes Krakatau, or drop you into China somewhere and get out again before I get a SAM sigmoidoscopy."

Lara chuckled. "You still take my calls. Why?"

"Who wants to die in bed?"

"The sane?"

"Naw! What I want, Lara—what I want is for a bunch of blokes to be sitting round the bar thirty years from now, shooting away, and one of 'em says: 'My pa, he knew this bonzo bloke, Shanks Muldoon, pilot, could fly a water heater if you stuck a big enough engine on it. You want to hear what the crazy bastard tried to do?'—and then they tell the story about how I snuffed it."

Lara glanced behind her, where Borg, whiter-faced than usual, was checking the fit of his seat belt. "I'll do my best to keep giving you opportunities to realize your dream," she said.

"That's the spirit. Now hang on; I'll try to set her down. We go ass over, the best way out will be the door in back."

He worked the flaps and throttle. The wave tops, not that far away to begin with, suddenly looked close enough to touch.

Shanks lifted the boatlike nose of the plane higher than he normally would, and Lara felt the first touch of a wave at the back of the boat. Then it was *smack-smack-smack-shushhhhh* as the ship cut through the chop and landed.

The seaplane rocked as the short waves hit the floats at the wingtips. Spray washed up on the canopy.

Shanks let the engines idle. "You want me back on the twenty-second, right?"

"It'll all be over by then, one way or another. I'll try and radio, but if you don't hear from me—"

"Come anyway?"

Lara leaned across the seats and kissed his stubbled cheek. "I was going to say 'use your judgment,' but that's playing jazz on a saxophone with a broken reed, isn't it?"

"The storms are tracking funny. Looks like they're going to circle this damn island like a couple of ballroom dancers 'round the glitter ball. I should be able to cut through the tail of the western storm."

"Christmas toddies will be on me."

"I'll be at Tongatapu waiting for your call, Lara. I'll put an order in while I'm there."

She squeezed back into the passenger-cargo area and shouldered her lucky backpack, placing her feet carefully and bracing with her hands so she didn't trip as the plane rocked. She put on her holsters, her guns wrapped in protective plastic bags to keep the ocean spray off. Shanks followed, forced to bend almost double because of his long frame.

They put the inflatable boat out the passenger-cargo door, tied it off, and inflated it. Borg, a little green from the motion, helped Shanks with the trickiest part, moving the little outboard from the plane to its fixture in the Zodiac. The little boat alternately lunged at the seaplane and fell away in the confused sea.

Lara made the difficult jump into the Zodiac, landed on her knees, and grabbed one of the sidelines. She pulled the Zodiac up tight to the cargo hatch, sea spray already speckling her wraparound sunglasses.

The balky boat jumped again; a wave forced its way between seaplane and Zodiac and hit her full in the face.

"Bollocks!" she spat as Shanks laughed.

"Temper, temper!"

She gauged the motion of the boat and seaplane, gripping a fold-out handle at the cargo door in one hand and the boat with the other, waiting for both to bottom . . .

"Now, Nils!"

With Shanks letting out the line wrapped around the outboard's rudder-propeller housing, Borg dropped the engine into the fitting. Lara let go of the plane and shot home the bolts that would secure it.

The hard part over, Borg and Shanks passed over the diving gear—she'd purchased some water wings for Borg—bags of equipment, her VADS harness, binoculars, a satellite phone with a solar recharger, food, and fuel. Finally Borg—still in his climbing arms; the Peruvians hadn't gotten around to forwarding his regular arms from the *Madre de Dios* canopy tower—tried the difficult transfer.

He fell in, wetting his lower half. A little Pacific never hurt anyone. She helped him into the boat, filled the gas reservoir, and started the motor.

She gave Shanks the thumbs-up. He returned a finger-waggling salute-cum-wave.

The cargo in its netting checked one final time, she let go the line going back to the seaplane and motored off into the chop. The ocean felt like a horse in a buck-trot beneath her, and Borg dry-heaved off the starboard inflatable.

"Got it bad?"

"Strange," he gasped. "I never get airsickness. But boats do it . . . *urp* . . . every time, even if it's just a little bit rough."

She squeezed his ankle, it being the only part she could reach as she worked the motor tiller.

In case of accident they stood by until Shanks lifted off. He gunned the wide-bodied craft, shaped like a white sperm whale with a wing and twin engines mounted high, and blasted through the wave tops until it took somewhat gracelessly to the air.

"A good man," Borg said.

"Storms or no storms, we'll see him again. Now let's get to the island." She nosed the Zodiac over and opened the throttle wide.

Borg groaned and closed his eyes.

* * *

They floated along the edge of the Tonga Trench, one of the deepest points in the Pacific.

The easy way to reach the atoll would be to motor through one of the many channels on the west side. But Lara Croft didn't want to announce her presence on the island. The Prime and his cult had been one step ahead of her since she first began to look into Ajay's disappearance. It was time for her to steal a march on him.

She pointed the Zodiac straight for the highest point of the island.

Borg sat where she put him, leaned when she told him, as the little boat skipped through the chop toward land. Though it was sunny, distant masses of cloud from the storm systems Shanks had mentioned sent spiraling arms across the skies like the two whales in the Chinese yin-yang symbol.

"You have any plan for action at all?" Borg inquired with a groan.

"Not the slightest."

"This doesn't worry you?"

She had to raise her voice above the engine; they were nearing shore, and the chop was turning into surf. "I'm at my best pell-mell. Besides, Sherlock Holmes always said it was a capital mistake to theorize before gathering facts. Experience has taught me to agree. I've no idea what we're going to find here, so how can I make plans?"

Volcanic rock, blue-black in the spray, rose above them. Clusters of green iguanas lay on the flatter prominences. Not quite a wall, but only the most charitable would call it a slope. More of a ridge than a peak, the mass before them was the biggest remnant of the volcano that had formed Capricorn Atoll millennia ago.

A line of rocks, occasionally appearing as the surf fell away before smashing into them again, ringed this side of the island. Once inside the ring, Lara and Borg would be relatively safe; there would be only the surf to contest their landing.

Lara turned the Zodiac and motored back out to sea. Either this part of the island had no beaches, or some combination of tide and storm had covered them.

"I'm going to try to get us past the rocks," she told Borg. "Try to get a piton in, and we'll tie up."

Borg nodded, looked in the magazine in his arm that held the pitons, snapped it shut again. "Just say when."

In response she let the little engine roar. Down a wave, up—

Something poked the bow of the boat from below: a rock. Lara threw her weight to counterbalance, and with the wash of a wave they were beyond the rocks, trapped in a little swirl with a gentle slope rising from the seaweed-coated coral.

"Now, Nils!"

Borg fired his piton, hooked the arm on it immediately and clung to the boat with his other limb. The sea dropped away, and the boat hung sideways. Lara hung on to the side lines until the sea came up again.

"Another piton! Here!" She pointed.

Borg fired again; a piece of coral bounced off her sunglasses.

Lara got a handful of climbing line from the cargo netting, looped it through the boat's side line. The sea fell away again, and they hung on. Then, when it came up again, Borg looped line around the boat as she fixed it to the pitons.

One more swell of the sea and they'd turn the Zodiac into an improvised shelf suspended from the pitons.

They didn't get it.

The next time the boat fell away from the wall, Lara saw a flash of flying limbs, and then Borg hit the churning green water, the splash lost in the roar of surf hitting the breakers and the mountainside.

She snaked a line around her wrist and dove into the surf after him. Bubbles and stirred-up ocean obscured her vision. She caught a flash of a leg and went after it.

Borg struck the volcanic rock bottom, tried to right himself, but was caught in the undertow. Lara shot after him, ran out of line, abandoned her tether. She got an arm around him just as another wave lifted them both—air!—and threw them against the cliff wall as they went down again, Borg kicking madly but trying to not interfere with her grip. She had the rhythm of the waves now, and the second time the ocean pushed them up she used the thrust to bodysurf back toward the Zodiac, now hanging inverted by a single line.

The ocean flung them against the lava wall with a smack, and Lara felt the skin on her knee tear. She grabbed on to the bow of the Zodiac, and this time, when the surf receded, the water didn't take them with it. They both gasped, catching up on oxygen for a moment. Lara looked at the last piton; it was holding well enough, but they'd lost some of the gear.

They hung on through one more wave, this time using the Zodiac as a fender. Then Borg shot another piton into the rock, and they pulled themselves out of the surf, clinging to the rock like lizards.

"Sorry, Lara," Borg panted. "I let go to fix a knot—"

"We're both alive. That's enough."

Borg climbed to an outcropping, sending a startled crested iguana scrambling away, and Lara, a line fixed to her, negotiated the Zodiac and surf to pass up what was left of the gear. She still had her lucky pack, guns, and VADS gear—she'd done everything but handcuff those essentials to the Zodiac—but they'd lost the heavy oxygen gear, climbing supplies, food, and the portable radio-satellite phone.

She tossed up the netting bag holding the flippers and masks anyway, and joined him on the rock. The surf was beautiful again, instead of a deadly menace.

Borg looked at the slope. "This is no worse than the Jungfrau. We don't need gear, except perhaps near the very top, and there's enough line for us to support each other."

On the next rock over, a feud broke out among a heap of crested iguanas. They bobbed their heads and opened their jaws at one another.

"Let's get to it," Lara said, helping Borg into his pack.

On the way up the two-hundred-meter slope, she kept reminding herself that the mountain only looked big. Set this volcanic heap against even the lesser peaks of the Alps, and it would shrink to insignificance. Here and there they were able to walk up the side, but most of the ascent was a four-limbed clamber over sharp rocks that made her grateful for her tough reef walkers and leather gloves.

"Does this ridge have a name?" Borg asked as they paused to suck air and water.

"The Nuku Hava." Lara couldn't say if she had even pronounced it properly.

"What's that mean?"

"I don't know and didn't have time to find out. Getting the Polynesians to say anything about this island is one flat down from impossible."

They chatted over the route for the next fifty meters, then started up again. Near the top, the cliff became sheer, with spots that would require an inverted climb if they didn't choose another route. Borg, who had a feel for mountains that rivaled a sailor's instinct for weather, found a chimney. He led Lara up it, climbing expertly and efficiently with his artificial limbs. Being at the other end of the line was like having a mountain goat on a lead.

Lara shrugged to herself. Nils Bjorkstrom's love for Alison was the only obstacle he couldn't seem to get over.

21

There is no good way to knock at a tent. Alex Frys settled for clearing his throat.

"Yes?" Heather Rourke called from inside.

"I've brought some dinner. I haven't seen you all day."

She unzipped the tent and let him in. The little nylon-floored household consisted of a cot, a bag of clothes, and some magazines scattered on the floor.

Heather took a pair of kiwis off the tray, sat primly on her field cot. "Last night's beach party was a bit much for me. Gassim is dying from the wounds Lara gave him at the canopy tower."

"I know." This was the second time she'd gotten her Irish up since he'd taken her, more or less forcibly, to Capricorn Atoll.

She persisted. "Gassim should be in a hospital. And that old trout, Mr. Van Schwellenkammer or Seven or however you say it, looks ready to keel over at any moment."

None are so blind as those who refuse to see. "I don't doubt it."

"Yet you've got them propped up, clapping along to the drums and pipes and that abalone shell horn like it's a summer Baptist revival."

"Different people choose different ways to say good-bye to earthly life."

"One other thing. In the lagoon last night, I saw . . . eyes. Sets of eyes, like those of cats or raccoons or something reflecting the firelight." She shuddered.

He'd told Boris to keep her away from the shoreline. But then Boris had been drinking last night. "Seabirds floating," he said.

The Prime reached into his pocket, felt the reassuring handle on the crystal. Heather didn't know how right she was. But, again, willfully blind. Still, she could be useful. Perhaps even fun. He'd woken up from an afternoon nap feeling randy, rested, and ready. He'd hoped to finally become intimate with Heather. But all this talk of death . . .

"Tonight is important," he told her. "The most important night of my life. I thought I'd get it off to a good start by dining with you."

"Why so important?" she asked, finally looking up at him.

"It's the solstice. A planetary tipping point. Revelations are at hand." Well, not at *hand,* if one wanted to speak precisely.

"You want me to see these 'revelations,' too?"

"Absolutely," he said, sitting on the bunk next to her. He poured her some wine. "It will be the biggest story of your career, and I'll be happy to guide you as you shape it."

"Shape it?"

"The world isn't quite ready yet for the full truth. We have to give it to them a little bit at a time."

"I've been a journalist since junior high school. I think I know how to report a story, thanks."

Frys raised the crystal on its ivory and brass handle. He practiced the gesture in the mirror a lot, trying to look like an eighteenth century gentleman with his monocle. Heather

Rourke's fuzzy outline was black as midnight, closed to him. "We could accomplish great things together."

He leaned closer, brimming over with lust. With other women, with Alison, it was the simplest thing in the world to pour it through the lens and into them, until they exploded into red-orange flame and fell back for the taking.

The same pinks and greens formed in his lens. "The wine is good," Heather said, and the pink grew brighter, then faded away again.

Frustrated, he took it from his eye. Kunai had told him there were people like this, people resistant or even immune to the effects of the crystal. But until now, he'd never actually met one. Heather wasn't immune, but she was highly resistant. And the more he used the crystal to influence her emotions, the more resistant she seemed to get. He would spend hours trying to coerce her with the crystal, only to develop a splitting headache. Instead of the passion he'd hoped to instill in her, she'd regard him with a kind of wary neutrality, as if she were using him as much as he was using her. The most perverse thing of all was that this only made his desire for her stronger than ever.

One of the magazines lying open on the floor caught his eye; the latest issue of *People*. He got off the cot and picked it up. It was open to an article about Ozzy Osbourne, but that wasn't what drew his attention.

The article had tiny black letters scrawled in what looked like crayon between the lines. He read aloud:

> Cults don't thrive on faith alone. It takes money, and in the *Méne*'s case the Prime can draw on bank accounts set up from Sydney to London, Tokyo to Rio de Janeiro. But money can only buy so much power. The true influence of

the *Méne* might be measured in the portfolios of ministers rather than . . .

That was as far as she'd gotten. He looked up. She was watching him coolly.

"Very resourceful," he admitted. "My men must not have searched your clothing thoroughly enough. Did you have a pen sewn in the lining?"

"No. Just an eyeliner with my makeup."

"This will have to stop." He raised the crystal again, looked at her shifting energies, now dark and closed. He tried to turn them white, a new, clean slate for him to begin on, but even with all the force of his will, she only sparkled a little, like the white dots of stars against an evening sky. And the black engulfed them as soon as he stopped straining. It was ironic. In his experience, journalists could be led around by the nose, even without the help of a piece of Deep Gods technology or magic or whatever the hell it was.

If he couldn't control her better, or if she couldn't be persuaded to behave herself, he just might have to give her a more active role to play in the coming ceremony.

From the top of Nuku Hava ridge, Capricorn Atoll became a paradise again.

Lara and Borg surveyed what they could of the central lagoon in the star-bright Pacific night. They might have been able to see more of the *Méne* camp, but their German optics were rolling around with more mundane forms of sand beneath the upended Zodiac. A few tiny figures walked along the beachfront, standing on a lava rock flow to look into the lagoon. The mass of stone, descending into the lagoon like a boat ramp the width of the M-4, had regular enough lines to make Lara think that it had been shaped.

Lara strapped on her VADS gear and readied her guns in their holsters, then tested the headset.

"What next?" Borg asked.

"I want a better look at their camp. We'll try and get in. I'd like a word with Alex Frys."

The trek down from the ridge was easy, the slope gentle on this side of the lagoon. When Lara finally saw the tents in the distance, she climbed a mango tree for a better look while Borg hid their remaining gear among its roots.

Lara saw a few casually dressed cultists and shirtless natives, muscular islanders who had shaved their heads smooth and covered their scalps with tattoos. Evidently the French frigate had not been as thorough in destroying the *Muwati* as the Fijians had believed.

"Any sign of Alison?" Borg asked when she descended again.

"No. One strange thing, though. The big tent in the center is a hospital. IVs, blood in ice coolers, two men who look as though they are attending to casualties. Either their plane crashed on landing, or they brought their injured with them."

"Interesting way to run an expedition."

"Maybe it's a healing," Lara half joked. "The plates we found are supposed to draw their gods, or allow communication."

"Lara Croft, the look on your face says we will find out soon."

"Exactly. Best way to learn about a religion is to observe the rituals. Barring joining, that is. I don't imagine you're interested?"

Borg ran his fingers across the rainbow arc of a red-tipped fern. "Over Frys's dead body, as the English say."

"That sounds more like John Wayne than Oscar Wilde. Not that I don't agree with the sentiment."

As the moon rose at the end of this, the longest day of the year, they had all the time they wanted to explore the *Méne* campsite.

It lay empty. They'd watched the entire camp pick up and file away, carrying tiki torches.

As the long arms of the twin storms reached for each other overhead, the evening became hazy, with confused winds blowing the trees first one way, then the other. A curtain of clouds boiled up on the horizon beyond the toothlike shards of volcanic rock at the eastern end of the lagoon.

The *Méne* had left their tents open and bags of waste lying around what had once been the hospital tent. Rats, the living residue on any island visited by shipping, nosed around in the trash, occasionally squealing and fighting for choice scraps. Lara even found a charcoal fire still alight in a cooking pit. Like many tiny streams joining to form a river, the individual tracks all led out to the beach, where they joined into one trail leading toward the volcanic rock ramp that led into the lagoon the French frigate sailors had named Blood Bay.

The *Méne* looked more like they were preparing for a luau than a sacred ceremony: no robes, no chanting, no strange arm movements and lifting of holy relics. Even the drumming had stopped.

Lara and Borg, hidden a hundred meters away behind a fallen palm on the beach, watched Frys lead perhaps thirty *Méne* from the jungle, walking, and in the case of the wounded and infirm, being carried on stretchers down the wide stone path. Ajay brought up the rear, hands ready on the machine pistols at her hips, searching the jungle around the volcanic ramp.

They looked, if anything, like a tour group off a cruise ship, save for the tiki torches they carried. Aloha shirts and shorts, sandals and boat shoes, cheap straw hats and leis adorned the *Méne*, and at their head Alex Frys wore swimming trunks and a loose-fitting souvenir T-shirt. Only the machine pistols at Ajay's hips and the occasional assault rifle in the group revealed that they were on business more serious. Even those nearest the water, each carrying one of the platinum panels taken from the Whispering Abyss, bore their treasures with all the reverence of boys toting schoolbooks.

Heather, easily spotted thanks to her red hair, stood among a mix of islanders and others. One of them might have been the Peruvian park ranger Fermi, but at this distance Lara couldn't tell.

Frys and a group of natives—she could now distinguish the black pseudo-omega symbols tattooed on their skulls—walked down the ramp and thigh-deep into the lagoon as the cloud-streaked sky turned orange. Frys raised his arms and began to speak loudly. The gusting wind carried away most of what he said; Lara caught only scattered words: "offering . . . not death . . . life . . . final threshold." And then the group parted and one of the *Méne* limped down, stripping a bandage from his head as he dragged his injured leg into the water.

Two natives steadied the injured man in the water, and another passed Frys a square green bottle. He handed it to the limping man, who poured the contents down his throat until it ran out the sides of his mouth and he sputtered for breath. Then the injured man left the steadying arms of the natives and continued to walk down the ramp, his arms stretched wide as though he were waiting for an embrace. Lara thought she heard a wailing cry, but it might have been seabirds.

Hip-deep, then stomach-deep—

He disappeared beneath the surface of the lagoon in a flash, as though he had stepped off an underwater cliff.

Lara waited for his head to break the waters of the lagoon farther out. She waited in vain.

"What the hell?" Borg whispered. "He drowned himself? That's seawater; his body should float."

"Something dragged him under. Current, or maybe a

shark . . ." She didn't want to think about other possibilities.

Seven more times they watched the ritual, seven green bottles used and then placed on the volcanic ramp. An old woman in a wheelchair; a wounded man on a stretcher who had to be floated out by the natives and then dumped in; an aging man who walked with the aid of two rubber-tipped canes; a young man with a shaved head who had trouble tipping his head back to accept the contents of the bottle and had to be tilted by the islanders; a man in a back brace; a woman who coughed repeatedly into a handkerchief as she waded in; and a couple who walked into the water hand in hand, wearing flowers about their necks as though they were attending a beach wedding.

Each time, as the water reached a level somewhere between their belly buttons and armpits, they disappeared in the blink of an eye.

Once, when the man in the stretcher was tipped in, Lara thought she saw a flash of something moving quickly just below the surface, but the torchlight played tricks in the rippling lagoon waters and she couldn't say what she saw.

"If they try this on Heather, we must fight them," Borg said.

Lara nodded. Or if even one of the . . . sacrifices or offerings . . . had resisted, she might have gone to their aid. But not one showed anything but eagerness to get into the water. And as far as she could tell, they were not drugged. They were, in fact, as she could tell by their bows to Frys, all members of the cult.

None of them broke the surface again.

The cultists waded back out of the water, and all, even Frys, turned to face the bottom of the ramp, knelt, and touched their foreheads to the rock surface. With that over, several in attendance embraced.

Including Frys and Ajay. Borg stiffened and growled at the sight.

The water took on a faint phosphorescence, brighter farther out in the lagoon than close to shore.

"What is that glow?" Borg asked.

Lara shook her head. "I don't know. There are single-celled organisms that live on the surface of the water that glow, but usually they're most visible near shore. I've never seen it that strong at a distance."

Then a metallic groan and a fierce bubbling from the lava ramp froze them. The *Méne*, led again by Frys, disappeared into the ground. Their heads did not bob as those of people walking down a stairway would have, but went down smoothly.

"My God!" Borg said.

"You couldn't be more wrong . . . C'mon!" Lara grabbed at Borg's shoulder and dashed for the tree line. They kept to the growth, running for the lava ramp and startling birds into flight right and left, but Lara didn't care. They had to reach that ramp in time to—

Too late.

The surface of the ramp closed with a last hiss of air. The bubbling in the lagoon to either side of the lava ramp trickled off to nothing. Lara watched, her ponytail flapping in the fluky but strengthening winds.

She probed and explored and went so far as to wade into the water where Frys had stood. Borg almost danced with anxiety on the shaped volcanic stone as she stuck her hands into the water, looking for some device to operate the door. All she could do was find the fissures marking the ramp. She thought of the counterweighted platform in the ruins of Ukju Pacha and ran up the ramp to the other end.

The ramp ended in a natural amphitheater. The hill wall had been flattened and shaped into a rectangle about the size of a movie-theater screen, and in the darkness she could make out a huge version of the pseudo-omega symbol worked into the stone, the carving filled with silvery metal. This one had arms longer than the others she had seen, and what could only be eyes bulging from either side of the elongated skull-like shape. In its size, the skill of its artistry, and its evident age, the carving would be a great discovery, but she had no time to admire it. Instead, she searched the inlaid rock and surrounding stone for a device or trigger for the ramp, but came up empty again.

The *Méne* had locked the door behind them and taken the key.

"The glow is getting brighter," Borg said as they wandered back down the ramp to the beach. With the strange ceremony over, Capricorn Atoll was once again a South Pacific paradise save for the growing wind kicking up surf and sand.

Lara had never seen a glow like that. And it wasn't at the surface; it was deep, coming up through the water as a uniform light, rather than as the flows and tendrils of the surface organisms which were caught by the currents and moved by the wind.

Borg rubbed his chin with a mechanical claw. "Lara, they all disappeared toward that glow. Ajay went down through a tunnel in this rock. But the others, the ones who waded into the water, perhaps they were going to the same place by a different path?"

"You could be right, Nils. Let's go get the flippers and masks and have a look."

They hurried back to their remaining gear at the mango tree. It took Lara a moment of casting about outside the *Méne* camp to determine under which tree they'd placed it. Lara cut a two-meter length of line and tied knots at each end. Then they slung the bags and ran back to the beach.

She watched him fit his mask. She spat in hers, wiped the

saliva around. The new plastics didn't fog, but she still did it out of habit. "You sure you want to try the lagoon? There could be . . . sharks. You saw what happened to those people. It looked like something . . . took them."

"I can go anywhere you will."

They tried an exploratory swim out into the lagoon. Lara helped Borg along by pulling him with her knotted line. Borg kicked with water wings on to compensate for the weight of his arms, the water growing clearer and clearer the farther they got from shore. The ground sloped away fast from the lagoon beach; the water here was a good deal deeper than in a typical atoll. Lara spotted a strange round shape below.

"Wait a moment," she told Borg, and dove.

Away from the surface, she could see better. The ocean floor sloped away toward the source of the bluish glow coming from the sea bottom. She saw more orbs like the one she had dove to investigate, only deeper down.

She looked at the nearest one more closely. The four-meter orb, like a crystal mushroom top, was tethered to the sea floor by a net of vines joining at a taproot and was open at the bottom like a diving bell. She swam farther down, saw row after row of sea grasses, but—and she thought this strange—no fish. She rose and broke the surface inside the sphere, took a small, cautious breath. It invigorated her like pure oxygen.

The translucent interior of the crystal dome glowed faintly from little splotches, like blue algae, growing on its outer surface. More roots clung to the interior walls.

Within the sphere, woven sea grass nets held little grape-like bulbs. The baskets had been fashioned, filled with the bulbs, and then hung there, but for what purpose she couldn't begin to guess. Curious, she reached up and gave one an experimental squeeze. It broke easily; milky liquid flowed down her hand. She felt a tug at her ankle, gasped—

Borg floated beneath. She kicked over, and he shot up into the air pocket. He'd partially deflated his water wings.

"What's this?" he asked, gasping for air.

"It's like a diving bell. They're growing stuff in here, or drying it, or preserving it." She pointed at the nets full of berries, or grapes, or whatever they were.

"I don't like this. I feel like these vines are reaching for me."

She plunged her face into the water; the taproots that held the spheres had masses of fronds waving back and forth in the lagoon current. They gave off tiny, champagne-sized bubbles which rose within the diving bell, evidently replenishing the oxygen supply. With her eyes, she followed the seafloor down to the glow, saw more of the crystal diving bells, then looked up again. "There's more of these. We can use them to get to the bottom of the lagoon. To the glow."

"You can dive that deep without a helmet?"

"I've heard of pearl divers who go deeper, just on what they can carry in their lungs."

"You'll need weights," Borg said, blowing his water wings back up. "My arms will do for me. I'm a fantastic sinker."

"I remember." They left the crystal diving bell suspended in its seaweed cables, and Lara led him toward the surface. On shore, they filled their flipper bags with rocks. Lara put her guns back in their plastic bags and secured them in her holsters, and then they turned and waded out into the lagoon.

"You ready?" she asked, kicking with her flippers to stay on the surface.

"I'll follow you."

"If you need to go back to the surface, just grab me and do

a dive kill." She demonstrated the classic throat-cut pantomime. "Just rise slowly and wait for me at the mango tree where we hid the gear."

They both took three deep breaths and plunged into the undersea world of Blood Bay.

They dove, Lara leading Borg with the knotted line. They rested and caught their breath in the first diving bell, then swam to the next in the direction of the blue glow at the bottom. The second held more masses of the odd bulbs, some as big as a healthy-sized lemon. They made easy adjustments to the changing water pressure thanks to the diving bells. The diving bells obviated the ear pain and the feeling of being wrapped up by a python from sinus cavities to diaphragm that made deep skin diving a mixed pleasure on the way down.

From the second diving bell they examined the lagoon-bottom glow. It came from a dome—almost a sphere. The top of it was perhaps thirty meters below the surface, the bottom sixty. The glowing dome rested upon an upthrust rock like a seer's crystal ball on its mount. The gash of a deep abyss ended at the upthrust. Lara had a hard time gauging the scale of the dome, but she thought it looked to be about the size of the Pantheon in Rome: roughly the same size as the dome at the Whispering Abyss.

Borg elbowed her. "Lara, at the bottom of the sphere."

A pair of figures with smallish flippers swam out from under the edge of the dome and disappeared into shadow at the lagoon floor.

"Next we'll head for that sphere," she said, pointing to a small one near the dome.

"Long swim, Lara. There is another one, closer, on the way," Borg said.

Lara spotted gray shapes in the blue glow, with odd T-shaped heads.

"Look around the base of it. Those are sharks. Hammer-heads. They can be dangerous, but their usual prey is stingrays—that's why their heads are like that, to pin the rays."

"I'd rather not get pinned. Sounds like my drowning dream. The far one it is."

They filled their lungs and dove again, a long downward glide. The sharks fled as they passed—were they afraid of swimmers here? Lara did not want to meet anyone who frightened a great hammerhead. Lara looked up at the diving bell they were bypassing. She saw feet hanging down. She waved Borg on and made a detour.

The diving bell held two bodies. She recognized both from the ceremony on the beach: the older woman and the first man in, the one with the bad leg and the head wound.

She took a quick breath of air and dove to catch up with Borg.

He hung about the bottom of the final diving bell. When he saw she was on her way, he entered and rose.

"What was that about?" he asked, after they'd taken a few breaths. This sphere was apparently unused or had recently been emptied; nothing hung within, though the taproot and undersea vines still kept it full of oxygen.

"Two of the people who walked into the water—their bodies ended up there."

Borg asked the question on her mind. "Where are the others?"

"I'm not sure I want to find out."

"Where to next?"

"The dome. At the bottom where it overhangs the rock."

"If we see other divers?"

"Avoid them. Maybe the *Méne* swim in and out of here all the time. If we can't find an entrance, we meet back here."

Nearer to the dome, Lara saw that the light came in patches rather than being uniform. The sandy floor looked like an underwater vineyard. Stakes held plant tendrils in place, and there was none of the riotous mix of corals, rock, and plant life of a typical near-shore bottom. Lara put her hand on the meter-thick crystal of the dome. The translucent crystal was faceted irregularly, as though it had been grown into the dome shape rather than cut. She looked beneath the lip and saw air trapped within, and waved for Borg to follow. They broke the surface among thick roots that reminded her of mangrove growth, stretching from crystal to rock seabed and back again in a tangled web. The light from the crystal gave everything a blue-green glow. She heard water lapping and dripping in a confusing mix of echoes—

Borg disappeared with a yelp. She felt something seize her foot. It dragged her down, she grabbed at one of the roots, but the pull was too strong.

Then she saw what pulled at her. She gasped involuntarily, losing precious air.

Three inhuman figures, web-fingered and flipper-footed, were pulling her down to the edge of the dome. Another three had Borg. Naturally green or made to appear that way in the light from the glowing dome, they had thick, swollen skin, great wattles under their necks, and faces reminiscent of the creature from the black lagoon. One of the three released its hold on Lara's leg and went for her arm.

Borg's piton arm bubbled as he fired into one of his attackers. The creature folded at the waist.

Lara drew her diving knife and stabbed at the clawed hands pulling her down. The creatures seemed immune to pain. She tried sawing at a wrist instead, and the grip released. She must have cut a tendon.

Borg sent his claw shooting toward the surface. Lara felt the pressure of its passage as it shot past her face. It fixed on something, probably a root, and stopped his descent. Lara stabbed at another of the creatures, but only managed a glancing blow. The blade opened a shallow wound in the swimmer's thick, sharklike skin, but no blood flowed. It won her a chance to grab on to Borg's cable with her free hand.

Borg pressed his piton arm to the forehead of the creature gripping his left leg. Lara saw an explosion of gray tissue as the piton shattered its skull.

Her lungs screamed for air. She almost severed another webbed hand, stomped at the one holding her leg, her flippers making anything but blows from the heel ineffectual. Borg fired two more pitons at one coming for her, jaws agape to reveal pointed teeth. Both pitons hit home, and the creature sank. But now Borg was in real trouble. One of the swimmers had gotten him in a bear hug and emptied his lungs with a Heimlich maneuver. Another bit Borg in the fleshy softness behind his knee.

Face contorted with pain, Borg looked up at Lara and used his piton arm to release his claw arm from its mounting before she could come to his aid. Freed of the pull, the arm drew Lara back up into the dome, away from Borg, as the monstrous creatures dragged him down to the caves. She shot past yet another swimmer coming out of the depths.

She recognized him—or it.

It was the wounded man from the ceremony who'd been tipped off his stretcher into the lagoon. Where wounds had been, she saw thick, pasty scabs of greenish skin. Thin wounds at his neck—*gills?*, she wondered—leaked blood into the water, and his eyes had a milky film covering them, so that just the vaguest suggestion of iris and pupil remained. Lara did not have time to make a more detailed examination; the cable drew her past him even as he reached out toward her sluggishly with hands that were now ragged claws. She surfaced back in the root forest.

Her lungs sucked in life-sustaining air. For an intoxicating second she forgot Borg, the swimming monstrosities, even the *Méne*, in the joy of simply breathing.

Then she scrambled up and out of the water, kicked off her flippers and turned, ready to stab anything that came up behind her.

Nothing emerged.

She clambered up the roots, into a honeycomb of smooth-skinned, fungus-covered wood, and found a place to hide next to the edge of the dome. She quieted the rage she felt at the loss of Borg by drawing her pistols. The VADS control screen, after some hesitation, glowed green to show that it was ready for action.

She heard water, lapping and dripping and trickling among the roots. The oxygen and clean salt smell made her feel strong and alert.

The crystal wall next to her diverted her for a moment. Unlike the outside, it was regularly formed from triangular facets about the size of her hand. She looked within the crystal and saw that blotches of tiny glowing growths clung together. Some bits floated, spiraling in the currents moving through the crystal. Evidently the dome was constructed like double-paned glass, with a space in between where water flowed and these organisms thrived. Animal or vegetable, she couldn't tell without a microscope, and interested as she was, she had a bill to settle with the *Méne*.

Alex Frys, the Prime, would hate paying the wergild on Nils Bjorkstrom's life.

The Tomb Raider picked a promising root and climbed up into the dome.

The space stole the Tomb Raider's breath away.

She crouched among the roots next to the dome wall, peering across the arena-like circular space. Frozen, hardly breathing, moving only her eyes, she tried to take it all in.

The floor at the center of the great dome was over half water, a gigantic moon pool such as divers use in undersea stations open to the ocean. The mangrovelike plants grew in a web up the sides of the dome, pressing against the luminous crystal. Thinner branches grew right to the top of the dome. Here and there they flowered. There was something vaguely familiar about those white flowers, and after a moment, the Tomb Raider realized that they had been cultivated to make a map of the night sky in the northern hemisphere. She marked Ursa Major and Minor, Orion, and several other constellations, all formed from the white blossoms. Here and there tiny buds grew.

She'd seen similar buds before, at Ukju Pacha. Was this a saltwater variant of the *Méne* plant?

At the center of the dome, a clear crystal cylinder the width of an ancient redwood ran down to the ocean. The cylinder housed another crystal within, shaped like a screw.

At the bottom, where the cylinder met the water, six long wooden spokes the size of palm trunks stuck out into the water, pushed round and round by thrashing creatures like the ones that had taken Borg.

It was a giant Archimedes' screw. It drew water to the top of the dome, where it sprayed out in a mist, feeding the tangled roots there as well and perhaps feeding fresh water to the organisms in the space between the two domes. The Tomb Raider looked at the plump leaves on the vines. Some, new and young and uncurling, were as thin as a fingernail. As they grew, they swelled, it appeared, until they turned into the grape-sized fruit pods she had seen earlier in the diving bells, gathered there for some unknown purpose.

At the edge of the moon pool the nine platinum panels she'd removed from the Whispering Abyss stood fitted into a ledge where the root-covered floor of the dome met the moon pool. The arrangement and spacing reminded her of how they had been placed in Peru.

At the center of an orderly line of fourteen older *Méne* facing the water, Alex Frys led chants with Ajay. Behind them, held by cultists of lesser rank, Heather stood with some others. Lara marked that they had plastic cuffs about their wrists—the sort of disposable restraints placed on protesters and political demonstrators.

The green-skinned swimmers at the Archimedes' screw left off their labors and swam to the edges of the pool.

"The Awakening is coming," Frys said. "Power and glory!"

"The Awakening is coming," his flock repeated. "Power and glory!"

"A new dawn is coming," Frys said. "In power and glory."

"A new dawn is coming in power and glory."

The slice of water Lara could see from her vantage point boiled and clouded as something rose from the depths. The Tomb Raider made out the crest of a bulbous head the size of a weather balloon. It almost filled the moon pool.

Then the eyes, the terrible, shining, multifaceted eyes, began to glow with a red light bright enough to turn the dome into an antechamber of hell. The hair on the back of Lara Croft's neck rose as she gazed upon the Deep God.

24

The Deep God extended a thin, rippled tentacle from the hanging, rootlike mass that trailed from the bottom of its bulbous head and rested the tip upon one of the panels. The Tomb Raider watched, transfixed, as Frys hurried over. He splashed into the water, and in his eagerness slipped and sat down hard.

The Deep God took no notice, but an irreverent chuckle or two broke out among the *Méne*.

"Behold!" Frys said. "Uhluhtc calls its fellow Deep Gods."

Whitish etchings on the nine panels began to glow. The patterns now looked like circuitry designed jointly by Intel and M. C. Escher, the artist who did the never-ending forced-perspective staircases. Lara felt the dome begin to vibrate.

The tentacle danced across the panels. Lara Croft saw flaps of skin atop the Deep God's head move, like flower petals opening and closing. When they opened, she saw fold after fold, ring after ring, of what looked like brain tissue. So the thing was called Uhluhtc? It was a fitting name.

"For the Deep Gods will wake, the Deep Gods will restore, the Deep Gods will rule," the assembly chanted. "Power and glory for ever and ever!"

"Hear the Call!" Frys shouted. His face was expressionless. The *Méne* were silent.

A faint rumble, like whale song played through a subwoofer, echoed in the dome. The frequency was too low for Lara to determine its source: Uhluhtc, the panels, or the dome itself.

With that, the *Méne*'s eyes went to the dome. The Tomb Raider's gaze followed. A single red flower opened to the left of the flower representing Rigel in Orion's Belt.

"The sign of the Cataclysm," Ajay called, pointing up at the red flower.

"Then the Deep Gods will wake, then the Deep Gods will restore, then the Deep Gods will rule," the *Méne* said as one. "Power and glory for ever and ever."

"Show your devotion through sacrifice," Frys said, his face blank, as though he were in a trance. Only then did Lara realize that the inhuman monstrosity was actually speaking through the Prime. Frys was somehow channeling Uhluhtc.

"Give Uhluhtc the sacrifices," Ajay barked to the *Méne*.

The *Méne* parted; the gun-carrying cultists shoved Heather and the other eight of the bound group forward toward the stairs into the ocean.

The screams of the sacrifices cut the misty air.

Long tentacles ending in three-fingered webbed hands the size of car doors reached for the bound figures. The captives screamed and kicked as the armed cultists shoved them toward the creature in the moon pool.

Lara had seen enough. She aimed her gun at the thin tentacle working the panels fifteen meters away. She flicked off the safety—

Three figures emerged from a dark archway of roots. Borg—soaked, bleeding, and bound, his piton arm removed—was dragged in by a pair of native cultists.

Alex Frys came out of his trance as he recognized Borg. "Croft," he said.

The Tomb Raider aimed. A shot echoed across the pool. The thin tentacle fell, twitching along its severed length.

A moan, a moan the like of which had not been heard in twelve thousand years, sounded and shook the ripening bulbs from the vines. Lara shifted her aim to Ajay—

HOW DARE YOU! The Voice exploded in Lara's head like a psychic bomb.

Through double vision, she saw Ajay draw her machine pistols.

LESSER THING YOU CROFT MAMMAL WOMAN PAY IN PAIN OUTRAGE!

Lara fought the drunken, painful sensation in her brain that threatened to paralyze her, pointed her other gun, tried to aim for the gigantic head, fired . . .

The lines of *Méne* dissolved into chaos.

"There she is," she heard Ajay shout.

PAIN! TRAITORS FOOLS WEAK STUPID VERTEBRATES DIE YOU SHALL DIE ALL DIE!

The Deep God disappeared in a whirl of water. The pain went with it, and Lara could see and hear and think clearly again . . . just in time to duck behind one of the lichen-covered roots as Ajay fired her machine pistol. One of the *Méne* guards fired his Kalashnikov at her as well.

"No, you fools, you'll damage the dome!" she heard Frys shriek.

Lara popped up on the other side of a mass of roots and took down the guard holding Borg with a .45 double tap to the chest. She fired at Frys as he dove among the roots at the edge of the dome, but missed.

"Kill her! Would someone please kill her?" Frys screamed from his hiding spot.

Ajay rushed toward Borg.

"Nils!" Lara shouted.

Borg raised the stumps of his amputated arms, but they did not slow Ajay. She grabbed him, pivoted, and suddenly he was in a headlock, held as shield between his former lover and Lara. Ajay fired a burst from her free pistol at Lara.

The old schoolmates' eyes locked.

Lara sighted on Ajay's right eye, placed her finger on the trigger. Ajay fired again, but Borg chose that moment to try to wrench free, throwing off her aim.

Lara wanted to shoot. *No, too much risk of hitting Borg.*

Borg, still facing Lara, butted his head backward and connected solidly with the front of Ajay's skull.

Alison Harfleur dropped senseless to the ground. Borg fell beside her.

The water in the moon pool boiled again. Dozens of gilled *Méne* horrors flopped out of the water, their greenish skin glistening like wet rubber, their wide-open mouths revealing rows of pointed teeth. They attacked anything that moved: *Méne* cultist, sacrifice . . . but the abominations did not stay to fight. Instead, they dragged their shrieking victims to the moon pool and dove in, pulling them under in a flutter of webbed limbs.

Frys tore himself from the grasp of one of the swimmers and fled toward the arched tunnel from which Borg had been dragged just moments ago. Lara ran around the edge of dome to intercept him, dodged an awkward lunge from one of the green servants of the Deep Ones, and fired at the Prime. He ducked into darkness.

Lara ran after him. As she ran, she saw a mutant clawing at Heather. The reporter blocked the blow with her bound wrists. The creature's webbed claws sliced open Heather's wrists—and the plastic restraint as well. Heather rolled, but the monster got a hold of her feet. Without slowing down, Lara shot the creature on her leaping run toward the tunnel mouth.

Lara pulled up just outside the dark portal, aimed her right gun down the tunnel. "VADS, left lumen."

As she reloaded her left gun, Frys popped out from around the corner of the darkened root-archway, an arm's length away from the Tomb Raider. One hand held a small pistol, the other the crystal on its ivory handle.

He fixed his gaze on Lara.

"Drop the guns, Croft!" he ordered, staring at her through the lens.

Lara complied. She wanted a better look at the monocle anyway; she'd been curious about it since first learning of its existence. She stared into it, saw a fuzzy version of Frys's right eye.

Behind her, more shots and screaming. It seemed unimportant now.

Frys stood, legs planted a little wider than his shoulders, one hand clutching the small pistol and the other holding the monocle between himself and Lara.

"Now pay attention, Croft," Frys said. He seemed tired, a hundred years old. "You've committed a terrible crime. We all must answer for our actions, sooner or later."

Lara agreed with that. Frys wasn't such a bad person at heart. He'd gone bad, that was all. A pair of fleeing cultists with a sacrifice following pushed past her, but she hardly noticed them, so intense was her concentration.

Frys continued: "Here is what you must do now. You'll dive into the moon pool and swim down, down farther than you ever have before. The Transformed will help; you've met them already. They will bring you deeper, where you will answer for your deeds and serve until your crime is expunged. This will take a lifetime, if the Deep Gods are merciful. If not, it might take several."

"Yes?" Lara asked. She stood before Frys, strangely relaxed as she saw him through the glass. All her doubts and reconsiderations vanished. She knew exactly what she must do.

The Tomb Raider held out her hand. "Alex, give it over." She didn't take her eyes from his face, slowly turning lighter in the little piece of crystal.

"What?"

"Hand me that, please. It's too dangerous a toy for the likes of you, I'm afraid." She opened and closed her palm.

Behind her, she heard Heather scream, "Borg, look out!" More gunfire echoed in the dome.

Lara didn't dare take her eyes off the Prime.

"Come on, I don't have all day. Hand it over," she demanded.

Frys's arm shook. He lowered the crystal from his eye as if fighting the impulse of his own muscles, placed it in Lara's outstretched hand. Then Lara put the crystal to her own eye. The wavy shadow that was Alex Frys pulsed. As her eye focused on him, the color drained away, and he became as white as a sheet of paper waiting to be written on.

As I thought. An empty space within. Tragic cases like his find solace in cults, either as followers or leaders. It fills a hole. What was it, Alex? A remote father? A lonely childhood?

"Alex, if anyone should talk to the Deep Ones, it's you," she said. "Humanity no longer needs to be numbered, weighed, and judged like cattle at auction. You'll go down and explain, won't you?"

"I'll go down and explain," Frys said, walking toward the moon pool stairs. Lara saw Heather empty one of Ajay's guns into one of the "Transformed" as Borg knocked another back with a powerful kick. Ajay lay unconscious between them.

Alex Frys stepped over the dead body of the cultist Lara had shot in the chest without even a glance downward. Lara picked up her guns as he walked away.

At the edge of the moon pool, a screaming elderly cultist hung on to one of the fixed platinum panels with his fingernails. He reached out a hand toward the Prime, but Frys ignored him. The cultist disappeared with a wail. Frys stepped down into the moon pool and submerged.

"I hope they're merciful," Lara said, and slipped the crystal into her lucky pack.

A flash of green—she emptied her right gun into another *Méne* mutant leaping from a hiding place among the thick roots. It showed no expression as it died; the creature just sagged and sat, its pupiless eyes vacant.

VERY GOOD CROFT.

The Voice was back in her head again. Lara felt her knees buckle.

What? she thought dully.

SUPERB EXTRAORDINARY OUTSTANDING YOU ARE TRULY ONE IN A THOUSAND LARA CROFT.

Go away.

HEAR ME YOU WON A CONTROL LENS WITH IT YOU COULD RULE THE SURFACE WORLD ULTIMATE POWER ULTIMATE FREEDOM THE WORLD FOR YOUR DESIRES WE ASK LITTLE TRIFLES IN RETURN.

I wouldn't know what to do with it, she thought back. *You keep to your world. Leave us ours.*

VERY WELL ONE THING CORRECTION YOURS IS OURS TOO OURS OURS OURS OURS . . .

The Voice faded away.

Nothing moved within the Dome now but the three passengers who had gone upriver on the *Tank Girl* on a trip that seemed to Lara to have begun a very long time ago.

Plus one would-be Tomb Raider. Ajay gave a groan.

"I think it's time we got out of here," Heather said, picking up a Kalashnikov. She pulled out the magazine, looked at the bullets remaining, and slammed it back into the gun.

"I thought you couldn't shoot," Lara said.

"I'm a quick study with monsters on my ass," Heather said.

"One of you must pick up Alison," Borg said.

"First I've got to take care of those plates," Lara said. "VADS: right nitro."

"No!" Ajay howled. She rose, drawing her other machine pistol. Her pupils gaped wide, her body trembled, sweat plastered clothing and hair to her body. Milky white liquid ran from the corners of her mouth. "You'll all join Alex at the bottom. Uhluhtc demands it. But first, drop the lens!"

"Lens?"

"The crystal on the stick!" Ajay screamed, her voice cracking. "Don't play dumber than you are. Lara Croft is going to return to England, oh yes, and take up residence in that fine estate, become a bit of a recluse perhaps, and have very few visitors, but she'll buy the Harfleur manor and fix it up properly—"

Lara reached into her lucky pack and took out the crystal. "Very well, Ajay. If you really want to be me so badly, catch!"

She threw it to Ajay, who lowered the machine pistol to grab the falling lens. Ajay caught it, held it for one second before Heather clubbed her across the back of the head with the Kalashnikov.

"I know Lara Croft, girl," Heather panted. "Seen her in action. You're no Lara Croft, and I'll accept no substitutes."

Lara nodded at Heather, bent to retrieve the lens, reached behind her, and put it back in her lucky pack.

Ajay's head came up, and she flung herself at Lara. Lara's pistols fell with a clatter as Ajay attacked her like a wild animal, hissing and gibbering.

It felt like wrestling a tiger. The Tomb Raider got her knee up, somehow forced Alison off her, and rolled over the small roots covering the dome floor, drawing her diving knife.

Ajay smiled and drew her own knife, a K-bar-style fighting and survival blade, complete with blood gutters. She waved it before Lara. Lara dropped into a defensive stance.

Ajay stabbed, powered through Lara's guard, bounced her blade off a rib as Lara just managed to turn the point. In return, Lara drove at Ajay's neck with her own blade, cut a piece of cheek instead.

The pair broke away and circled through the water, blood glistening on their knives.

"What if we kill each other, Ajay?" Lara asked. "Would you call that a tie?"

"I'll take it," Ajay said, lunging at Lara. "All I ever wanted was to be your equal."

Lara stepped in, feinted, and swung her empty fist at Ajay's jaw. Ajay brought up her guard hand and caught Lara's arm. Lara brought her knife across Ajay's exposed forearm, going for the tendons at the wrist, but only cut Ajay's muscle. Ajay swung with her own blade, and Lara felt a hard thump at her back, waited for the pain and the horrible feeling of a lung deflating, but realized Ajay had buried her knife in the Tomb Raider's lucky pack. Then she felt warmth inside her wet suit, and knew that Ajay had gotten to at least some skin after all.

Lara used her leverage to throw Ajay across her hip, judo style. Ajay rolled over in the water and rose again, knife held toward Lara like a lance.

CROFT! The Voice exploded in her brain like fireworks.

Lara fell back, stunned.

The Deep God lunged out of the pool, tentacles reaching for her. Some had fingers, some had hooks, some even had what looked like eyeballs. A thick-fingered one knocked Ajay aside.

Borg kicked one of Lara's pistols over to her. She snatched for it, knowing that whether she would live or die could very well depend on whether the pistol was loaded with illumination shells or explosive. She grabbed it as it slid past and felt the custom grip of her right-hand gun with a thrill of triumph—

—then felt the world jerked away from her. The tentacle lifted her into the air, and for a moment Lara thought it would dash her brains out against the housing of the Archimedes' screw. Instead, it pulled her over the moon pool.

A tooth-lined mouth big enough to swallow an SUV opened beneath her. She saw pieces of what had perhaps once been Alex Frys in the circular rows of teeth.

HUMANS UNDERSTAND NOTHING the Voice cackled in her head.

It dropped her, but she clung to the tentacle with her left arm and fired her pistol into the maw of the Deep One.

A howl of pain and anger tore at her mind, and she nearly dropped her gun.

HURT YOU EACH SHOT AS HURTS ME came the Voice, gloating through its pain.

One more psychic blast like that, and Lara knew she would fall unconscious, easy prey for the Deep One. It was time for

Plan B. She swung herself around and aimed with her right hand for the crystal screw housing . . .

Blam! Blam! Blam! Blam! Blam! Blam!

WHAT?

Explosions ripped across the crystal housing of the Archimedes' screw. Great shards of crystal fell away.

Blam! Blam! Blam! Blam! Blam! Blam!

STOP! NO!

The screw's mounting shattered in a shower of water and crystal.

Lara saw the screw begin to drop. It spun as it picked up speed.

Lara looked down at one of the Deep God's red eyes as it brought up a second tentacle to grab her.

She used her free hand to wave bye-bye and slid down the tentacle. She kicked out and fell into the moon pool instead of the God's mouth. The forest of tentacles turned for her.

The redwood-sized screw plunged out of the shattered crystal housing, spinning like a rifled bullet. The screw struck Uhluhtc, tearing through its flesh even as its weight dragged the Deep One back to the depths it had risen from.

Water cascaded from cracks in the peak of the dome where what was left of the screw housing descended. More and more water forced its way in as the dome gave way to damage and water pressure.

Borg ignored the falling seawater, patting Ajay with his stumps, trying to waken her. Ajay moaned.

"Now?" Heather asked, tossing Ajay's knife and gun into the moon pool. Fluid from the Deep God covered the surface like an oil slick.

"Almost," Lara said, retrieving her other USP Match. "VADS: both armor."

She loaded the armor-piercing magazines, stepped over to where she had a good view of the nine plates from the Whispering Abyss, and went down the line, riddling the platinum plates—or were they circuit boards?—with bullet holes.

"What was that for?" Heather asked above the sound of falling water.

"Just hitting the snooze button," Lara said.

Ajay rose, looked wide-eyed at the destruction all around. She glared at Lara, snarled, and rose.

"Ah-ah," Lara said, pointing her right USP. Borg put himself between the gun barrel and Ajay.

"No, Lara," he said.

Ajay ran for the edge of the dome and jumped down among the twisting roots. Borg rose and followed.

"Now," Lara said, looking at Heather.

"Make for the diving bells, Borg," Lara yelled as Borg jumped down among the roots.

Lara and Heather ran together, under a monsoonlike downpour of seawater. The ocean rose to meet them, welling up from the moon pool and the edges of the dome as air escaped out the top.

Lara filled her lungs, grabbed Heather's hand, and plunged in. Heather kicked off her shoes and breaststroked next to Lara as they swam out under the lip of the dome.

Far above, Lara glimpsed Ajay frantically kicking for the surface, felt a stab of regret. Whatever *Méne* potion she had taken to enhance her physical abilities, it had interfered with that wonderful brain of hers. Borg followed, just a couple of meters ahead of her and Heather, not rising as quickly with just his legs to power him.

Lara yanked on Heather's red hair, pointed toward the nearest diving bell. She got her point across. When Heather swam for the sphere, Lara swam after Borg and caught up to him easily. She grabbed him by the wet suit and pulled him toward the diving bell by main force. Borg pointed toward the distant figure of Ajay, but Lara shook her head and continued hauling him to the sphere.

They broke the surface together.

"Lara!" Borg protested with his first breath. Heather looked like a doused Irish setter, and did nothing but breathe as Lara struggled with the armless Norwegian.

"We have to rise slower than our bubbles or we'll get decompression sickness. Understand, Borg? You know what that is."

"Of course," he said. Then his eyes widened. "Ajay!"

"Too late," Lara said.

Borg plunged anyway.

"Slower than your bubbles," Lara said to Heather, took a breath, and went after him.

Borg kicked her all the way up, but she managed to retard his rise. Heather helped restrain him, grabbing him by a leg.

It might have been the most awkward ascent in lung-diving history. But at last they reached the surface, bursting into the pure, clear, life-giving Pacific air.

They bobbed under the stars. The arms of the storm were breaking up, revealing the night sky above. With nothing to compete with the stars, each sparkle of diamond dust stood out bright and clear.

Shanks would have no trouble bringing the floatplane in. Lara had some flares in her lucky pack to signal him.

Heather and Borg both sputtered; he'd taken in some ocean, evidently, but floated easily in the calm of the lagoon.

Lara heard a faint cry. She swam swiftly to the source, found Ajay, her eyes two bruised wells. Blood ran from her ears.

Decompression sickness. Nitrogen bubbles expanding in the bloodstream, wreaking havoc with soft tissue as they did.

She got an arm around Ajay and followed the others to the shore, making for the tiki torches at the camp. One final time, she dragged Ajay's body out of darkness.

Nils Bjorkstrom, on his knees in the wet sand, looked through his wet hair at Ajay. He let out an anguished cry and staggered to his feet, sank down beside her, cradling her in his stumps.

Ajay's bloodied eyes were open, but Lara doubted she could see Nils. Alison Harfleur keened weakly. She was dying . . . and painfully.

Lara unholstered her left gun, ejected the illumination magazine, and put in one of the spares from her lucky pack.

"You're going to shoot her?" Heather asked, disbelieving.

"No!" Lara said. "I'm going up to the camp. Try to find a radio or a satellite phone. But if any *Méne* have escaped up the tunnel, I'm going to be ready for them."

"Are you going to radio for your ride home?" Borg asked, tears in his eyes.

"I'm going to call for a plane to get Ajay to a hospital," Lara said. "We've got to get her in a pressure chamber as soon as possible."

Heather followed her as she trotted toward the tents. "I've done enough scuba diving to know that she'll be dead before a plane can get here. It might be kinder to just shoot her."

Lara flicked the safety on her gun, handed it to Heather. "Be my guest. I'd rather give her a fighting chance, no matter how small."

"Why?"

"Because that's what I'd want."

"Do you really think she can make it?"

"No. I don't. But she's proved me wrong before, Heather."

"You almost sound like you admire her."

"Not at all. At least, not now. Not after what the Alison I knew turned into."

"Surely it was Frys. The crystal. He just about had me with it. He tried to use it on you."

"No, Ajay wanted it, in the end. She was 90 percent there before she even met him, I expect. Just a tiny nudge and . . . She wanted to be the Prime. She didn't need a crystal to encourage her to overreach."

Heather pursed her lips. "Still, nasty thing, that crystal."

"Yes, that's why I'm going to destroy it."

"I think you mean it."

Lara searched the ground, picked up a rock. "Von Croy would have been surprised to see this. He was a collector, and I became one, too. Now I think Frys—the father, I mean—was right. There are some things that human beings are not yet ready to know." She took off her lucky backpack, rummaged in it for the crystal, then began to laugh.

"What?" Heather asked, pulling her wet hair out of her eyes so she could see. "On a night like this, what could possibly be funny?"

Lara held up the shattered crystal on its ivory handle. "Ajay did the world a great service after all. She must have smashed it when she tried to stab me."

She looked up at the stars, bright and close enough to touch—which reminded her that she'd have to ask someone at the Royal Observatory to keep an eye on the vicinity of Rigel.

EPILOGUE

Heather Rourke checked her Bulova watch for the umpteenth time.

Outside it rained, a typical dreary English winter day. She'd been battling a head cold all week. She'd even considered canceling, but in the end she hadn't. She knew that she needed closure.

She'd spent a half hour examining the pub from beams to bogs, nursing a whiskey and soda. Croft was late. Somehow, that didn't surprise her.

"Set me up again, please," she told the bartender. The barkeep left off his talk with a beer drinker at the other end of the bar.

A motorcycle rumbled outside, and she heard tires screech.

Lara Croft had arrived.

She entered, smelling of leather, auto exhaust, burnt rubber, and just a hint of Armani.

"Hot lemonade, please," she told the bartender.

"Hot lemonade?"

"Hot water. Lemons. A little sugar." She revealed her brilliant teeth.

"Yes, but we don't—"

"Tea then. Black and strong. You've got that, don't you?"

"Strong enough to stand a spoon up in it, miss."

Lara Croft slid onto the stool next to Heather. A sheltie trotted up and gave her motorcycle boots a sniff. She reached down to pat its head.

"Thanks for finding time to meet with me," Heather offered as a greeting.

Lara laughed. "If I'd given you an hour a month ago, the whole *affaire d'Méne* might have turned out better . . . for you, anyway. Or maybe not. You must have gotten a terrific story out of it."

Heather shrugged. "I wrote it up. Everything that happened to me. Everything you told me. And you know what? It *was* terrific. Best thing I ever wrote."

"I'm glad. When is it going to be published? And where?"

Now it was Heather's turn to laugh. "Are you kidding? SNN won't touch it without video. Gave it to an editor I know at the *Atlantic*, and she advised me to try a publication called *Weird Tales*. When I showed it to *National Geographic*, they did everything but have security show me out. Wish I had that magic lens. It would make my conversations with editors so much easier."

"Better that you don't."

Heather downed a gulp of her new drink. "Agreed."

"Hope it doesn't hurt your rep in the journo world."

"Seems the theory being whispered in Washington is that I got dehydrated in the jungle and went a bit delirious. You can have the article if you want it. For your archives."

"Thank you. I look forward to reading it."

The bartender put down a tray holding a pot of tea, sugar, and an empty cup. She poured her tea and took a sip. Then slid a five-pound note across the bar and told the bartender to keep the change.

"Any news from Borg?" Heather asked.

"He's got his cable show back, I understand," Lara said. "One of these days, I'll have to watch it. But somehow I never seem to have the time to curl up in front of the telly."

"He took it hard, losing Ajay like that. A terrible way to die."

"She was lost to him a long time before that, Heather."

Heather thought back to the journalistic wolf packs up and down the East Coast, in Washington, D.C., New York, the Cape, and the Hamptons. She had run with those packs. But the whiff of fresh blood she'd scented at a Georgetown soiree a year ago struck her as pale and pointless now. Would she ever have the same rush, sitting at a polished table opposite some egotistical president or prime minister, after seeing the face of a Deep God?

She thought not. In a way, she understood Ajay. "Legend hunting might be addictive. I'd like to try it again. Any chance of you teaching me to be a Tomb Raider? I don't quit easily." She was only half joking.

Lara Croft's eyes went moist, but no tears fell.

Heather realized belatedly what she'd said, whom she'd reminded Lara of. She looked away, offered her friend silence as an apology.

The trill of Lara's cell phone broke the quiet.

"Excuse me, please," Lara said, standing and striding toward the door.

Heather finished her second whiskey and paid the bartender for both drinks. She put on her camel hair coat and walked outside.

The Tomb Raider she'd seen in action in Peru and on the Capricorn Atoll stood next to her cycle, the earpiece of her cell phone held in by her finger, microphone hanging in front of her mouth.

"When's the next flight out of Heathrow? Good. Tell him I'll be on it. I just have to run home and pick up my bag. No, Winston, you'll do no such thing. Jamaica is paradise this time of year, and you're going to spend a fortnight there if I have to put a chlorpromazine dart into you and have you shipped as cargo." She clicked the phone closed.

"Going somewhere special?" Heather asked.

Lara grinned as she replaced her phone and earpiece. "Smelling another story, Heather? Sorry, dear, no room for tagalongs on this trip."

"I learned my lesson; don't worry. But you will promise to at least tell me about it when you get back, won't you? Off the record, of course."

The Tomb Raider put on her helmet, zipped up her jacket against the drizzle. Heather could still make out the dazzlingly beautiful brown eyes, shining with excitement behind the smoked plastic. The lioness had caught the scent of game. "It's a deal, provided you write it up for my archives."

Lara Croft didn't wait for a reply, but flicked on the twin headlamps and gunned her Triumph motorcycle, sending pebbles flying. Heather watched her drive out of sight, trying to imagine herself on that motorcycle, a Tomb Raider in the tradition of Lara Croft, speeding into the cold rain down the public highway toward an unknown destiny. Then she laughed, shook her head, and walked over to where she had parked her car. One Tomb Raider in the world was plenty.

As long as that Tomb Raider's name was Lara Croft.